hello
(from here)

hello
(from here)

CHANDLER BAKER & WESLEY KING

Dial Books

Content notes: Please be aware that this story touches on topics such as parental death, COVID-19, AIDS, generalized anxiety disorder, panic disorder, and racism.

Dial Books
An imprint of Penguin Random House LLC, New York

First published in the United States of America by Dial Books,
an imprint of Penguin Random House LLC, 2021

Visit us online at penguinrandomhouse.com.

Library of Congress Cataloging-in-Publication Data is available.

Printed in the United States of America

ISBN 9780593326121

1 3 5 7 9 10 8 6 4 2

SKY

ISBN 9780593407653 (International Edition)

10 9 8 7 6 5 4 3 2 1

Design by Cerise Steel
Text set in Alda

For all those who missed the expected moments

We hope you found your bright spots

hello

(from here)

chapter one

MAX

Conventional wisdom suggests that, when the world finally does begin to fall apart, love will be the only thing left that really matters. Petty grievances will fall away. You won't remember who called you Maxi Pad for the entirety of sixth grade (Logan Bennett) or how much money is in your bank account or the hours spent studying for that one calculus exam you almost failed. Instead, you will spend time with loved ones. Hold them close. Be present. Let them know that you care. And so, I guess, that's more or less how I came to be price-comparing boxes of condoms for my seventy-seven-year-old customer, Mrs. Phillips, at the start of a global pandemic.

This is what it's come down to. Me, standing in the Family Planning aisle of the grocery store debating the merits of flavored versus colored versus ribbed varieties—trust me, I am so not qualified for this—and guarding my grocery cart like a lion over its kill. I first took an after-school job as a personal grocery shopper eight months ago and never have I seen Vons like this. It's only been a couple hours since Governor Newsom announced a shelter-in-place order effective tonight, but already the checkout lines stretch past the soda aisle, and if you want hand sanitizer that badly, you might not want to get too attached to your kidneys.

The canned beans shelves—wiped. Frozen pizzas—wiped. Cleaning products—wiped, wiped, wiped. It's as if there's a hurricane, a wildfire, and a blizzard all hitting at once and the entire county has decided to doomsday prep.

I run through the lists of today's clients, circling the items I still need. Listen, I'm not here to judge anyone's life choices, but, Mr. Culver, are three different types of soft cheeses and organic pomegranate seeds, like, really priorities right now? I make my best guess for Mrs. Phillips, which is all I can do, given the woman still doesn't know how to text, and make my way through the maze of shoppers who are demonstrating the whole spectrum of concern levels. I weave around a woman sporting those rubber yellow gloves meant for washing dishes and a dad in shorts and flip-flops licking his thumb and wiping food from his toddler's mouth all in one aisle. When I can't get through a traffic jam in front of the garbage bags, I take the long way through cosmetics toward the back of the store.

"Miss!" someone calls out from somewhere between canned goods and chips, and I'm 99 percent sure that he's not talking to me because I have a messy bun and a hole in the armpit of my favorite T-shirt and *Miss* is some country club shit. "Uh, miss. Hello, I'm talking to you. Excuse me. You can't do that." A boy taps me on the shoulder and when I turn around, I see that we are the exact same height, looking eye to light blue eye, a detail that I only notice because, first of all, I'm not oblivious, and, second of all, he is all up in my business.

"Excuse you," I say, but with attitude, and while trying not to notice the passersby staring me down like I'm trying to shoplift an entire case of frozen pizzas. "Social *distancing*." I shoo him back.

He hooks his palm around the back of his neck and stares down the Salty Snacks aisle. "Oh, um, sorry, but you're not supposed to hoard . . . toilet paper."

"I'm not." I lean my elbow on the cart handle, mentally tap-tap-tapping as a frantic shelf-stocker in a black apron and an "Ask Me about Super Savings" button rushes between us.

I know you're not supposed to judge a book by its cover, but I'm sorry. I have this guy pegged. My age, floppy red-brown hair, nice teeth, those techie catalog glasses, and real collared-shirt energy—so much that it's like *hi, yes, you're obviously from around here and own at least one leather item that's been monogrammed.*

"Actually, you've got six packages." He says it like it pains him a little to be the one to point this out. And yeah, I made sure to score a load from Lou in Inventory as soon as I arrived because I read the news. "The shelves are empty," he says, "and it's just—well—you're only supposed to take what you really need. So that there's enough to go around."

I eye his basket: a wheel of brie, Clorox wipes, and two bottles of sparkling water.

"So that's what you really need?" I reach up and pull my bun tighter. "Not that I need to explain myself to you, but this is my job." Like it pains *me* a little to be the one to point this out. "I deliver groceries."

His mouth forms an O as he drags his fingers through his nice haircut. A bright shade of pink swallows up the freckles on the tops of his cheeks and I almost feel bad because, well, the absolute truth is that he's kind of adorable, if you're into that sort of thing. "I—wow—okay," he says. "I'm sorry." He coughs, which is so not the thing to do right now. Everyone within earshot looks at him like he's Patient Zero in the zombie apocalypse. "I'm—can we just, like, start over? I'm Jonah and I'm really kind of desperate here."

"I'm Max and that's really not my problem."

"Look." He shakes it off. "I can pay you for the toilet paper." He reaches into his back pocket and pulls out a (monogrammed!) leather wallet, fishing a handful of bills from it. "How's forty dollars sound?"

He holds it out and I stare down my nose, not wanting to admit to this boy who has at least a hundred just sitting there that, to me, forty bucks sounds really, really good. "I don't want your dirty money," I say, with more conviction than I feel.

He frowns. "I'm not, like, in the Mafia. I got it in a birth-day card from my grandma."

"I mean germs. Cash is covered in them."

"Oh. Right. Those." He nods once, returning the money to his wallet. He rocks back on his heels before jumping out of the way of an oncoming cart with a squeaky wheel. "Okay then. Well, I'm sure we can negotiate a deal."

"Oh, so you're a lawyer?"

"My dad actually. M and A. That stands for mergers and acquisitions."

"I know what *M and A* stands for." I don't. "So what do you propose?"

He looks down at his basket and I see that he bites his nails. So do I. "Trade sparkling water for toilet paper."

I tilt my head, all *you've got to be kidding me.*

"Oh, come on," he protests. "Someone on your list defi-nitely ordered sparkling water if they're from Fountain Valley, and I got the last two bottles." He holds one up and shakes it as enticement. "Oops, probably shouldn't do that," he says.

"No deal."

"Okay, okay." He holds up a finger. "You drive a hard bar-gain. I'll throw in the brie too."

I begin walking away with my cart. No thank you.

"Fine," he calls after me. "*Fine* and the Clorox wipes." I stop. Wait. This just got interesting. "Look," he says once he has my attention. "We can make it official and everything."

He has his palm up like a stop sign, like *hear me out*. "I, Jonah Stephens"—hand on his heart now—is he for real?—"in exchange for toilet paper and . . . other good and valuable consideration, yadda, yadda, yadda . . . do hereby agree to transfer all of my . . . *assets* in this here grocery basket to you—what was your name again?"

I roll my eyes. "Max."

"Max." He grins, pleased with himself. "This agreement constitutes the entire agreement with respect to the matters set forth herein and may not be amended without the mutual consent of the parties hereto. How's that?"

I sigh. "Think I can get that in writing?"

"*Actually,* that's a common misconception. Verbal contracts are *just* as binding."

"Learn something new every day." I make my eyes wide and innocent. "Okay then. You've got yourself a deal."

"Really? Awesome. That's great! I would shake your hand, but—" He gestures at the madness going on all around us in the store and instead unloads the brie and sparkling water into my cart. He'd been right. They'd been on my list.

Slowly, I take a pack of toilet paper and use the only nail whose life my teeth have miraculously spared to rip into the plastic, selecting a single roll. "Catch," I say, and throw it over to him.

"What's this?" He squeezes the roll.

"Toilet paper." *Obviously.*

"Yeah, but I—"

"You didn't say how much." I pause a beat for him to catch up. "The contract simply stated that I owed you toilet paper. Period. Frankly, I think I'm being generous. It's a double roll."

"Okay, but I clearly meant—I mean—this—"

"Sorry." I shrug. "Verbal contracts are binding, I hear."

I turn as I'm walking away with my loot. He's standing on his tiptoes. "Come on. It's not like you can give someone an opened package!"

"That was from *my* stash," I yell from the end of the aisle. "Pleasure doing business with you." I salute. Shopping lists complete.

chapter two

JONAH

"I'm still confused as to why you have a single roll of toilet paper."

Olivia stares at my pitiable offering, tapping her fingernail on the Carrara countertop like a small but suitably disdainful gavel. Her expression reads, as always: *What the hell is wrong with you?* It should be ironic, since she's wearing an aquamarine bathrobe she hasn't removed in at least three days—it looks . . . hard—and she has her chestnut hair in slowly unraveling space buns. But my older sister can look judicial, and by that I mean deeply condescending, even without regular hygiene.

"Well, it turned out we didn't really specify," I manage weakly.

I'm still trying to remember *how* that happened. We were negotiating and it seemed to be fairly equitable . . . and then I was looking at her big green eyes and the way the right corner of her lip moved when she smiled and then I had no toilet paper and yeah it all makes sense.

"Do you know what an Unconscionable Contract is?" Olivia asks.

"I can speculate," I mutter. "It's not a big deal. I got another brie—"

"Not a big deal! Do you know how many times a day I poop, Jonah? Don't give me that face. This is not embarrassing. My intestines are like an active volcano." Olivia has been away for the last year at UCLA, but the pandemic forced her home even before the shutdown. Olivia has Crohn's disease, which, for her, is basically a constant inflammation in her bowels, and it puts her at greater risk. The occasional brie is one of the few fatty foods she'll allow herself. That and Chips Ahoy! chewy chocolate chip cookies, but only when under duress. "I'm going to have to origami my toilet paper for who knows how long. Death by a thousand tiny wipes."

"I bought you some moist towelettes at the gas station," I proffer, then sigh. "They only had one pack, though. And it's travel-size."

She takes a deep breath and examines me. Her eyes are sharp and small and hazel like our mom's had been . . . minus the warmth. "It all just seems a little . . . odd for you," she says finally, picking at her teeth.

"The embarrassing handling of a negotiation—"

"No," she corrects, analyzing some residual broccolini. We had that for dinner two days ago. "That's standard fare. I meant the actual gumption to negotiate with a stranger. You screamed 'Stranger Danger' every time someone walked by us in a parking lot until you were twelve. You're neurotic."

A *diagnosed* neurotic, in fact. First came the GAD: generalized anxiety disorder. That one sucks, but it's the panic disorder that truly kicks my ass. I earned that label in eighth grade following my first public panic attack. They kept going from there, chipping away little pieces of me. And they led, of course, to the big one.

"I wanted toilet paper—" I murmur.

"Jonah."

"Okay, I wanted to keep talking to her," I admit. "I . . . well . . . I think we had a moment."

It was the loose strands of hair falling around her cheeks. It was the way she spoke . . . the confidence and the easy lopsided smile and the way her eyebrows arched and fell in a second conversation that was surprisingly easy to decipher: *vaguely amused, this boy is an idiot, vaguely amused, this boy is an idiot . . .*

And yeah, they never indicated: *Oh, he's cute.* Or: *I wish he would ask for my number.* God, I wish I'd asked for her number. A last name. A chance. All I have is *Max.*

Olivia is rubbing the bridge of her nose. "I hate when you slip into reverie. *Jonah.*"

"Sorry," I mutter. "I just can't help but think she was the one. Except less melodramatic. But also possibly not, because I keep picturing her turning around and I think I can hear music."

"It's a pandemic, dickwad. Not the start of *Twilight.* I am *immunocompromised.*"

Olivia overenunciates this like I've never heard the word. Like Kate hasn't already said it to me four hundred times this week, as if we are protecting the last Siberian tiger. It wasn't exactly helping my stress levels in the grocery store. Kate sent me in because she was on a work call, and she told me to be careful and not to touch anything but, like, that's what shopping *is*.

"I know," I say.

"And you're not exactly a pillar of stability—" she starts.

"*I know.*"

Olivia gives one last gavel tap, takes her glasses off, and begins cleaning them with her disturbingly brittle robe. I await my sentence.

"You're a dipshit," she pronounces.

"Thank you."

"This is a horrible idea. Forget about her. Join me in my super bubble and wait out the apocalypse in isolated, heart-numbing misery like an intelligent young man."

I wave her on impatiently.

"Fine," she says. "*You* want to see her again. *I* need toilet paper. I think we can solve both our problems in one fell swoop. You said she worked as a personal shopper. So, we simply find out which company she works for, procure an order from said Max, and *voilà*. I can wipe my ass, and you can make one of yourself."

I frown. "This sounds a little . . . stalker-y."

"I prefer *sleuthing*, but call it what you will."

"Don't you think she's going to figure out the incredibly unlikely coincidence?"

Olivia pauses. "Possibly. But I want toilet paper. Do you want to see her or not?"

"Well . . . yeah . . ."

She starts down the hallway, her aquamarine bathrobe fluttering out behind her like a cape. "Follow me."

"Where are we going?"

"To do some sleuthing, my dear Watson. Watch and learn."

Thank you for shopping with Shop4U. I've begun your order and will be sending through messages on preference, changes, and substitutions.

Maxine M.: How ripe do you like your avocados? They have a decent selection.

I stare at the message, beaming . . . and concerned. This is kind of creepy. Okay. Very creepy. Olivia is disturbingly good at stalking people. The actual Vons shopping service didn't turn up anything, so she then googled all the third-party services offered in the area and checked their Instagram pages for followers named Max, or as I described her, the prettiest girl I've ever met, which was probably not helpful.

Sure enough, she found a *Max Mauro* following a local company called Shop4U, and even though Max's profile was private, that tiny little smiling circle was more than enough for me to shout: "Holy shit, you are an evil genius!"

But she wasn't done. Olivia downloaded the Shop4U app, ordered and canceled until MAXINE M. popped up, and then strutted out of my room, spouting some sort of Victorian adage and a few additions to my otherwise well-curated shopping list.

Now I have a message.

And more importantly, a chance to redeem myself.

Max doesn't know it's me yet, since we had to use Dad's AMEX and have his first name on the profile, but she will certainly figure it out when she gets here and sees me doing . . . Push-ups? Reading *Anna Karenina*? Somehow pretending my sister didn't just stalk her and *Oh hi Max I was just pruning these marigolds look at me I'm all aflutter!* Oh god.

I look at the blinking cursor on my phone.

Okay, let's review. Don't use the word *merger* ever again. Don't banter about toilet paper. *Definitely* don't admit your sister just tracked her down . . . I chew my nail feverishly, trying to think.

I always suck at this, but I suck even more lately because my last relationship ended *not well* in a very public, humiliating setting involving a preposterously muscular ass. Moving on.

I try to focus. Okay. Just say the first clever thing that comes into your head.

Customer: The softer the better! I am making a guacamole, or ahuacamolli, which was loosely the Aztec word for "avocado soup."

Okay, it's pretentious. And I admit I googled *avocado fun facts*. But it was either that or how they have more potassium than a banana, which is good to know, but . . .

I stare at my phone. No response. The seconds tick by.

Shit. I should have gone with the potassium—

Maxine M.: I will keep that in mind for my next hipster Instagram post. Ahuacamolli toast.

All the pent-up air in my lungs whooshes out again. My stomach is no longer a churning mass of regret and day-old brie rinds—Kate ate most of the actual cheese. She really is evil.

Kate is my stepmother, by the way, and an estate planning attorney. I call her the Wicked Witch of the Wills. Or, I would, if I weren't deathly afraid of her. She takes Muay Thai three times a week and apparently her instructor told her to "ease up" because she broke some dude's nose.

Usually I can rely on my dad to temper the evil, but he's in Madrid for some major corporate acquisition or something . . . and hopefully catching a plane back soon. Really soon.

The one-two punch of Kate and Olivia is draining my soul.

I flop onto my bed and message Max back. The fact that she would reply like that to an anonymous customer just reaffirms what I already suspected: Max Mauro is kind of a badass.

Customer: Exactly. *"Just living my best life with my ahuacamolli."*

Maxine M.: Educational flex. And yes, I got the waxing strips.

I sigh inwardly. The order *had* been well-curated until Olivia got her hairy mitts on it.

Customer: Those are for my sister.

Maxine M.: Don't ask, don't tell. I should go. Your order will arrive soon.

I put down the phone, grinning. I don't support Olivia's tactics . . . but Max is coming! And also holy shitballs, Max is coming like . . . soon. Now what? I want to run out and talk to her in person, but the app said *very* clearly that all deliveries were now to be left outside the door with a notification, and that it was better for everyone if clients stayed inside their homes and only retrieved the groceries after the driver had left.

But how am I going to say hi from inside? I turn to the window, pondering.

Oh. That could work.

I pace around my bedroom, through its lounge area and the attached bathroom and back around again. And again. And again. It smells like mint and gardenia . . . Kate filled our entire house with potters, so I basically live in a conservatory.

My bedroom also doubles as a shrine to all things cinema: a continuous loop of classics on my TV, alphabetized stacks of Blu-rays because I'm a traditionalist, walls plastered with posters of my favorites: *Butch Cassidy and the Sundance Kid*; *The Good, the Bad and the Ugly*; *Greed and Glory* . . . basically a bunch of cowboys deadpanning me while I have anxiety attacks. I'm a massive Westerns fan, which is ironic, because I'm terrified of horses. I got bit once on a field trip. Long story. Actually, the horse just bit me on the shoulder for no reason.

Many of the posters have tears and crinkles. These are the movies I watched with Mom, and I tore them all down in the weeks after everything in a hail of hardened Sticky Tack and peeling greige paint. They went into the bottom of my closet with the photos and keepsakes and that amazing Death Star stress ball she bought me that brought back painful memories with every futile squeeze.

But I slowly put them back, over the last year or so. Baby steps, maybe, like the ones Dr. Syme is always talking about. That, or I'm just a masochist who craves grizzled disdain.

I sit down at my desk, trying to distract myself with some always productive YouTube rabbit-holing, but my eyes go instead to the navy blue folder sitting beside my laptop: the official welcome package to *Esprit Brillants*.

It's been displayed there for months like a nerdy trophy. I won the uber-competitive competition for the summer semester abroad in Paris, which made sense, since I prepped for that interview for a solid year. I *needed* to win.

Esprit Brillants was supposed to be the turning point. Now the sight of the folder makes my stomach roil. What if things don't clear up? What if I can't travel? What if things *never* go back to normal? The thoughts wrap their invisible fingers around my throat.

I check my phone again.

It's been twenty-four minutes since I got the last notification: Shopping complete. I'm getting a little too antsy and I know it. I inhale slowly. Deep in. Hold. Deep out. The little nagging questions try a more urgent angle of attack: Does my breathing feel different today? Did I already catch the coronavirus? What if I give it to Olivia? What if she dies and it's my fault again and—

I hear a bass rumble from the street and run to the window just as a car pulls up to the curb. *Car* might be a stretch, since that thing is rapidly devolving back into steel and rubber. The bright red beater looks very out of place against our pristine front yard and sculpted hedges, matching white Benzes in the driveway, and a truly repulsive cherub fountain that Kate picked out last year to spit recycled love and water to some gigantic Koi fish at the base.

The muffler spews smoke and sparks(?!) as it comes to a stop. Is that legal?

The door swings open, and Max Mauro walks around the hood, hair the color of chocolate tied back in a messy bun. A few loose strands blow over her face. White tank top and one-strap-on overalls. She's freaking singing. I press my face against the windowpane.

She comes to the porch, and I belatedly notice she has AirPods in. I pat my hair down—needlessly, since it sits flat by default—and knock on the window. She keeps walking. *The AirPods* . . . she can't hear anything. I knock again, louder this time, but Max disappears below my line of sight. My plans. My message. My chance at redemption—they're all strolling away with her. I open the window, lean out, and shout at the top of my lungs:

"Max! Max! It's me! *Ahuacamolli!*"

I see a surprised old man with a Yorkie jump on the sidewalk, squint, and look up at me. Mr. Finney. He hates joy. Max seems to notice the scowling Mr. Finney and turns back to me as well. We meet eyes. I don't know what the hell to say. My brain is broken. I just . . . stare. I think my mouth moves, but nothing comes out. Speak! Please! Something!

Max smiles, waves, and then gets into her ramshackle old Civic and drives away, sending up a trail of smoke and fading sparks. I watch her go, sighing and retreating inside.

On the window is my sign, carefully written on the glass with a blue permanent marker:

HELLO (FROM HERE)

chapter three

MAX

"Did you wash your hands?" my mom asks by way of greeting. She has her cell phone to her ear and is pacing in the kitchen of our second-floor apartment. On a normal day, the drive from Fountain Valley back to Huntington Beach is twenty minutes, but today, it took exactly one hundred and fifty-two thousand times that. It's like all of California simultaneously thought, *But this might be my last chance to eat In-N-Out Burger* and hightailed it to the freeway. Like, *You know what might be fun? To give purgatory a test-drive.*

"I literally just walked in the door, Mom."

"Shhhh!" She draws pinched fingers across her lips. A beat. Then—"Sing two happy birthdays while you scrub. Don't stop." She gives me The Look.

"You're talking to me now?" I run the faucet and pump soap into my palm.

"Uh-huh. Yessir. I can arrange for them to be available—I can't hear you." Mom snaps her fingers and points at the faucet. She's back on me apparently.

It's amazing. My mother can be having two legit conversations at once and it's up to me to know when it's my turn.

She calls it her Single Mom Superpower. She has lots of them—like finding the best thrift store furniture and tuning out any questions with the word *dad* or *father* in them.

"Happy birthday to you, happy birthday to you . . ." I have a bad singing voice. The kind that would get me singled out as a national laughingstock if I ever auditioned for a reality TV singing competition. I glance at my mom. We both have the kind of pasty white skin that doesn't tan, just burns. Her long dark brown hair—same as mine—is pulled up into a ponytail. She's still wearing her Mauro's Dry Cleaning polo with *Rae* embroidered above the logo—a clothes hanger bent into the shape of a crown. Barefoot, the hem of her old Dickie's tucks underneath her heels.

"Did you take off your shoes?" My mother sets her phone down on the peeling laminate countertop and ticks through the mail pile.

We've been in this apartment through four consecutive lease renewals, the longest I've lived anywhere, and even though it's not the nicest place we've called home, I like that we've hung around long enough to paint the walls a buttery yellow and for it to smell like my mother when I walk through the door.

We share a bathroom, our toothbrushes side by side in the medicine cabinet next to the sink, and I swear the fact that not all of our apartments have come with washer-dryer hookups is the main reason why Mom started a dry-cleaning business.

I try not to think of that kid Jonah's house, of the massive lawn, of the scaling walls, of the working fountain in the front, because it seems wild that he lives there and I live here and we both call these places "home" like they belong in the same category. For the record, I'm not in the habit of comparing my life to those of rich Fountain Valley kids. I mean, what's the point and who cares? I'm proud of how far Mom and I have come and the best part is, we have nobody to thank for it but ourselves. It's just that when the whole world is supposed to "shelter at home," it's hard not to clock the differences in what that word can mean.

I dry my hands on a dish towel and then wiggle my pink-socked toes to demonstrate my shoeless feet. "Who was that?"

"Just one of the two dozen clients who wants to know how the heck they're going to get their clothes now that everyone's supposed to stay put." She pushes bangs off her forehead and collapses into the kitchen chair that our cat, Sir Scratchmo, uses to sharpen his claws. Mom worked at Ricky's Cleaners for eighteen months before Ricky announced he was going to retire and planned to close the place. We had six months to scrape together savings and bank loans and google *how to run a cleaning business,* but Mom said we wouldn't get an opportunity like this again to have something that's ours. I don't think stains are exactly a passion of my mother's, but people will always need their clothes cleaned, and we Mauros are practical like that. "You know they say that we should be stocking up on cash in all of this too," she says.

"Who is 'they'?"

She takes a long sip from a glass of water. "I saw an article on Facebook."

"Mom, what have we talked about when it comes to Facebook articles?"

She waves me away. "Mm. Was it wild out there?"

"You know *Walking Dead*? Well, like the entire first season of that, but with better hygiene." I do the bored stare into the open fridge, letting the artificial air cool my cheeks. "What's for dinner?"

"Sorry, M 'n' M, you'll have to fend for yourself. I've got more calls to make."

Coincidentally, *Fend for Yourself* would also be the title of the sitcom version of my life. Sometimes I think the majority of my childhood was one long afternoon sitting way too close to the TV and eating boxed mac 'n' cheese. Not that I'm complaining. Rae Mauro works harder than anyone I know, and for as long as I can remember it's been just the two of us, which means often it's just me.

I dump two pepperoni Hot Pockets on a plate and shove them in the microwave. Three minutes later, dinner is served, and I tiptoe past Mom, who's deep into strategizing her customers' wardrobe deliveries using our coffee table like it's a Risk board. Honestly, I don't even understand why anyone *needs* their dry-cleaned clothes during a lockdown except that I guess cashmere is pretty soft, if you can swing it.

I tuck myself beneath a mound of blankets and balance the plate on my lap before searching the covers on my bed for the remote control. Sir Scratchmo judges me from his perch on top of my dresser, flicking his scruffy tail. Sometimes Scratchmo watches me with such disdain that I think he sticks around only on the off chance I might choke on a pizza roll and he'll get to feast on my carcass.

I check my delivery app—sixty-two dollars in tips today. Not too shabby. I mentally tally the Berkeley fund. I think even my mother's starting to believe it might happen. A four-year business degree from one of the best colleges in California. Two years ago, I would've said I'm destined to be a community college kid, at least for the first two years, because universities are crazy expensive—like, fifteen *thousand* dollars a year expensive. But think what kind of boss business ladies Mom and I could be with a school like that on my résumé.

Exactly.

If you work hard, if you make sacrifices, if you stick to the plan, you'll get ahead. Mom and I are like two horses in the Kentucky Derby. For most of the race, we've just been out here trying not to get trampled in the pack, but then slowly, slowly, inch by inch, we pushed up, and we pressed and pressed even when we were bone-tired, even until just recently, and we nosed ahead enough to get our photo finish. And as my mom likes to say, the finish line is really just the beginning.

The cheese from the Hot Pocket still manages to burn the

roof of my mouth, so I have to use my hand as a fan while my jaw hangs wide open, like no wonder I'm single. I watch one episode of *Hannibal* and then half of another, take my plate to the sink and wash it while my mom is still talking with great passion about camel hair and mothproofing on the phone. Outside is the usual racket of the dumpster lid opening and closing and cars locking, the guy next door playing his bass too loud, and footsteps from the apartment above ours.

I belly flop back onto my bed and stare at my Mickey Mouse alarm clock—eight thirty. For the record, lots of things sound like a good idea when you're really, really bored, and almost none of them can be considered your fault. Like eating an entire package of Oreos or starting a blog or attempting to dye your hair blond. Or in this case, unlocking your phone and finding that you forgot to click "delivered" on your last order of the day and so you still have access to a certain pre-pre-*pre*-law-slash-L.L.Bean-model-wannabe's phone number.

Maxine M.: So you could have told me that you were the customer I was shopping for earlier.

CUSTOMER: And RUIN the element of surprise?

Maxine M.: Wait, this *is* the guy from the grocery store, right?

CUSTOMER: Jonah Stephens, the one and only.

Maxine M.: . . .

Maxine M.: Yeah ran a quick fact check on that and I just found like 13 of you on Facebook alone so . . .

CUSTOMER: Did you friend me?

Maxine M.: No

CUSTOMER: Why not? You were right there!

Maxine M.: Because . . . we're not friends?

CUSTOMER: Details

Maxine M.: Yeah you're not big on those I seem to recall

CUSTOMER: OK OK not friends got it.

CUSTOMER: Do you think that's permanent?

Maxine M.: Nothing is permanent Jonah. Time is ephemeral. The ice caps are melting and Criminal Minds is canceled and Prince Harry moved to America so hey anything is possible DREAM BIG

CUSTOMER: says the girl to the boy with a predisposition for existential crises

Maxine M.: says the boy to the girl with a susceptibility to ennui

CUSTOMER: ennui. Fancy.

Maxine M.: This is weird, by the way.

CUSTOMER: Which part?

Maxine M.: . . . texting you

CUSTOMER: Yeah, but the whole world is weird so it's like a double negative. It cancels out.

Maxine M.: That logic is airtight.

CUSTOMER: Waiting for an emoji. I can't tell if you're being sarcastic.

Maxine M.: Oh I don't believe in emojis.

CUSTOMER: They aren't Santa Claus, Max. Emojis exist. They are a reality. Like climate change.

Maxine M.: What I mean is that I've taken a principled stance against emojis. Like if there were enamel pins that could support the fight against emojis, I would have five pinned to my jean jacket because enamel pins, unlike emojis, I freaking love.

CUSTOMER: OK, wow, a lot to unpack here. So did you have a traumatic formative experience with an emoji? Is this like a scary clown type thing? Max, are you afraid of emojis?

Maxine M.: I'd rather not say.

CUSTOMER: This is a safe space. I can recommend resources. Start a support group.

Maxine M.: . . .

Maxine M.: . . .

Maxine M.: OK, fine.

Maxine M.: I was dumped via emojis.

CUSTOMER: Serious?

Maxine M.: Dead.

CUSTOMER: It's settled then. I'm never using emojis again. Out of solidarity to those whom emojis have harmed.

Maxine M.: Thanks.

Maxine M.: Moving on. So . . . are you, you know, worried?

CUSTOMER: Max, worry is my permanent state. I worry about the soccer goal I missed at an away game 3 years ago. I worry about my SAT score. I worry about that one time my voice cracked when I raised my hand in AP Euro. So yeah I guess you could say I'm worried

Maxine M.: Not really what I meant. But anyway. I can't keep my eyes open.

CUSTOMER: That's lucky. I can never get mine to shut.

CUSTOMER: Hey, do you mind if I save your number?

Maxine M.: Yes.

CUSTOMER: OK . . .

Maxine M.: I mean no!

Maxine M.: I mean I don't mind.

Maxine M.: Good night Jonah Stephens

CUSTOMER: Good night

Maxine M.: zzzzzzzzzzz

I wake to the sound of my mother's voice talking loudly into the phone. My Mickey Mouse alarm clock reads 6:00 a.m. and I roll face-first into my pillow. Sir Scratchmo jumps onto my back and begins kneading it, sneezing twice like he's allergic to me.

My best friend, Dannie, had strong-armed me into a joint New Year's resolution to start mornings off with "mindful meditation!" and "gratitude journals!"—in my defense, I'd been three glasses of sparkling cider deep—and now the first thing I think when I peel open my eyelids each morning is: *How . . . dare . . . you, Dannie.* Which, when I told her, she somehow took as a compliment. Like: *Thinking of you too, XOXO!*

My sleeping laptop trills from the corner of the bed where I fell asleep with it half open. It trills again. Relentless. Sir Scratchmo gets the boot and I wriggle sideways to reach my keyboard, jostling the screen to life.

"Hiya." My friend Imani's face pops up the moment I click on the Google video chat. The third side of the Max-Dannie-Imani triangle. Imani and I know each other from way back when we started at the same day care down the road. Then we met Dannie when Mom and I lived at the Crescent Moon Complex circa fourth grade. There was a community pool. Times were simpler.

Imani has a glowing sheen of sweat on her dark brown skin. She's wearing a sports bra and sipping from a green smoothie. "I had to finish my Zumba video before Sweets starts watching the *Today Show,* and I knew you had to work, so." She shrugs like this should be a perfectly good reason to contact someone before sunrise.

I grunt, my chin still smashed into the comforter.

"Oh grouchy Max. You know I love grouchy Max. Not as much as hyper Max but definitely more than in-her-feelings Max." She uses her hands to weigh the options. "You're just so cute when you snarl. Grrr. Yeah, like that."

I pull a blanket over my head.

"Okay, so I came up with a whole quarantine to-do list and I want to run it by you to see what you think."

"Already?" I peek out from underneath the blanket.

"Yeah. It's been like two days. Get with the program." On-screen, Imani flourishes a notebook. "First, learn to knit. Second, Marie Kondo my whole closet. I want to spark major joy over here. Third, train for a marathon, but not if I've gotta wear a mask, shoot, I didn't think of that, and fourth—I'm struggling with a fourth."

"Read *War and Peace*."

"I guess I could, but—"

"Oh my god, I was kidding. I think one through three will keep you plenty busy. It's not like this will go on for an eternity."

"I just hate the idea of having nothing to show for this time, you know?"

"Really? Because my only goal is survival."

"You're *working*. That's so important." The Athleta store where Imani has a weekend job had announced its closure two days ago. "Speaking of which, could you pretty-please snag some Aleve and fiber gummies for my grandparents?" Imani and her parents have been living with Sweets and Big Paw since two Christmases ago. It's a long story with a mostly happy ending, but she can't get away with anything around Sweets, and her apartment's so crowded that when she comes over here, she's just excited to get fifteen minutes alone in the bathroom. "Oh and Dannie needs some packs of frozen fruit. She's scared she's going to get scurvy by the end of this. I think that's the thing people get on ships."

"Done and done." Technically, I'm not supposed to do any personal shopping while on shift, but who am I kidding? "I better get a move on. You know what they say: Early bird gets the good canned soup."

"Godspeed. And maybe run a comb through that hair? There's enough fear in the world right now without you scaring the good citizens of Fountain Valley too."

I log off and tug at the blinds cord before prying open my sticky window. Sunlight is just starting to seep into the sky and palm fronds rustle in the breeze. On the best days, I can smell the ocean right from my room. Today is one of those days. I poke my head out and take a deep whiff. There's salt in the air. A skateboarder rolls down the middle of the quiet street below, the low hum of his wheels on asphalt close enough to hear.

Reluctantly, I slide off the mattress and spend the next twenty minutes trying to become human. By the time I've washed my hair and brushed my teeth and rubbed lotion into my face, I'm at least not snarling anymore. Openly.

I pour myself a cup of coffee from the half-full pot waiting for me and clutch a mug with both hands, sipping slowly. "Did you sleep?" I ask Mom. My dad left when I was four years old, which, no matter what anybody says, is late enough for me to remember but apparently easy enough for him to forget, because after he took me to Disneyland that one time when I was six, I never heard from him again. The day after Disney, Mom took me to sit by the ocean and said, "See how big the ocean is? That's how much I love you, which is plenty." She had a point.

"A couple hours," she says. "Early shift today?"

"The world is ending. The people need their shaved Brussels sprouts."

"Be smart out there. You hear me?" She pushes a granola bar into my hand with the same gravity with which she might hand over a loaded weapon, as though *granola* might protect me. This is the part where I'm supposed to roll my eyes, but even though this might not sound "cool," I actually like when my mom goes all mama bear on me. It makes me feel lucky. Maybe not a thing you think to appreciate unless you came close, like we did, to losing everything, even each other.

"I will. Text me if you need anything while I'm out, okay?"

Something triggers: *Text*. Last night. That guy from the grocery store.

That guy who has a name.

Jonah.

Oh right. So, that happened.

And it wasn't terrible.

I grab for my phone and see that there's a new message on-screen, sent at 2:01 a.m. *All the better to ignore me by* followed by a link to Spotify. My mouth does a little twist.

"Don't forget these."

I look up. Mom forks over a plastic bag. In it, hand

sanitizer and the Clorox wipes I'd conned Jonah out of. At the door, I push my feet into my worn-out shoes and lace them. I slide on latex gloves. I swipe hair out of my eyes. I put in my AirPods. I hit play on the first song. Listen. Grin. Type.

Oh . . . so you're *that* guy?

Jonah's Greatest Cannot-Debate-It *Essential* (get it?) Playlist

7—Catfish and the Bottlemen

Rill Rill—Sleigh Bells

This Year—Mountain Goats

Loving is Easy—Rex Orange County

We are the People—Empire of the World

Ready to Let Go—Cage the Elephant

Making Friends—Joey Cape

Mass Pike—The Get Up Kids

Waiting for the End of the World—Elvis Costello

The Kids Don't Stand a Chance—Vampire Weekend

Big Jet Plane—Angus and Julia Stone

Such Great Heights—the Postal Services

Maps—Yeah Yeah Yeahs

chapter four

JONAH

A panic attack is the classic chicken vs. egg scenario.

I am having a panic attack because I am afraid of having a panic attack because I had a panic attack last week because . . . it's the circle of (a miserable) life. My therapist said to stop asking which came first. Just do the steps, Jonah. It doesn't matter where anxiety starts—only where it ends. Apparently, *I* get to decide that part.

Of course, I suck at making decisions. So, naturally, I am in my bedroom having a panic attack with my hand on my cell phone ready to call 911 because my heart is pounding and I can't breathe and maybe this one is it and I am actually dying and . . . It isn't.

I see it out. I breathe deeply: in through the nose, out longer and slower through the mouth. The attack passes without pressing the call button, or having a heart attack, or whatever the hell else I'm afraid of. The aftermath leaves me feeling like a deflating balloon.

I used to turn to my mom. Warm eyes and an easy calm and that wry smile that pushed the dark away. But these days I turn to, well, me. It's not quite the same.

I catch sight of myself in the mirror. Bedraggled auburn hair from my own grasping hands, glazed blue eyes, shoulders slumped forward in defeat. I look awful. I feel worse. Every panic attack leads to the slow creep of derealization . . . that numb *I'm looking through a screen* feeling where there is no past or future or anything but this deeply shitty now. I manage to get to my bed and flop there, staring up at the ceiling. My phone was pinging a couple times through the attack, and I finally check my messages. It's my best friend: the enigmatic Carlos F. Santi.

P.S. He actually writes *Carlos F. Santi* for everything and even introduces himself that way, so I just gave up and went with it.

Carlos F. Santi: DUDE I am so bored come hang out

Carlos F. Santi: At least play COD with me. I have gossip. I won't tell unless you play

Carlos F. Santi: OK fine Emerson messaged me today. Like . . . now you want to talk?!

I sigh. He's been trying to get me to hang out for days now, but Kate keeps giving me a hard no. And to be honest, I would be worried anyway for Olivia's sake.

Carlos and I talk about fifty times a day—most of it involves his ever-changing love life—but it feels weird not to see him. He's clearly having a hard time with all this too. I'm about to message him back when I hear the familiar ominous clacking of heels outside my doorway.

"You look like hell." The Wicked Witch of the Wills is wearing a striped gray pantsuit, even though she is working from home. Her ponytail is pulled back in that *Maleficent* look, which matches nicely with her crimson lipstick and cold, dead eyes. No wonder her clients just sign shit and leave. I know I sound awful, but like, she broke a dude's nose doing Muay Thai. She could kill me on a whim.

"I know," I mutter.

"Do we need to make a virtual appointment—"

"Yes."

My biweekly appointments have been put on hold, of course, but Dr. Syme is apparently opening up some Zoom calls. He already says I space out a lot during regular sessions, so this should go well. In fairness, things have gotten better in the last two years. After . . . Mom, I was spiraling hard. Panic attacks twice a day. Not sleeping. Not eating. *This*, by comparison, is an improvement.

She nods. "Good. I'll set one up. Are you doing your breathing exercises—"

"*Yes.*"

"Hmm." Kate examines the room. "You know, Charla can't come for a while. You'll have to clean this place yourself. No more towel swans and throw pillow roses."

"I'll survive."

"We all have hard times," she said. "When I lost my husband—"

"Didn't you divorce him because he wanted to be a surfer?"

She nods unabashedly. "We met in law school. He changed."

"What's the point of this anecdote?"

"I was sad. But I picked myself up, got back to work, and look at me now."

I glance at her. "You want me to wear pantsuits and feed on old people's souls?"

"You're impossible." She pauses. "Your father didn't catch his flight today. Has to wait it out . . . A few people at the firm tested positive. He's stuck in the hotel. He'll call later."

I sit upright, snapping back to reality. "How long until he can leave—"

"I don't know. He has to monitor for symptoms. Spain has a lot more cases than we do."

"Can't he just get on a plane anyway and—"

"*No.* I'll book the next available appointment. Have a shower, Jonah. You stink."

Then she's gone, mercifully, leaving me to wallow in brand-new anxieties about my father. And my stench. I run my hands down my face, pulling my bottom lip with them. I really do need a shower and a distraction. Kate is evil. Max has gone radio-silent.

That leaves only one other woman in my life.

I watch helplessly as Olivia completes her dominion in Settlers of Catan. She gave me a free choice of games in an attempt to level the playing field—UNO was a complete disaster—and then still kicked my ass. This is supposed to be my specialty too. I beat Carlos in like twenty-five minutes when we played. Granted, he thought it was called Settlers of Canada even after the game was over and questioned the inclusion of deserts, but still.

"Well, that was fun," Olivia says. "You *almost* had me. Napping, I mean."

"I thought you've never played this game," I mutter.

"I haven't. I am simply superior in every facet of life. Including settling."

"That is true," I agree, eyeing her. "You were born to be quarantined."

She's in her petrified bathrobe again. Her hair has become a chaotic, possibly sentient mass atop her head, and she has abandoned all pretenses of teeth-brushing, semi-regular bathing, and socks. The last one troubles me the most, since she puts her feet up on the coffee table where I eat lunch. I make a note to give it a thorough Lysol wiping.

Olivia snorts and goes to the fridge. "Pretty much. Though Crohn's at twelve really sealed the deal. Trust me, there are worse fates than staying home."

"Are we out of anything?" I ask as she paws through the fridge.

"Here we go," she groans. "I don't know. Yes, I suppose. We could use milk."

"Milk, huh . . ."

"If you're debating whether calling your crush to deliver you milk in the midst of a pandemic is a questionable romantic gesture, then the answer is yes. Thoroughly . . . *yes.*"

"It's been two days since I've seen her. She . . . didn't message me back yesterday."

Olivia sits back down with a glass of water and a stack of chocolate chip cookies. It's nine a.m. "Where did you leave off?" she asks, sounding deeply bored already.

I pause. "Well, I sent her a playlist—"

"Oh, god. Did any of the songs include the words *crush, love, longing*—"

"Only in passing," I murmur, burying my head in my hands. "I liked the songs."

"Well, you're all in now. You might as well propose."

"What do I do, Olivia?" I look up at her. "Save me from myself."

Olivia curls one wayward strand of hair around her finger. "Well, considering I have self-respect, I would dig a deep hole and hide in it. Of course, you, on the other hand, don't. So do something romantic. Get her here in a way that doesn't scream *Where is my liver pâté?* And by here, I mean *outside,* ye of always questionable judgment."

"Hmm."

"Think while you clean the board, serf."

"You know, I'm astounded you don't have a significant other."

"Me too," Olivia agrees, downing her water in one gulp. "I'm such a treasure."

I ponder that for a moment. "Do you like scavenger hunts?"

"I'm not ten years old, so no. Let me guess: You did one of those for Ashley."

"Okay, ow."

"It probably sent her running to that goalie. *Save me, Adam.* Ha!"

I stand up, mind racing now. "This could work."

"I'm embarrassed for you already."

"Hey, Max . . . do you want to play a game?" I put my hand over my mouth in horror. "I heard it as it was coming out."

"Should I call the police now or wait an hour?"

I run for the stairs. "I won't say that!"

"Good. Hey! The board is not clean! Jonah! Not! Clean!"

I drop into my desk chair and pull out my cell phone. Here goes nothing.

chapter five

MAX

Jonah: Hey Max. I have a mission for you (should you choose to accept it).

Max: I don't.

Jonah: Don't what?

Max: Choose to accept it.

Jonah: OK. That is not how I pictured that going.

Max: Really?

Jonah: But you haven't even heard what it is yet. You're making a completely uninformed decision.

Max: All right. Hit me with the facts. You've got 1 minute.

Jonah: OK!

Jonah: You know what? Let's just pretend there was no exclamation point there.

Max: Can't. I already pictured you clicking your heels together when you said it.

Jonah: Moving right along. Let's get back to the mission, shall we? Dares.

Max: Dares?

Jonah: You don't sound impressed. See I think the problem is you were supposed to imagine it with jazz hands.

Max: You really should have sprung for the exclamation point that time.

Jonah: So what do you think?

Max: I'll pass.

I pull my sunglasses down onto my nose. A scented mini surfboard swings from my rearview mirror. I pull up my next delivery address while the car idles with the windows down. It's a sunny seventy-two degrees. Outside, sprinklers chug water onto the empty golf course that's peeking out from between the houses here. Two down—I reach across to the passenger seat and strike *Rivera* from my crumpled list—four to go.

Jonah: It'll be fun!

Max: I'm working.

Jonah: Right. No. I totally get it. I mean maybe some other time.

Jonah: Or not. Not is good too.

Jonah: You know I'm just going to say it: this is when an emoji would really come in handy. Because it's totally cool. Could not be more cool.

So yes, I opened a can of worms. My bad. It's not like I meant to, you know, strike up an unlikely friendship or anything. This isn't some weird community outreach program in which I volunteer to spend quality time with the richest, preppiest kid I can find.

Though if it were, let the record show, I'd be straight crushing it.

Anyway. I generally prefer my worms in the can, thank you very much. It'd be so much easier to ghost him if I weren't halfway enjoying this exchange. And if I didn't have a secret thing for slightly neurotic boys with pretty hair who look really cute in glasses. Still, don't think the idea hasn't crossed my mind—when I want to, I can go full on specter. Happy Halloween in March.

Max: Serious question: Do other girls fall for this stuff?

Jonah: Is that a trick question?

Max: I hope not.

Jonah: There are no other girls

My hand is on the gearshift. I've only got another five minutes before someone in this nice neighborhood calls the cops on my "suspicious-looking vehicle." That's counting on twice the usual amount of time, given that every residential street I've driven down today looks eerily deserted. No one balancing coffee cups on top of their cars, wrangling kids into car seats, dragging trash cans to the curb. It's spring break, but everyone says it's bound to last at least an extra week, and it's not like anyone's rushing off to ski or sip drinks with tiny umbrellas or whatever it is people in this neighborhood do on vacation. Instead, the sky is robin's-egg blue and the sun is perfect and there isn't a soul in sight to appreciate it except for me.

It's not that I'm lonely. Because Max Mauro doesn't *get* lonely. I am perfectly content being a solo artist. My favorite card game is solitaire. But, it does strike me that in a world that has suddenly and unexpectedly stopped spinning, there may be plenty of days exactly like this one up ahead, and so, purely from a practical standpoint, it might not be the worst thing to break up the monotony. If the opportunity were to present itself.

I remove my hand from the gearshift.

Max: How bored are you?

Jonah: My body has molded to the sofa so that's an interesting development

Max: For the record, there's no such thing as "Dares." That's not a game. It's called "Truth or Dare." We can play that. If you want. But! You have to be 100% honest with me no avoiding the question no holding back. Do we have a deal?

Jonah: Deal.

Jonah: And I'm happy you changed your mind.

Max: I mean. I'm obviously going to blackmail you. I need a retirement fund.

Two seconds later my phone vibrates. "You did not just FaceTime me." I stare down at Jonah, who has apparently relocated so that he's propped up against an expensive-looking headboard.

"Clearly I did. That's what we're doing right now. We're FaceTiming. See? Hi!" He smiles, and, yep, the glasses are working on me. "I haven't been outside in three days. I want to make sure the world still exists."

"Do I look like your avatar?" I say.

"Think of me more like a co-pilot." He holds his hands to his face like aviator goggles.

I stare out the windshield at the curve of worn tire marks in the cul-de-sac's dark gray paving. "Fine," I say. "Then, off we go, I suppose."

"Hold up, hold up." He waves his hand at me. He's wearing a polo shirt. To hang out at home. "I have to turn my camera off."

"What's the point in that?"

"The point of *that* is safety," he says, and this time he sounds a little annoyed. I must look low-key confused, because he adds, "I just—I knew someone who got into an accident texting and driving and it's a whole—we don't have to get into it. Just—"

My screen goes cloudy and the word *paused* appears across it.

"Better," Jonah says.

Honestly, I'm not loving the idea that he can see me when I can't see him. I resist the urge to cover my face in my hands. I don't have on an ounce of makeup and an angry zit is taking up residence on my chin. "Okay. Whatever." I nod once and hook my phone into the dash holder. "What's our first challenge?"

. . .

"No." I spear him with one of the Mauro women's patented looks.

"I didn't peg you for a chicken," he says.

Mrs. Phillips lives in a pink stucco house nestled back behind a massive iron gate.

"I'm not." I lift my chin.

"Great. Then press the intercom. It's just that *little* button right there by the gate." Jonah, un-pausing the camera, uses the cap of his pen to point it out for me.

"I know which button," I huff.

"Oh, okay, so you're stalling." He gives me a pleased-with-himself grin. "I wasn't sure."

"Does it have to be that song?"

"Excuse me, '*that song*'? *That song* is a—"

Before he can finish, I lean out the window, screw my face up tight, push the intercom, and channel my inner Lionel Richie:

"Hello, is it me you're looking for?

I can see it in your smile, these groceries drive you wild."

"—Max?" Mrs. Phillips voice crackles through the speaker. "Is that you?"

I slap my hand over my mouth. I haven't sung around anyone other than my mother since I was a kid and I'm reminded once again why. My singing is a straight-up travesty.

Jonah disappears from frame, but I can hear him laughing. Squealing. Oh my goodness, Jonah Stephens *squeals*.

I snort-laugh and clap both hands over my mouth.

"Max!" he erupts.

"Shhhhh!" I say.

"Is there a pig out there, honey?" asks Mrs. Phillips.

Jonah mouths *pig* to me.

"No, I, um, just had the sudden urge to sing. It happens sometimes. It's uh—it's a condition. Melo . . . dono . . . nophyism?"

I pinch the skin between my eyebrows. I cannot look at Jonah right now.

"I love it, dear! What guts! Come on in. Did you get the lubricant this time, by the w—"

"I got it!" I say. "Coming up to the porch now."

"Oh my god, please let me meet her," Jonah begs as the gates creak open.

I drive up the pavers past the pruned topiaries. "Mrs. Phillips? I don't think so. But, now that you mention it, I do have someone I could introduce you to later. My favorite customer. *If* you're good." I open the car door to get Mrs. Phillips's groceries. "For now, you have other things to focus on. Like how you're next."

chapter six

JONAH

"I am so jealous right now," I say, watching as Max devours a burger.

I Venmo'd her lunch for "driving" me around today, and now I wish I'd ordered something too, because I am eating a pear and it's definitely not the same.

"I'm jealous that you get to lie in bed while I deliver condoms to rich people."

I pause. "Fair."

She's parked outside In-N-Out, worn-out Keds propped up on the dash, chewing thoughtfully and washing it all down with a prodigiously sized double chocolate shake.

"How did you start delivering anyway?" I ask.

She shrugs. "Had a car, a pressing need for money, and a mom who wouldn't let me be an Uber driver. Plus I turned down all the usual options: VP of sales, hedge fund manager . . . I did almost take that ambassador job in Sofiya . . ."

"Point taken. Well, at least you get to meet interesting people."

"Oh? Like who?"

"Uh, Mrs. Phillips, obviously. Also a certain Lionel Richie . . . enthusiast."

"And what a coincidence that was," she drawls, eyeing me as she pops a fry into her mouth.

"You love Lionel Richie too? 'Dancing on the Ceiling' is like—"

"No. What I meant was, one moment I'm getting mansplained over TP in the grocery store, the next I'm *delivering* it to the very same mansplainer screaming *ahuacamolli* from his bedroom window."

I feel my cheeks burning. "The . . . world is a mysterious place?"

"So is the internet. Actually, it was kind of impressive."

"It was Olivia," I admit. "My sister. I was just . . . really excited about the avocado soup." There's a pause. "Hey listen, I'm sorry. I should have told her no. Was it"—I wince—"even slightly endearing?"

"Not really. If you'd had an adorable dog run out and greet me, maybe."

"I wish. Kate won't let me have one. It might attack David Copperfield. Her cat," I clarify. "Not the 1980s magician with the fabulous hair. Unfortunately."

"Wow. I was kind of thinking of the Dickens book."

"Oh yeah. No. He's just a really pretentious cat. Judgmental eyes."

"I feel your pain," she says. "I'm pretty sure my cat, Sir Scratchmo, can read minds. Think of whatever it is you want him to do and then he'll do the exact opposite, it's uncanny. Sometimes I threaten him with a puppy, but again, he's got the whole mind-reading thing, so he knows I'm lying. My mom's all kinds of allergic."

"A dog would have been my request number one on *Step into Our Family*."

"Jonah Stephens," she whispers, leaning toward the screen. "He of boat shoes meets polo shirts meets I have a weird cupid statue on my front lawn . . . watches cheesy reality television?"

"I may have caught an episode or two."

She gives me a scandalized look. "I just binged it for like three days straight. I mean, we really *should* get to pick our parents' suitors. My mom's dating life is a mess."

"Thank you! Like, Dad, ignore the evil lawyer—this other lady has three cocker spaniels. It's amazing how the kids always think to google people. Remember the one where that dude turned out to be in a bike gang and went by Big Rex?"

"I thought he was kind of awesome. My mom just went on a first date with a guy who randomly FaceTimed his mother halfway through dinner to introduce his new girl-friend."

"Wow. Step—"

"*Out* of our family!" We finish it together. Max laughs like she means it: Her eyes disappear, her shoulders scrunch up, and it's, like, really loud. It's maybe the best laugh ever.

"We should watch it sometime," I say. "I could definitely re-binge it."

Her eyebrow shoots up.

"You know . . . virtually," I clarify. "Or in person in some non-dystopian-hellscape future?"

"I don't even know you," she says, though the right corner of her mouth twitches and drags the rest into a smile. I notice a little crinkling around her green eyes when she smiles. I make a note of that, because Olivia told me we'll all be wearing masks sooner or later.

"Then let's change that," I say. "Truth."

"Hmm . . . well, it has to be something deeply personal or embarrassing," Max says, tapping her chin. "Preferably both, since I sang into an intercom and got called a pig."

"It was a legit snort, in fairness."

"All right, I'll take the low-hanging fruit. Have you dated anyone recently?"

I lean in. "Max Mauro . . . is this a roundabout way of asking if I'm single?"

"Answer the question."

"Somewhat," I say hesitantly. "We broke up a few months ago."

"What happened?"

"That's technically a new question—"

"I sang into an intercom, Jonah."

I groan inwardly. This is number one on *Things I Don't Want to Talk About with Max*.

I take a despondent bite of pear and put it aside. "I walked in on her making out with this guy on my soccer team, Adam Fredow, at a team party. Without clothes on. I have a very distinct memory of his flexing haunches. And sweat. It was all very sweaty."

"They were *naked*?"

"Stark," I reply weakly. "He had his back to me, so I could see her surprised face and his butt and I didn't know which one to look at. I kept going back and forth like a Telemundo soap."

"Way to paint a picture. And?"

"Well, I got mad, I guess, and the whole team came in. I mean, she was dressed by then. But there was lots of shouting and laughing and stuff. And then . . . well . . . Ashley told me we should go on a break."

"*She* said that to *you* right in front of everyone? After *you* caught her in bed with another dude?"

"Yeah. It was sort of a public breakup."

"You have to admire her gumption."

"Oh, I do," I manage, trying and failing to sound unaffected.

"All right, sorry, not funny. Well, hilarious, but only for everyone else." Max puts the shake down and sighs. "Ugh, okay, now I feel guilty because you look all—mopey. It's my turn. But I want to finish my fries, so I'll take truth."

I brighten. I have about ten thousand questions for her and try to parse through for something revealing in a *Do you have a crush on anyone and also is it me?* sort of way. But I keep seeing Adam Fredow's exposed, pimply butt and it's really hard to think straight. Ugh. I'm lying. It wasn't pimply at all. It was the richly tanned ass of a soccer Adonis.

I decide to go for the most direct and optimistic question I can think of.

"Why did you agree to play today? I mean, really?"

She takes a long sip of her shake, eyes blinking in mock innocence. "Boredom."

"A friendly reminder that the game demands *truth*."

"Fine," Max says. "That mixed with a teeny-tiny bit of curiosity. I figured I might find out why you're still texting me, even after I deprived you of all pomp, circumstance, and toilet paper. Don't make a big deal out of it."

"We really did need toilet paper."

"I doubt you *needed* toilet paper. It was clearly a panic buy."

"Well, Olivia has Crohn's disease . . . she really does use a lot of toilet paper," I say. "I was kind of afraid there would be a national shortage or something. Which totally did happen."

Max pauses. "Oh. So . . . you were getting it for your sister?"

"Yeah. I got her some moist towelettes, but admittedly, they felt underwhelming."

"Why didn't you tell me that?!" she demands, letting her hands flop to her sides. "I would have given you the whole pack. Now I'm like a toilet-paper-stealing con-artist monster."

"That was always the case," I point out.

"Wow. Okay, so you were actually being sweet, even in a very annoyingly pretentious way. Plot twist. Tell you what . . . whenever I see toilet paper, I'll snatch some for Olivia."

"Max," I say seriously, "you're the best personal shopper I've ever had."

"I try. But you still have to pay for them. I'm too broke for reverse philanthropy."

"Deal. Now, can we return to my original question? You wanted to know why I was still texting you, and . . ."

She cocks an eyebrow again. "*And* the playlist wasn't half bad. You have good taste. For someone so buttoned up."

(Take that, Olivia!) "Thank you . . . sort of."

She pops the last fry into her mouth. An errant strand of black hair wisps down, almost brushing the top of her lips, and she tucks it back around her ear. "Well? You're up."

I'm distracted but try to make an informed decision. "I'm stuck in my house. If Kate catches me doing anything remotely fun or dangerous, she will knee me in the solar plexus."

"And Kate is your—"

"Evil stepmother, yes. I told you I should have been on the show."

"Wow. I don't even know where to start. Do you sing to birds too?"

"*Truth*," I say.

"Ugh," she groans. "I need a good one." She checks the clock and puts her food aside. "Actually, hold that thought. We have one last delivery."

Max is parked at the base of another massive driveway. A huge, white-bricked home with a turret sits in the background, wreathed with beautiful rose gardens and shapely boxwoods.

My camera is on again, and she glances down at me.

"What are you smiling about?" she asks.

I can't seem to stop smiling but I don't think "because talking to you makes me happy" is appropriate for our first real hangout, so I try to think of a redirection. "Oh. Nothing. I don't know. You—have nice eyebrows."

She lifts one. "What is a *nice* eyebrow?"

"I don't know. One attached to a nice face?"

"You are a modern-day Romeo. Truly. Dearest Juliet, thine radiant face be . . . nice."

I lean in, lowering my voice. "Are you saying this is now an official courtship?"

Max grabs her grocery bags with her free hand. "No. *This* is a job. Watch and learn."

"Hey, I know about jobs—you think I don't know about jobs? I teach at the sailing school every summer."

"Why does that not surprise me?" she says.

The view goes all *Blair Witch* for a moment, and then the

world swings around and lands on an elderly man standing on an enormous covered veranda with a large, perfectly coiffed black poodle at his side. I honestly can't tell which of the two looks more distinguished.

The statuesque poodle has been trimmed as expertly as the boxwoods lining the walkway and seems to consist of three separate poufs: one on the tail, one on the body, and a particularly shapely pouf atop the head. Not to mention the fact it's wearing a polka-dot bow tie for some reason.

Not to be outdone, the old man is rocking a hot-pink sweater vest, crisp white pants, and polished brown loafers, along with luminous ivory-white skin like he just got a facial. He adjusts his small, square glasses, as if readying a professorial lecture on the merits of exfoliation. He also looks vaguely familiar, but I can't quite place him.

"Guten Tag, my dear! Someone looks very happy today. Smiling from ear to ear."

He has this pronounced, almost lyrical German accent. I frown. Even his voice sounds familiar. But, far more importantly, Max looks extra happy today!?

I grin and Max's face goes beet red. "Nope," she says. "Normal smile."

"Hmm," he says. "And who is the boy in the box—am I finally meeting the famous Rick Hutton?"

I feel my smile vanish. I don't want to make it obvious that it feels like another sadistic horse just hoofed me in the stomach but also I can't really breathe. *Rick?* Who is

Rick? Why is he famous? Is he the emoji dude or a dude *after* the emoji dude and oh god I didn't ask her if she was dating anyone. I just assumed she was single because I was really hoping she was but, come to think of it, why would she be? She's smart and funny and gorgeous and—

Max looks down at me.

She clears her throat. "No. This is just a friend." And in a stunning turn of events, the same horse has now head-butted me in the trachea. "Jonah Stephens, meet Arlo Oxley. Former Hollywood producer, current master gardener, and fashion icon. Also, my favorite client."

I'm still trying to figure out exactly where, when, and *how* I got the automatic friend designation, and also, you know, still trying to breathe, but I am nothing if not polite. So I sit up and extend a hand toward the phone, mocking a formal shake. "Nice to meet you, sir."

Despite everything, I am kind of intrigued by the Hollywood producer thing. It explains why he seems familiar . . . his name definitely rings a bell. I'm a big enough movie buff to know a lot of the big producers by name, but Arlo is like eighty and I'm still reeling from the emotional ass-kicking, so I can't place him. Still, I feel like I've seen him before.

"Charmed, dear boy in the box," Arlo says, bowing.

There's a moment of silence and Max glances down at me, and I wonder if I should just say I have to go and spare myself any more embarrassment. Wow, did I misread things. I thought it was going well. We were laughing and talking and it was so easy and, yeah, I guess that does sound a lot like starting a friendship. Not exactly what I was going for, but then again, I have notoriously bad aim—there was a whole incident that involved archery in summer camp. But I do love talking to her, and even if she doesn't want anything else, I'll take what I can get. So brave face. I give her a smile.

"All right, treats for the boys," she says, finally looking up again and pointing the camera back toward Arlo and that majestic beast of a dog. "Lamb and a slab of foie gras for Arlo, baby carrots for Chester."

"You spoil him, my dear Max," Arlo says, scratching Chester behind the ear. "Mind you . . . the foie gras is for him too. Wednesday is our fancy night. We wear hats. Bring the carrots up here, dear, and come say hello!"

"*No*, Arlo," Max replies, a disembodied voice behind my view. "You need to socially distance."

Arlo holds a hand to his heart. "I'm too old for change."

"Be smart!" Max tells him. "Chester, here."

She tosses Chester a carrot and laughs when he jumps up and catches it. He is *très gracieux*. I soak it in, even as I remind myself I might not get to hang out with her again, period, even on FaceTime. She might have a boyfriend named Rick who might just be metaphorically famous in that she talks about him all the time, but that's even worse. The thought of this being a one-off *really* sucks. It makes my stomach roil.

"I'm leaving the bags over here again," Max says, setting them down on the pristine white-stone walkway. "Wash your hands after you bring them in. And I love you, but you really shouldn't be ordering every day. You're supposed to be *isolating*."

"I know, I know," he says. "I'm being careful. This is my second pandemic, my dear. And, as luck would have it, I am once again at a high risk."

There's a slight pause. "What do you mean?" Max asks.

Arlo smooths his sweater vest. "I lived through the early years of the AIDS pandemic. And I remember the same confusion, the same fear. Of course, isolation *cost* me a loved one then." He moves as if to get the grocery bags, Chester following dutifully.

"Arlo!" Max says, her hand shooting up past my view like a crossing guard.

Arlo stops, frowning for a moment like he's lost. "Ah . . . sorry. Old habits and all that."

"I just want you to be careful," Max says fondly. "And what do you mean isolation cost—"

Arlo waves a hand as if to shoo away the question. "It's nothing," he says.

He smiles again, but it doesn't travel across his face like it did before. There's something else in his expression now.

"Bye, Arlo. And I know you're a gossip . . . but stay away from the neighbors! And no more visits to the dog park. Don't try to tell me you're not still going. I'm onto you."

He juts out his lower lip. "I can't give up my walks, dear.

I'll keep my distance. Though we do get chatting . . . Linda Mulgrave has this little Shih Tzu named Mimi that Chester and I adore—"

"Arlo . . . just . . . be careful," Max says.

"See you tomorrow, dear!" Arlo calls after her. "Auf Wiedersehen, boy in the box!"

Max climbs back into her car, propping me up on the dash. "So, that's my rich bachelor."

"To be honest, that pink vest was killer," I say in my best *I am fine/I don't care who Rick Hutton is* voice. It's a little pitch-y. "I'm curious what he meant by that whole isolation thing, though."

"Me too. I've never seen him like that . . . sad." Then her eyes roam an inch up and she covers her mouth in horror. "Shit," she says. "*Shit!*"

"What?!"

"We've been talking for over two hours."

"And that's a . . . bad thing, I'm gathering?"

She isn't laughing now. "For my data overages it is."

"Data . . . overages—ohhhh, yikes. Yikes, yeah," I say, slow on the uptake. I probably sound like a complete idiot.

"Sorry, Jonah. This is costing me a—"

"I mean, of course. God, I'm so sorry—I should have—I—"

But now we're doing this weird dance thing where we aren't in step and we're talking over each other and—

"I've got to run."

"Right, I totally get—sorry," I say, wishing this weren't

the end of this day, wishing I weren't this much of an idiot. *Say something about a future hangout without terrible data overages!* my inner freak-out voice is yelling because I feel terrible about the overages but also this could be my last chance and I don't want to seem like—I don't know—like I don't want to talk to Max if there's a Rick Hutton in the picture, like I'm the kind of guy who only wants to talk to a girl if there's a chance of the two of us dating, like—"I'll talk to you later . . . buddy."

Oh my god. *Buddy*? I don't even *say* buddy.

I try to think of something—*anything*—to salvage this—

But she ends the call.

chapter seven

MAX

"I mean, it's just so obvious. It was a preemptive strike," I say.

"*Obvious* might be a strong word," Dannie singsongs from one of the three frames on-screen. She's wearing a bandanna around her blond hair and her middle school reading glasses on her pale face—the thick ones that make her hazel eyes look like they belong to an insect.

"Yeah, I mean maybe he calls everyone buddy. Like, 'Hey, buddy, how about that game last night?'" Imani makes her voice go low so that she sounds like a cross between Arnold Schwarzenegger and Santa Claus. Also: She knows absolutely nothing about sports.

"*Exactly*," I say. "Which is fine. I'm just annoyed that he felt like he needed to make sure I didn't get the wrong idea. He might as well have taken out a billboard in Times Square. Like, I get it! I wasn't sitting around pining for him. I texted him one time. Once! And I didn't even like him. Or I don't think I did. Not the point. The point is that *he* called *me*." Though, in truth, he had made it crystal clear that he was bored at the time. "And then he thinks he gets to *buddy* me. I don't think so. Not on my watch. *Buddy*."

I realize at some point I probably turned the corner from miffed to bonkers conspiracy theorist who calls in to radio shows at two a.m., but in my defense, I haven't had a snack yet. There are still red indentation marks from all the grocery store bags that hung off my arms as I schlepped them from car to front door. And while, yes, I do recall that I introduced Jonah as a "friend," that was clearly because— *hello*—manners, and also not the same as buddy-ing a person. Not even close.

So there.

"Okay . . ." Imani comes to us from her kitchen table because she's stuck with that hulking desktop she not-so-affectionately refers to as T. rex. She's got her hair in thin black box braids with dark red extensions. "So what are you going to do?"

I flop back onto my pillow. "I was considering holding a grudge indefinitely."

"You are really good at that," Dannie says, half listening, half messing with her lighting. She's an aspiring director and, through a number of well-curated Christmas lists and Craigslist ads, has managed to amass a selection of movie-making gadgets. Think Mindy Kaling if Mindy Kaling made low-budget horror films.

"Real good," Imani agrees. "You could put it on your résumé."

What are the odds that will impress Berkeley?

"Use your *words*," says Dannie, who has been babysitting her two-year-old half sister, Scarlett, while the day care is closed and, well, it shows.

"That's what I'm doing," I tell her. "Using my words to tell you how *annoyed* I am."

"I don't get it," says Imani. "I mean, he sought you out and ordered groceries from you, so like, what's the deal, bro?"

"That's what I'm saying." Because finally somebody is on my same page. "Maybe things are different in Fountain Valley." I use my most posh accent, which is so *not*. "I mean, I don't even think we speak the same language. When I mentioned data overages, he looked at me like I was from another planet."

"My kingdom for an unlimited plan." Imani raises her palms like, *Hallelujah*.

"Anyway." Staring at my ceiling, I brush my hands together—good riddance. "I've got you guys and that's plenty. No new friends."

Which is a thing we used to say back when we were in middle school and it felt like all we wanted was for things to quit changing—to stop moving apartments, moving schools, our parents' jobs, sometimes even our last names. Things are more stable now. We've got our shit together. We get each other birthday presents. We plan regular game nights. Imani and I each keep an extra toothbrush at Dannie's. But I still remember what it felt like before. I lift my head off the pillow to catch Dannie mouthing something to Imani and doing a hand signal like she's a catcher in a baseball game. "What?"

"Nothing," says Imani.

"What was that look?"

"We didn't have a look." Dannie tries to appear innocent, but good thing the girl wants to be behind the camera, because she is a terrible actress.

"Uh-uh. Why are you guys acting weird?" I prop myself up on my elbows now.

"We're not acting weird." Imani shakes her head.

"*Anyway,*" Dannie says pointedly. "What have *you* been up to, *I-man-i*?"

Imani glares back. "*Well.* I just finished organizing my closet. It's color-coded. Looks like a freaking rainbow in there. Highly satisfying. Next, I'm taking on my drawers."

"Watch out," I say, but real slow like I'm making sure nothing between them is getting by me. "Somebody's getting wild."

"I found five dollars, so how about that." Imani serves the attitude right back. "Also." She checks over her shoulder. "Sweets says that if you've got nothing to do, you're likely to do some mischief. I'm on my fifteen-minute break."

"Sweets is right," Dannie sighs, apparently deciding to let whatever beef she's been trying to cook up with Imani go. "If I even try to run to the bathroom without Scarlett and it gets real quiet, she's a thousand percent into something she shouldn't be. Yesterday, it involved a bowl of water and our remote controls."

I don't even like kids, but Scarlett is a plump, redheaded cherub, and I do not know what Dannie is complaining about.

"She's napping for the first time in two days," Dannie says, "and, guys, I keep telling myself, I have more willpower than a toddler, but honestly, I'm not so sure anymore. Also, I just heard that they're officially extending spring break another week. But after that I have no idea how I'm going to do Zoom classes and watch Scarlett too." She frowns.

Sir Scratchmo comes over to rub the side of his face on my socked toes.

"They canceled graduations, sports seasons, dances and everything too," says Imani.

"The one year I buy a dress," I say. I'd actually been excited. I've never been much into girly stuff, but now I think that was because it was easier not to want what I couldn't have. A month ago my mom announced that she'd run the math and this year was the year of dress shopping. Next thing you know, I'm watching YouTube makeup tutorials and it's kind of fun. So, of-freaking-course it's canceled.

"This whole thing is honestly crazy banana pants. I mean, what's it like being out there delivering groceries in all this anyway?" Imani wraps a braid around her pointer finger. And then stays that way. And stays that way. And stays that way and—

"Shit. I think you guys are frozen." I sit all the way up and hit my keyboard a couple times, like that's ever helped. Imani's voice comes out in starts. "Hang on." I crawl off my bed and walk around the room holding my computer out in front of me. Still frozen. I scramble over my mattress to the window and prop it open. It's the thick of day outside. A homeless man with a leather tan sits on our corner holding a sign that reads: "Stop the Panic Open CA."

"That's better," I finally say.

"Still sharing internet with your neighbor?" Dannie's reappeared with a giant bag of pretzels in the time I spent wrestling with my Wi-Fi.

"Yes. And they've got this uncle staying with them who is obsessed with *Call of Duty*. It kills our connection. Anyway. I've gotta get going. I have an evening shift."

"Hold on. You're not working full-time now, are you?" asks Imani.

"Just while school's out. Not to brag, but I've almost saved up for two whole semesters of the business degree. If I take enough extra shifts, then I can make a serious dent in sophomore year." I cock my head, thinking. "You know what? Scratch that. *To* brag. I think I'm entitled to brag a little." I dust my shoulders. "You know, like I say, if you work hard, you get ahead." Imani looks like she's about to say something about that, but right then Jonah's name pops up all casual on my phone like: la-de-da. I grimace. "You've got to be kidding me."

"What?" Dannie asks, rummaging noisily around the bottom of her pretzel bag.

"You-know-who texted."

"Voldemort?" Imani asks.

"Close. Jonah."

Imani has really perfected the eye roll. "So don't respond if you don't want to respond."

"That's the trap," I say. "I have to respond. If I act annoyed, then he'll think I care. Which, as a reminder, I don't."

I clock another look passed between my two best friends, one that again does not include me.

"Clearly," Dannie says.

I know I'm being dramatic. But a girl's allowed to be at least a little annoyed. "I better go." I'm already imagining what might be in that text message. *Hola, amigo. What's up, old chum?* Or, I mean, it *is* Jonah, so maybe "Ahoy, matey" feels more on brand. You know, just so I don't get the wrong idea about us. I wish I could borrow Imani's eye roll.

There's a shriek from inside the screen. Dannie's eyes go even bigger behind her glasses. "The beast awakens."

And then the meeting closes to an empty white screen. My phone buzzes again.

Jonah: Um, hello, you failed to mention that Arlo won an OSCAR

Max: What are you talking about?

Jonah: I'm talking about how your rich bachelor is a living legend. You're really burying the lede there.

Max: He is?

Jonah: OMG. Have you seriously never googled him?

Max: Why would I google Arlo?

Jonah: Don't you google everyone you meet? I thought that was just standard

Max: So you're saying you've . . . googled me

Jonah: I think we're getting off topic, which is, as a reminder, how you've been sleeping on my boy Arlo Oxley. He has an IMDB page three miles long. You have no idea how many exclamation points I want to use right now, Max.

Max: Wow, someone really does have a lot of time on their jazz hands.

Jonah: Do you realize that you just introduced me to the man behind Greed & Glory. I have the official poster on my wall, Max. Arlo Oxley's name is ON that poster. It's in super tiny font which explains why it took me a while but it's on there.

Max: Is that a movie?

Jonah: Is that a movie? she says. IS THAT A MOVIE???

Jonah: My family only watched it literally a thousand times when I was a kid. (Read: exclamation points)

Jonah: Not just that but I'm like 92% sure he dated Winter Robbins. Who, by the way, is staring at me from said poster as we speak, chewing on a stalk of wheat no less

Max: That can't be a real person

Jonah: *sigh* Hold on, sending you a picture of them together

Jonah: . . .

Jonah: did you get it?

Max: That's Arlo? MY Arlo? He looks like James Bond

Jonah: Yeah and he was dating WINTER ROBBINS—the coolest fast-talking cowboy in the west.

Max: cowboys . . . what are you five? Do you have a thing for dinosaurs and rocket ships too?

Jonah: Westerns. I have a thing for westerns. But now that you mention it, dinosaurs and rocket ships are empirically cool. So.

Max: Wait what makes you think they were dating?

Jonah: There were a bunch of pictures of them on red carpets around the time of the movie and I did a deep dive. Apparently they caused quite the stir. They were one of the first gay couples to walk an actual red carpet together at a movie premiere

Max: Wow, props to Arlo

Jonah: OK, first of all, you should know that the Academy Awards are like my Super Bowl. My family used to have this whole fantasy bracket the way other people do for football.

Max: You mean like normal people?

Jonah: Excuse me but there's a trophy and everything and you are texting with a THREE time champ! Also because they only happen once a year we'd go back and actually watch past seasons the way other people watch reruns of like Friends or something

Max: Again, normal people?

Jonah: I'm getting to the important part. There's this famous line in Greed & Glory where Winter says, "None of this matters anyway." That line apparently wasn't in the script. Legend has it, Winter was out of character and actually talking about something else entirely. They just happened to catch it on film and the director decided to use it. My mom and I had an ongoing debate about it . . . we watched that scene a hundred times.

Jonah: And now my thumbs are tired.

Max: OK . . .

Jonah: OK???? So you have to ask Arlo for me. What really happened?!

Max: Um, I don't have to do anything. Except get back to work. That I have to do.

Jonah: Sorry. What I meant was: please can you pretty please ask Arlo what Winter was like for me. And what the real story was with that line? Please? With a cherry on top. This could settle a long-running Stephens family dispute.

Max: . . .

Max: Has anyone told you that you're kind of high maintenance?

Jonah: Constantly. Is that a yes?

Max: Sure, Jonah. I mean, after all, what are friends for?

• • •

I put my phone in the cup holder, turn the ignition, and am greeted with a feeble sputter. It's two hours later and my car won't start. "Seriously?" I ask it. "This is what I get for not texting and driving?" I try it again. No dice.

The thing about my car is that it likes a bit of special attention. You can't just *open* the door like some kind of door-opening maniac. It takes a practiced touch. Two half-pulls followed by one solid yank. And—bingo presto bango—you're in. The gas pedal tends to be a *touch* fussy, so it's best to keep your foot on it unless a blatantly red light absolutely demands a hard brake. The air-conditioning will fall within an eleven-degree range of the temperature at which it's set, but it's an art, not a science. And the radio is a joke. That's why I use my trusty and insanely expensive AirPods.

But now I've done it. And despite threatening, coaxing, and ultimately begging the old beast where it's stalled out in Fountain Valley surrounded by homes that look like Barbie Dream Houses, it won't budge.

I kick the tires. I think about calling Imani. But what's she going to do? Come get me and my mountain of groceries on her brother's bike?

I think about calling Dannie, but she's got Scarlett.

I think about picking up the phone and calling Jonah.

But then I *un*-think about calling Jonah. I am not some damsel.

What I am is sweaty with a trunk full of groceries in danger of going bad. I scan the area. Only a few blocks away from my next two deliveries. I tuck my phone into the back pocket of my jean shorts, loop five grocery bags over each arm, and start walking.

Grumbling, I trudge past skinny palm trees, red tile roofs, and the hint of glittering blue pools that peek out from the well-trimmed spaces between homes.

I drop the first seven bags off on the porch of a yard littered with trampolines, Razor scooters, and abandoned chalk. I remember not to ring the doorbell, as most of my clients with kids prefer it, and knock and send the text alert instead.

Plastic digs into my arms as I walk the curve of road shaded by thick hackberry trees and ghost gums all the way to the apparently famous Arlo Oxley's house. My knock-off Keds slap against the stone steps on my way up.

"You made it." Arlo grins from one of the upper balconies. I'm turning into such a softie. "Hold on, dear, I'll be right down."

"Arlo, wait." But he's already disappeared behind the reflective glass door. Chester begins to bark when I set the groceries gently down on the doormat and back away.

A few seconds later, the door unlocks and a blur of curly black fur bounds up to sniff my shins. Without prompting, Chester hikes himself up to stand on two legs. Today his bow tie has cute little palm trees printed on it and, I mean, I'm a practical person and all, but even I'm like, *Yep, that's money well spent because it's straight-up adorable.*

I let him hug me and he sweetly rests his chin on my shoulder. I swear this dog has no clue he's not human. He's bougier than Sunday brunch uptown.

Arlo stoops in the doorframe, about eight feet away.

"You should be inside," I say, but only half-heartedly because it's not like he'll listen. Arlo has been a weekly part of my life for more than six months now. I don't know when our conversations became a regular thing, but I do know that he started them. He always has questions for me. Who's the meanest kid at my school? (Dale Singer.) What's my earliest memory? (Throwing up peanut butter crackers in my mom's bed.) Who would play me in the movie version of my life? (Millie Bobby Brown.) Things like that. And even though this probably sounds way sadder than it is, when you have a mom who has to work as much as mine does because—you know—food and shelter and whatnot, it's kind of nice to have a grown-up ask how you did on that chem test the other day and what your favorite movie is right now.

"No, no," he says, when I urge him back into the house. "I'm not cut out for this screen time communication rigmarole."

I lower Chester's paws off my shoulders and he twists around to sit on my feet. Sure, make yourself comfortable. "Some might say you practically invented screen time." I relent and scratch Chester under his chin. "Good boy. You're so handsome."

"Bah." Arlo swats at the air. Even from a safe distance, I can make out the blue veins running beneath his knotted knuckles as he readies to pontificate. "Making movies is about *people*. Being together. Telling stories."

"Speaking of which, Arlo, I had no idea you won an Oscar."

He teeters out to hold the railing. His eyes sparkle, a hint of a younger man so close to the surface that if I look at just the right angle, I feel like I might catch him. "It was a long time ago." But he winks and it occurs to me that winking isn't really a thing that guys can pull off anymore.

"Still. That's incredible. And, okay, this might sound weird, but Jonah—you know that guy I introduced you to— well, I promised him I'd ask you something about this line Winter Robbins said in one of your movies. You probably don't even remember. I think it was, like, 'None of this matters anyway' or I don't know, something like that."

I've never heard anyone *guffaw* in real life before, but Arlo does it.

"What?" I cock my head, smiling.

He shakes his, eyes squinting, and says, "I haven't thought about that in ages."

"So, was he supposed to say it?"

"Definitely not. I think he forgot he was on a live wire. He was probably venting. Sometimes he got that way. Winter had a . . . tenuous relationship with his craft."

"So, the line was about acting, then? He thought acting didn't matter?"

Arlo shrugs. "At times. Though, ironically, Winter pushed for it to be in the movie. I have no idea why, but he was insistent. My writer told me it cost him the Best Original Screenplay Oscar that year, but I don't think this writer was ever going to win, to be honest. Winter carried that movie far beyond the script." Arlo smiles, eyes drifting. "He was a genius, really, for all his self-doubts."

"So you two were close?" I know I'm leading him, but Jonah's right—this is kind of fascinating.

"We had . . . chemistry," Arlo says, his eyes drawing back to mine. "Like you and that boy in the box."

"Jonah? No way. Jonah and I do *not* have chemistry. You won an Oscar and, from what I hear, dated like a sort-of-cowboy movie star. You've been holding out on me."

"Ah. Well. That's because I prefer stories with happy endings."

Before I can think, Arlo thanks me and steps inside, saying, "See you tomorrow, dear Max," but not with his usual gusto. I stand there for a second, then turn, feeling bad leaving him all alone in that great big house. He's got Chester, and Chester is very excellent, but I wish there was . . . I just wish there were more I could do for Arlo than a quick conversation squished within the few minutes I can spare between deliveries. I wish all this time I'd shown as much interest in him as he'd shown in me. Then I wouldn't have needed someone like Jonah to tell me about his career.

But I will. From now on.

· · ·

By the time I make it back to my car, we've both managed to cool off. The engine rumbles and groans back to life.

Max: So . . . I have to know. What ever happened to Winter Robbins?

chapter eight

JONAH

I walk into the living room and feel something collide violently with my thigh. A baseball bat? A truck? It doesn't matter. The result is the charley horse to end all charley horses. I am on the floor, my mouth open in soundless dismay, wondering what sort of self-respecting burglar robs a house at ten a.m. during a very publicized statewide lockdown.

I manage to look up at my attacker and—*"Really?"*

Kate is bathed in sweat. She has on a white hachimaki—hello, cultural appropriation—with the ends trailing down over a sopping wet tank top and honed, spray-tanned muscles.

"You have to watch out when I'm training, Jonah," she says, extending a hand. "I'm doing spinning leg kicks today. You're lucky I didn't catch you in the neck."

"Why?" I manage forlornly, massaging my thigh and ignoring her hand. "Why *here*?"

"Dojo's closed as of yesterday. Tiger told me he was going to hold out as long as he could, but they're done. As if we're going to catch coronavirus amongst peak performers."

I pull myself onto the couch. "I thought you were all about stay-at-home protocols?"

"For you and Olivia. But I'm an athlete. I have the lung capacity."

"I play soccer! And also that's definitely not relevant."

She waves a hand in dismissal and faces the TV again, where a shirtless white dude is elbowing a mannequin in the face, shouting: "Catcalling? Boom! You want my purse . . . not today! Boom!"

"Do we even have any sanitizer?" I ask, still unable to stand. "What about masks?"

"I am *not* wearing a mask."

I throw my hands up. "Where did this all come from? You were the one laying down the law." I tick them off: "No friends, no soccer, no parties. Can I go outside and frolic, then?"

"No. You have no need. But they closed my dojo, my hair-dresser, my *Freshii*—" She is punching the air with each new closure. "My office! Maybe we all just need to push through, you know? Just get the disease and deal."

She is a whirlwind of elbows and knees now, spitting each word.

"Does that apply to Olivia?" I ask, scowling.

She pauses. "Of course not. I'm just—upset."

"Yeah, I still feel the pent-up rage in my thigh. Did you talk to Dad last night? I thought I heard a call. He sent me an email but didn't have any info."

"Nothing yet," she says as she murders the figurative

owner of her nail salon. "He's still stuck there for the fore-seeable future."

"But can't he just get on a plane—"

Kate turns back, lowering her fists. "Oh."

"Oh what?" I ask suspiciously.

"You didn't see the news yet. All flights to and from Europe are grounded."

"But—"

"Your dad can get home. Repatriation is allowed. But you aren't going to Paris, Jonah."

I stand there for a moment. I guess I knew it was coming: the death knell of *Esprit Brillants*. But I had a crazy hope that it might go ahead. That I might have to be extra safe and wear a gown and mask on the flight and, sure, even in my photo in front of the Sorbonne. It didn't matter. I would still be in Paris. Like her. I would still be a "Brilliant Mind" like she was.

"You okay?" Kate says.

"Fine," I mutter, shuffling up to my room. "No sweat."

But upstairs, I sprawl out on my bed, feeling the weight of something heavier than canceled flights. I can almost see her, hear her voice, thin lips curled into a smile above the rim of her coffee mug that morning, telling me, "I struggled in high school. Bad. I'm afraid I dropped all this fun stuff on you, Jonah. I had bad anxiety and depression . . . the whole works. You know Grandpa. You can just imagine my home life. I was lost. And when I won that competition senior year . . . I almost didn't go. I mean, you got the flights and housing and a little bursary, but it was still going to cost something real to spend two months in Paris, and we didn't have much money. Your grandpa wanted me to stay and work for the summer and save for undergrad and dental school like I had planned and . . . I went anyway."

I was sitting across the kitchen table, watching the steam tickle the freckled nose she'd passed down to me too.

"I found something there. I found it in the art and the culture and the language and the people, and I stood in the Louvre and felt . . . better. It was the perspective shift maybe; the realization that broken people could still make beautiful things. I came home and did art history and got a job as a curator . . . and, I met your father. And we made two *very* beautiful things."

I remember wrinkling my nose. "One thing. Olivia is a Jackson Pollock at best."

She laughed. "*Two* beautiful things. I'm telling you—go for it senior year. Or something else entirely. But make it something risky and different and scary. Take a chance and find your shift, Jonah. Find the good thing that makes the bad times worth it, and they don't seem so bad."

It had been a completely random talk. A morning coffee before school.

Two weeks later, she was dead.

I was fifteen.

Her death cut all the mooring lines. I drifted. The bad

things got worse. The anxiety. The depression. I feel them right now, like someone sitting on my chest, fingers pressed against my windpipe, reminding me that I'm still broken and haven't made a thing.

I remembered the conversation a few months after her death when they announced the program that year. I was too young for it then . . . you had to be at least a junior. I applied the second I was eligible. It felt like an emergency anchor. A chance to reconnect with her. To follow in her footsteps. To find my own big fix, just like she did.

I feel the anxiety building now and know that an attack is coming. The fear creeps up my spine in little static bursts. A vise squeezes my lungs. How did she phrase it? "You need to find the good thing that makes the bad times worth it, and they don't seem so bad."

But what about now? What about when you can't leave your house? When it's just you and your brain and you don't always get along because your stupid brain keeps pulling the fire alarm—

My phone buzzes. It's Max. I start messaging her back and smile and I already feel better. And . . . yeah. What if it's *her*?

Jonah: I am googling as we speak. Headset. Spinny chair. Stay tuned.

Max: I don't even know if you're joking anymore

Jonah: My chair really is pretty spinny

Jonah: P.S. Did he show you the Oscar??? Is it heavy? Please tell me you gave a mock acceptance speech. I would like to thank Jonah for his googling prowess . . .

Max: He didn't have much to say other than he prefers stories with happy endings?? It was all very cryptic

I frown and start fishing with increasingly smaller nets: "Winter Robbins and Arlo Oxley," "what happened to Winter Robbins," "why is Arlo Oxley not happy about winning an Oscar." (You never know how specific you can get. Turns out, not that specific.) And I see lots of stories about movies and some flat-out hate speech about them attending premieres together and . . . a lot of stories about HIV and AIDS in Hollywood.

But the stories are general, not about either one of them specifically. I look through their respective careers for clues and see that Arlo spent most of the late eighties and early nineties on international film sets. And Winter? He just disappears.

I find an article: "What Happened to Winter Robbins?" but the writer seems to legitimately have no clue. No obits. No honorary Academy Awards. He just . . . vanished. I eye the poster plastered on the wall above my bed. Winter's flat eyes drift off to the side, hand resting on his revolver.

My mom loved the movie as much as I did. Winter was one of her favorite actors. She thought he was a dreamboat (her word, not mine). I always thought it was hilarious that my mom, the art curator, shared my love of gritty old

Westerns. She said she loved the simplicity. The open canvas of the landscape. The characters with clear goals and priorities. The distinct split of good versus evil that was so much easier than real life. It's partly why we were both so fixated on Winter's line. "None of this matters anyway" seemed so . . . fatalistic. So un-cowboy-esque.

My theory was that even if it *was* an ad-lib, Winter meant that his character's path to vengeance was doomed—nothing would bring back his burned farmstead or stolen herds. Mom didn't like that. She was a perennial optimist, and she wanted the same from her cowboys. She thought it represented some grand insight . . . that all the feuds and gunfighting were unimportant. We had a million debates about it. It was our thing. Our big mystery. It feels even bigger now.

Speaking of which:

Jonah: I don't suppose you asked Arlo about the line . . .

Max: He said it was Winter's ad-lib, and that Winter was probably just venting. I guess he had some self-doubts about his acting or something? But apparently Winter is the one who wanted it to be included. Arlo didn't know why but he said Winter was pretty insistent.

I squeal in excitement and *almost* open Reddit to share the news. But I fight the urge. I don't know if Arlo shared that in confidence or not. It was also incomplete. Even if Winter was complaining about acting, as Arlo said, and it had nothing to do with the story, why did Winter push for it to be in the final movie? What was he trying to say by leaving it in? That was what Mom and I wanted to know. But maybe only Winter himself can answer those questions.

I think back to our nights watching *Greed and Glory*. Mom mouthing all the words, her face flashing blue in the TV's light. I feel a wave of grief. Stomach squeezing. Pressure behind the eyes.

I push the thoughts away, focusing instead on the cowboy. The mystery. Arlo. Max.

Jonah: Well this is a dilly of a pickle

Max: You know . . . I often check to make sure I'm not texting an elderly client

Jonah: Sorry. I will start using more dudes and bros

Max: How about buddy?

Jonah: . . .

Jonah: My radar could be way off here, but am I sensing some hostility?

Max: No

Jonah: . . .

Jonah: OK . . .

Max: OK

Max: I'm just saying that, for the record, I didn't think we were, like, a thing.

Jonah: A thing?

Max: I didn't think we were, you know, talking

Jonah: But we are talking. That's what we're doing right now

Max: Not talking. TALKING talking.

Jonah: Is this a weird autocorrect situation or . . . ?

Max: I just think it was a little presumptuous to think you needed to "buddy" me or else I'd get the wrong idea.

Jonah: Wait, you think, *I* buddied *you*?

Max: Trust me, it's not like I was sitting around doodling your initials on my folder

Jonah: I know. I'm totally aware that your doodling is reserved for Rick Hutton. I'm not trying to interfere with that. I swear.

Max: What are you talking about?

Jonah: Oscar winner, Arlo Oxley, knows about the apparently famous Rick Hutton. I did not know about Rick Hutton, but I get it. We've hung out once. It's not like I'm going to know about every Rick Hutton in the world.

Max: . . .

Max: . . .

Max: I'm going to say this thing and you might be like: whoa, I don't care, didn't even ask. But . . . Rick's not famous to me anymore. He's D-List. C-List at absolute best. We grew up together and yes, I've known him since the third grade, and yes, we dated. For two years. But that's it.

Jonah: That's . . . it?

Max: And you *do* know about Rick Hutton. Stage name: the emoji bandit.

Jonah: The emoji bandit is a guy you dated for two years?

Max: It's kind of humiliating.

Jonah: So . . .

Max: So what?

Jonah: So does this change anything? I mean there was my formal introduction

Max: What introduction

Jonah: You introduced me to Arlo as—and I quote—JUST a friend

Max: I did not say JUST

Jonah: Oh there was a just

Max: But it wasn't capitalized

Jonah: . . .

Jonah: . . .

Max: I have to run. A new order just came through.

Thirty minutes later, I open the front door to Max Mauro standing on my driveway, groceries already on the porch.

Okay, so I totally pretended I wasn't waiting for her. And I wouldn't have come out to see her. Honestly. It was already kind of a questionable tactic and yes she approved the order, but that didn't mean she wanted to *see* me. So I just quietly sat at my desk and stalked a 1980s film cowboy like a normal young man.

I was sort of freaking out that she would drive away without sending me a delivery confirmation text, which, ironically, would confirm an awful lot, but then, instead:

Max: Hello (I'm here)

And then I ran for the door like a maniac. And she is *here,* at my house, standing halfway down the driveway.

"You literally ordered while we were still talking," she says, but not like she's mad.

"Yes. But it's for a good reason. I have updates."

She doesn't hightail it to her car, which I take as a sign that I have her attention, or maybe that she even *slightly* wanted to see me too.

"So, Winter Robbins falls off the map sometime in the late eighties," I report.

"He *died*?"

"I don't think so. Maybe went into hiding? Maybe just quit Hollywood and became a real cowboy. I have theories. But worry not—my internet sleuthing has only just begun."

She chews on her bottom lip. "Is this weird? Should we drop it?"

"Possibly. But to be honest, I kind of need something to do right now. And, I don't know, it seems like a good time to do something . . . *nice.*"

I don't say the rest. About how finding Winter Robbins feels like a connection to Mom right when I lost *Esprit Brillants.* How much she would love the idea of finding a link to one of her favorite film stars right in our own backyard. Or how *maybe* one love story can lead to another. After all, if Max and I have something to do together—like find Winter—then it would only be natural for us to keep talking, right? And then, if all goes well, maybe Max and I can—I don't know, just spinning ideas here—ride into the sunset. Except six feet apart and on bicycles.

"We're going to kick 2020 right in its soul-crushing balls." I pluck the mega-size cherry blasters from the bag, where they're nestled between three bags of chips and a two-liter cola. "Oh, and thank you."

"I have grave concerns about your nutrition," she mutters.

"Totally justified," I say, popping a candy into my mouth and making what must be a really not attractive *shit this is sour* face.

I take a step toward her, not thinking, and she takes a step back.

"I'm watching you," Max says.

"Of course." I cup my hand like a loudspeaker. "Are we far enough away?!"

"Probably not!" she shouts back.

I can see my neighbor across the street, the chain-smoking Mrs. Clodden, frowning at us from her front porch while she singlehandedly puts a hole in the ozone layer.

"I really did have fun the other day!" I say, still shouting.

"So did I! Even though I did all the work. Typical!"

"I'll plan something better for next time! I promise!"

Her eyebrow is like a built-in question mark.

I feel my heart dropping. Play it cool, Jonah. "Virtually! Whatever! How about tomorrow!"

Yeah, my voice is really pitch-y now. I spot more of my

neighbors watching us from their verandas, most of them sixty-five-plus and living on a neurosurgeon's 401(k) or something. Max looks around, and she must see the spectators too, because she lowers her voice . . . slightly.

"I'm busy!"

"The next day!" I say, still shouting. That'll show the neighbors you're not crazy, Jonah.

"I'm kind of always busy!" She screws up her face like she doesn't know what she's supposed to do with me other than laugh—*with* me, *at* me, does it matter?

"I like you, Max!"

Max goes red. "I . . . better get going."

She isn't shouting anymore.

Uh-oh. The joke is over. The moment is over.

I feel my stomach fall through my socks as Max opens her car door, ready to hop in.

Then she pauses, glancing back at me.

"I like you too," she says. Her eyes go up over me to my house, to my window with its big blue words fading in the afternoon sun, and she smiles in a way I can't quite read and says, "But . . . from here."

chapter nine

MAX

I know there's a thing with teenagers about an empty house—keg parties, illicit sex, smoking weed—but let me just say that most of the time, it's not that great. Actually, it kind of sucks.

The most conversation I'll have with my mom today is this note stuck to the refrigerator with a gas station magnet. I peel it off. We both have terrible penmanship and are the only two people on the planet who can consistently read each other's handwriting. It's sort of like having a secret code. Sometimes we'll leave notes about the characters in our building. She might write: *Weird guy with the pet snake has a girlfriend!* Other times about work: *Found CIA badge in Ms. Landon's coat pocket. Secret agent?* We spent a lot of notes plotting where we would buy a second home if we were rich. My choices: *English countryside* or *Aspen*. Hers: *Bahamas* or *Sonoma*. But today the note just says:

Need $100 to cover electric.

I read it twice and turn it over to look at the back because I'm half thinking this note is garbage—something that was dug out of the back of my closet from three years ago and got stuck on the fridge by accident. Only I'm not sure how that would happen. The more likely scenario is that this note is real.

And the sensation of a cold finger running the length of my spine is that niggling "what if" trying to worm its way to the surface. Like: What if that old saying is true? What if history is destined to repeat itself?

My eyes travel the apartment. The old bookcase with my mom's paperbacks, white lines creasing their spines. The cool rug in the living area, the only one my mom and I could finally agree on and that fit in our price range and that therefore we both believed was some sort of very specific miracle rug sent from god because, like Imani's grandmother Sweets says, he does act in mysterious ways. And our new couch from Ashley Furniture that only took us six months of payments before it was 100 percent ours, free and clear.

And I try to remind myself that these are all proof that our life's different now, that we are okay, that the thing that happened before isn't going to happen again. Because we worked hard and *we got ahead.*

I click the mobile app to the bank account I opened as soon as I got my first job at fifteen. It's linked to our family account, just in case, and in two years, there hasn't been a case, an instance where we've needed to dig into my personal funds. But, if the last week of a worldwide pandemic has made me think about anything, it's how one case can quickly become a whole lot more. But this is different. I punch in my password and push the money over in one go.

We're in this together, I remind myself. I'm bigger and older now. They can't take me away again.

Jonah: So Winter Robbins wasn't his real name. Shockingly. It was really Ernest Ralph Robbins.

Max: I have to say: he definitely upgraded.

Jonah: And I found out where he was born: Miami.

Max: They don't even have a real winter.

Jonah: Exactly. The average temperature in Miami in January is 79. Even we don't get that.

Max: What else?

Jonah: Did I mention the average temperature in Miami?

Max: Jonah! You tracked me down in like five minutes with just a first name and that's all you've got?

Jonah: OK that was 99% Olivia and it was still like an hour. What's our end game here anyway? Like what if we find Winter? What then?

Max: I don't know. I just keep getting the feeling that Arlo is lonely and I hate that. I guess . . . is it a total invasion of privacy to want to find Winter and try to reconnect them?

Jonah: You want him to have a happy ending, don't you? OMG, do you like rom-coms? You love rom-coms, don't you? This is so unexpected.

Max: OK. Fine. I love rom-coms!

Jonah: Exclamation point! You know, I like you even more now that I know you're really just a sentimental, hopeless romantic in disguise

Max: Sure you don't want to put that in all caps? That seems more your style.

Jonah: Au contraire. See the problem is that I usually play everything so cool. Like: what's he thinking? He's such an enigma. What an international man of mystery. So that's why I took it upon myself to *shout* my feelings at you in my driveway.

Max: Oh so it was a public service. That's why you made it so . . . public. I see.

Jonah: Can I ask you a serious question

Max: . . .

Jonah: In the interest of clarity, your answer was meant to imply *emotional* distancing, not just social . . . right? i.e. I like you OVER THERE

Max: Wow.

Jonah: Do girls still like confidence?

Max: You better hope not.

Max: *social* distancing. But just in the interest of clarity

Jonah: So like six feet apart outside? That kind of thing?

Max: In theory . . .

Jonah: Great! I have the perfect spot. Jazz hands.

Max: Wait

Jonah: Coordinates to follow.

Jonah: Don't wear heels.

Max: What about a cocktail dress?

Jonah: Let me think.

Jonah: OK, yes, that's acceptable. I'll see you soon.

By my calculations, there's a less than zero percent chance that Jonah Stephens is planning on murdering me.

I mean, he didn't *seem* like a serial killer, but I hear that's sort of serial killers' whole plan. Contrary to what teen slasher flicks would lead one to believe.

Honestly, though, I could use a distraction. I'm still sticky from the end of my shift, not to mention a hundred dollars poorer. Wisps of hair cling to my forehead and the back of my neck as I follow the virtual pin that's been texted to me. There's no one around. It's like someone has turned the world upside down and shaken out all of its people. The shadows grow long across the sidewalks while my flip-flops slap at my heels.

"Arrived," says a soothing voice from my phone.

I survey the potential crime scene, which, in fact, looks like it could be an actual crime scene. Limp yellow caution tape wraps pathetically around the perimeter of an empty playground. Dome-shaped jungle gym, dangling swings, merry-go-round, blue slide. I can't remember the last time I've been to one of these.

"Bonjour."

It's then that I see Jonah sitting on top of the monkey bars, shoes dangling off one side. He looks less Jonah-y, but in a good way. Like maybe he's decided to go wild and unbutton his top button, that sort of thing.

I cross the spongy mulch to look up at him. "Are you sure we should be doing this? It looks *kiiiiind* of off-limits."

"I assure you this playground has been sanitized to comply with the highest possible standards of cleanliness." I stare at him blankly. "I basically poured a bucket of sanitizer over everything."

"That seems . . . wasteful?"

"My summer trip to Paris was canceled. I know there are much bigger things, especially right now. But I won this scholarship to a program there and, well, it was sort of a once in a lifetime deal. So, yeah, I kind of needed to get out for a hot minute."

I nod, like I understand. "So then this is your *Arc de*"—I cock my head and shield my eyes from the waning sun— "what's the opposite of *Triomphe*."

"Defeat?" he offers gamely.

"Arc de Fail." I like that better.

He swings his feet back and forth like a little boy. "Well, climb aboard the Failure Ark, skippy."

I don't budge. "Two things. One—*skippy*?"

"It's a nautical term. Short for *skipper*."

"So that explains the boat shoes."

He pulls his chin back, all *Excuse me what?* "Boat shoes are a classic American style. Like Ralph Lauren."

"Uh-huh." I feel the corners of my mouth pull up ever so slightly. Because the funny thing I've noticed about Jonah is that sometimes he doesn't even know when he's being funny.

"There was a *two*?" he says.

"Two is, I'm watching you." I point my finger at him. I'm going for formidable.

His eyebrows skyrocket. "You think I'm just going to lunge at you? That I can't contain myself around the gravitational pull of Maxine Mauro? That I lose all self-control, restraint, and abstemiousness?"

He clutches his chest. And it's all fun and games. I mean, obviously. But also, what the hell is *abstemiousness*?

And I don't know him well enough to know his tells. To know if his lip twitches when he's trying not to laugh. Or if his ears are always pink. Or if the something behind his eyes is, in fact, something or nothing. Because it *feels* like it might be something.

"We're on a playground. Kindergarten etiquette applies. I'll keep my hands to myself." He makes it sound reasonable.

I nod once, satisfied. "Well, as long as that's settled. And as long as you'll clean the playground good as new after we leave."

I wipe my hands off on my black denim shorts. If this is the most rebellious teenage activity I partake in, then I figure I'm probably doing okay. I grip the sides of the ladder up to the monkey bars—the far side, just to be safe—still warm from the day's sun.

I forgot that there is no "grown-up" way to get to the top of monkey bars. I try planting my foot on the side to wedge my way up, but just as I push, my flip-flop slips and my chin knocks the top bar and I yelp.

Then Jonah's hand is wrapped around my wrist. It's cool and surprisingly strong. He's leaned practically all the way over, reaching across to me, and our eyes are nearly level. Bits of gold and green catch the late afternoon light. And it's a beat too long before I look down at our hands. Clasped together.

"Shit," I say.

"Shit," he says.

I withdraw my hand without another word, sliding back onto the top rung. It's silent as, this time, I remember that the way to get up on top of monkey bars is from underneath. I swing my feet up through a pair of the bars. My shirt slides up to my bra, exposing my bare stomach, and I pray that Jonah isn't looking as the blood rushes to my head. I elbow my way through and push up gracelessly so that finally I'm sitting seven feet in the air.

Jonah has scooted over to a safe distance again. We both stare straight ahead.

"It's okay." He breaks first. "It was just one touch. It was two seconds. We're fine."

"We're idiots," I say.

"I've been called worse."

I smile at that. He's probably right. Or probably wrong. Both seem just as likely.

But there's no rewind button. No turning back the clock. The moment's gone and what's done is done. There's a twist in the pit of my stomach that I can try my best to ignore as I pull out the miniature hand sanitizer tucked in my pocket and spread the gel over my palms while Jonah does the same. The whole thing is weird.

He's trying, at least. And I'm letting him try, which is . . . something. And even if he doesn't know it, seeing him takes away some of the anxiety sparked by my mom's note, by the recurring worry that has suddenly reared its ugly little head again that our life depends on balanced finances, and our finances? They might be starting to lose their balance again. So yes, does being around someone as Jonah-y as Jonah help ease my apprehension? Sure. Someone as sheltered and adorably nervous as Jonah—I wouldn't mind a bit of that rubbing off on me.

But then I touched him. And—hello—there is a whole other level of unease in play now and I guess the question is really whether one cancels out the other.

I shake my hands dry over the rails. "I'm sorry your trip got canceled," I tell him.

"*C'est la vie.*" He has a nice French accent.

I look sideways at him. Jonah's face is tan. There's a hint of blond peeking through his hair, a small constellation of freckles at the far point of his right cheek and across his nose.

"Why do you need a scholarship to go to Paris anyway? I mean, can't you just, like, go later?"

"Not for that program." He leans his weight back on his hands and I notice his elbows are double jointed, bending just a little too far the wrong way, and noticing something dumb like that actually makes me feel like I know him.

"I'm saving up for a business degree. My mom took over a business a few years ago and she had to learn everything while it was happening and it was . . . it was a lot. I bet I could learn how to franchise it. And someday when I start my own business, I'll know what I'm doing and I can hire people to help and I won't be gone all the time." Most of that plan was all me, but I'll admit that it was Arlo who pushed me to be specific about what I wanted. He told me everyone should act like the protagonist of their own life and that every great heroine needs a specific goal, not a mushy one.

"Max Mauro, famed tycoon. Has a nice ring to it."

"Maybe. I don't know." I kick off my flip-flops and let them plummet to the ground below. "It's more like . . . Okay, when I was seven, child protective services took me away from my mom. It was a whole thing. I set off a smoke alarm by burning a bag of popcorn in the microwave and a nosy neighbor found out I was home alone every day after school while my mom worked and then they took me and put me in foster care for a month until my mom could set up a plan to get me back."

"Wow. That sounds . . . wow. Were they nice at least? Is that a stupid question?"

"They were probably nice. I wouldn't know. I didn't talk to them for the entire month I was there."

Jonah turns his face to meet mine and his eyes crinkle at the corners. "You took a vow of silence at seven years old?"

"I can be pretty stubborn, I guess."

"You don't say."

I look down at the ground, which feels farther away than it should. "Anyway, my point is, I want to be successful enough, have enough money so that bad things like that can't happen to us anymore."

"I'm not sure it works like that." He turns his face so that he's once again in profile.

"What about your mom? You said you two like to watch Winter Robbins movies. Sounds like you actually get to do the crazy thing of—gasp—spending time together," I say.

The breeze ruffles the hair that's growing too long over the tops of his ears. I notice they aren't pink anymore.

"Jonah?"

"What?" he asks, coming to. "Oh, yeah, she's—yeah, she's cool."

I swallow the sense of something down. Earlier he'd seemed excited to talk about his mom, but now there was a definite wedge between me and the subject.

"And anyway," he says, but I think he forgets to finish the sentence. He just kind of spaces out all over again. And then, "You know . . . it's not Paris, but the view's not half bad."

Together, we look out. The sun is nothing more than

a line of gold behind a row of low-slung vacation rentals in the distance. Leaning palm trees are dark silhouettes against an orange-and-violet sky. Streetlights blink on. Somewhere up the 405, beyond view, is a measure of ocean so vast, I can never quite comprehend it. Like a math problem with no solution.

"There are definitely worse places to be stuck," Jonah says, looking not out at the horizon, but directly at me.

I wonder what my tells are.

Maybe there *are* worse places to be stuck, I think. But, when I consider my tiny apartment in Huntington Beach, my mom's and my toothbrushes side by side, a coffee table for her office, I think that some universes are bigger than others. And Jonah and I, we aren't really stuck in the same place at all.

One day later, I decide to initiate Jonah into my universe. "Trust me," I tell him. "I'm doing you a favor." I have the apartment to myself while Mom checks on the storefront, and I have the afternoon off and several hours to kill, plus a Wi-Fi connection that momentarily doesn't suck and, so, minus the risk of data overages.

"A T-shirt," Jonah says over FaceTime. "That's what's going to make you happy."

"No," I say. "That's what's going to make *you* happy." Jonah looks skeptical. "Okay, look, if I were forced to enter a . . . marathon for boats—"

"A regatta."

I pull a face. "You made up that word."

"It's Italian."

"As I was saying, if I were forced to sign up for a regatta, you'd be the first person I'd call." I take out a plastic barrel of neon-orange cheese puffs from the shallow closet we call a pantry and untwist the top because we buy this stuff in bulk.

"Thank you."

"But quarantine, now here is an area in which I have expertise. I've been training my whole life. You are speaking to the master." I give a small bow and then eat a cheese puff.

"And now I'm concerned you're convincing me to join a cult," Jonah says from the comfort of his bedroom, and I do mean comfort. There's a couch in there and an attached bathroom.

"Put on the T-shirt, Jonah."

It's kind of sweet that he steps off-screen to change his shirt, returning in one with the LA Rams logo on the front pocket.

"I didn't know you were into football," I say.

"I won it in an Instagram giveaway." He looks down at his new outfit. "I have to be honest, Max. It feels the exact same as my polo, but I look less put-together."

"That's the point. It's a state of mind. Prepare to do . . . nothing." I, for one, am fully prepared. I'm wearing a tie-dye shirt, my big gray sweatpants, and slippers with synthetic sheepskin lining the inside. Game on.

He closes his eyes and takes a deep breath.

"Step two," I instruct. "Sustenance." I wait until Jonah has had time to make the commute—yes, actual commute—from his bedroom down to his kitchen. There are stairs involved and it takes every ounce of self-control I have not to remark on the life-sized oil painting of a young Jonah that he passes in the hall. Here's what I can make out of Jonah's kitchen. An island, which isn't only reserved for tropical vacations apparently; a refrigerator big enough to hide not one but two dead bodies; and a bunch of shiny appliances that are probably really expensive and do only one specific thing each, like slice hardboiled eggs or fry zucchini—honestly I have no idea. "Okay, so like with all great chefs, I have a philosophy when it comes to cooking and it's this: If you aren't eating stuff your dentist would be mad about, you're not doing it right."

Jonah literally writes this down on a notepad.

"You'll need flour, sugar, milk, cocoa, more chocolate, preferably in the form of chips, but I'm not picky, and some baking soda and vanilla and whatever kind of oil you have. Got it?"

"Should I go ahead and preheat the oven?" he asks with the innocence of a young babe.

"God no, that would take forever."

On our opposite ends of the world, Jonah and I gather the same set of ingredients. I nod approvingly. "Now, dump them all in a coffee mug," I say.

"A coffee mug?"

I demonstrate mine, which is shaped like Winnie-the-Pooh's honey pot and acquired during that one ill-fated trip to Disneyland. Jonah selects a pretty blue-and-white one that he swears his sister made.

"Now we just pop it in the microwave for three minutes and voilà—chocolate mug cake." We click our microwave doors shut in sync and set our timers and then we just kind of stare at each other.

There are worse things.

"Were you ever mad at your mom for leaving you alone all the time?" he asks, a question I don't think anyone has ever asked me before.

"Yeah," I answer honestly. "For a while. Other kids had parents picking them up from school or bringing cupcakes for their birthday. I knew there were kids who got to do gymnastics at the Y and take swimming lessons, and I felt kind of trapped. I didn't have a way to get anywhere. It sucked."

"I feel kind of trapped now," he says. "This whole lockdown thing sucks."

"Totally sucks," I agree. "No parties, no formals, no reason to get dressed, let alone dressed up. I have a bomb dress hanging in my closet and nowhere to wear it to. Which sucks. "

"I miss restaurants," he says. "Takeout kind of sucks. My cooking sucks even more, though."

"Zoom classes are going to suck."

"Try being stuck for days on end with my stepmother. That sucks."

"I just started wearing a mask all day and trust me that—"

"Sucks," Jonah finishes for me.

The microwave beeps and we both break eye contact simultaneously.

"Hold that thought. We're not done with our culinary lesson yet," I warn.

I talk him through my famous nacho popcorn made spicy with crushed Flaming Hot Cheetos.

"Really, how you haven't received a Michelin star yet is beyond me." Jonah taste-tests his, which is sadly devoid of Cheetos.

"Do you at least have whipped cream?" I ask.

He rummages in his fridge and sticks his arm all the way to the back. "It's probably old."

"It's fine. It's just chemicals anyway."

"That's . . . comforting. For the cake?" he asks, shaking it.

I grab my own canister. "No, it's for our mouths. To 2020." I cheers him and then tip my head back and spray a big dollop of whipped cream straight into my open mouth. "The year in which everything sucks. Except for cake."

"Except," he says, mouth half full of whipped cream, "for you."

chapter ten

JONAH

"You may enter."

Olivia's voice is oddly sonorous, and for some reason a little British, and as I push open her bedroom door, I am assaulted by a truly baffling assortment of smells: clay earthenware, wet socks, sandalwood, something acidic (malt vinegar?), and the tang of leftover salmon.

She is in the middle of the room, her hands sliding up and down a hardening, misshapen mass spinning on a small wooden pedestal. She has no glasses on, her hair is streaming down around her face and shoulders, and she seems to be in a sort of spiritual trance, mumbling along to the tinkle of New Age music playing from her MacBook. It's two o'clock in the afternoon, though you'd never know it since the curtains are all drawn.

"What in the hell—" I start.

"The ancient art of pottery," she says, eyes half closed. "I received the kit yesterday from Amazon. It's my sixth new hobby since I returned, but I find this one particularly stimulating. I did order the ingredients for a charred

Mesopotamian flatbread. Might try that on an open firepit in the backyard tomorrow."

Discarded clothes have formed a new sedimentary layer across her entire bedroom . . . most of them tangled, deeply wrinkled, and either black, gray, or a lighter black.

"How did you use so many clothes?" I ask, amazed. "You don't even change."

"I try different arrangements for sleeping, then throw them off in overheated fits."

I push some jeans to the side and settle onto the couch—is that a french fry?—and turn back to my sister, who has since created the rudimentary shape of a vase, eyes still aflutter. I watch her with increasing concern. Olivia has always been a little eccentric, but things are escalating fast. The bathrobes, the cookies . . . yesterday she painted an accent wall in our basement.

"Have you considered taking a walk? Maybe a light jog at a time when there aren't a lot of people around—"

"Why?" She looks up at me, brow furrowing instantly.

It's surprisingly sharp . . . even for Olivia.

"No reason," I say quickly. "Kate wants me to put a grocery order in . . . you need anything?"

"Do you? Or just a visit from a certain *Maxine*."

She really drags out the name. Max is probably somewhere cringing.

"That would have been nice, but she's booked up, I guess. I checked. Only some dude named Claudio is available today. But apparently we urgently need lamb shanks and polenta for tonight . . . and it can't wait."

"Poor you. How *do* the Max visits work? Does she stand below the windowsill and cry, 'Jonah, Jonah, let down your hair'?"

I frown. "Are you okay? You seem particularly embittered today."

"And what if I'm not? The earnest young man in the throngs of courtship cares not for the plight of the world, nor for his older sister's heartache. He cares only for love and lust."

"Why are you talking like that?"

She nods toward the desk, where *Wuthering Heights* sits half open. Olivia has a habit of picking up the dialect of whatever book she's reading. We suffered badly through Chaucer.

"All right," I say. "What heartache? Did you actually have a girlfriend at school?"

"She was but a fever dream. There and gone. Now sheltered safely back in Delaware."

"What was her name?"

"Delaware. Her parents have an unusual affection for the state."

I rub my forehead. She really does make my brain hurt sometimes. "What happened?"

"I met her in Environmental Law. Delaware Von Dover. We connected instantly." Olivia is still swaying with the music. "I can almost feel her Swayze-ing my forearms as we speak."

"I have no idea what you're talking about."

"Shocking. But our affair was cut short."

"Why?"

She draws her hands back and examines her work. "The coronavirus."

"Ah."

"I told her I was vulnerable and had no choice but to cut the proverbial strings."

"I'm . . . sorry."

"She understood. And when I left for home, we made no promises to resume our relationship. For what is a promise in an uncertain world?"

She lifts the vase and heads for a small pottery oven plugged into the corner.

"Is that safe?" I ask, checking the room for fire alarms.

She nods toward the far wall, where nine other vases stand in a line, all expertly crafted and painted with animals and hieroglyphs. They look like legitimate ancient artifacts.

"When did you last sleep?" I say incredulously.

"No clue," she says, sounding like Olivia again. "The point is, I didn't *like* Delaware any less. It wasn't about our relationship. It was about a world going to shit, and I wasn't selfish enough to think that my hormonal desires overruled that. Timing matters."

She turns back to me, cleaning her hands on her shorts.

"And I'll take a box of cookies. The—"

"Chips Ahoy! chewy chocolate chip," I mutter. "Got it."

"Make it two. Now please exit my sanctuary . . . I must prepare my painting supplies."

I head for the door, stop, and look back at her. "I hope it works out with Delaware."

"Oh, I made her up, you idiot. Delaware Von Dover from Delaware? Really . . . it's like your brain stops working when you have a crush. It was a parable. I was at school. I had no time for flings."

"So—"

"So *keep your distance* from Max. Love story or not . . . give me the coronavirus and I'll kill you."

She shuts the door behind me and I sigh. Next time I'll just text her.

But her warning about Max lingers as I head downstairs. I want to say it's ridiculous. Of course I'm not going to get the coronavirus from *Max*. But . . . why? Because I know her? Because I really, really want to be close to her? The truth is . . . Max is out there. She's an essential worker and in the grocery store every single day and doing deliveries, and as shitty and unfair as it is, she is simply more likely to catch it than we are huddled up in the house. And Olivia knows that.

I know that. But it's Max. She's smart and careful and we're being careful too, minus a brief monkey bar incident, but . . . What if we weren't? What if she showed up at the house today and knocked on the door and said: "Jonah I like you too and want to be your girlfriend." That seems like a moment you kiss. What if *she* went in for a kiss . . . what would I do? Run away? Say no? It's *Max*. I can barely think straight when she's a disembodied head on my phone. I would definitely kiss her back.

And . . . Olivia probably knows that too.

So, yeah, I get her concern. We'll just have to avoid any temptations. Like, you know, being within ten feet of each other, because let's be honest, I would have kissed her on the monkey bars if she'd wanted to and . . . Shit. I really am an idiot.

I head downstairs to make sure Kate doesn't have any further additions, and I hear soft crying.

I jump off the last few steps and peek into Kate's home office. Sure enough, she is sitting at her desk, cell in front of her, and she's crying. I didn't even know she *could* cry.

"What is it?" I ask, feeling my heart lodge itself in my throat.

She looks up at me. "Your father isn't coming home."

The three of us are gathered around the kitchen table. Dad is on Zoom, wearing a crisp suit in his hotel room (I'm pretty sure he sleeps in one), Olivia is picking at her teeth, and Kate is alternating between long breaths and then sudden, violent bursts of prosecutorial arguments.

"But why can't you just work from here—" she starts.

"Company policy," Dad cuts in calmly. "They just want us to wait it out for a bit. Besides, the merger isn't done. Andy is sick and I'm not, so I've got to run the show over here. Once I'm cleared we're resuming meetings—socially distant—and getting this done. Besides, I can't just ship out when Andy is sick. I've got to see it through."

"For how long?" I ask, trying hard to be more understanding than Kate.

I'm annoyed but not at all surprised. I love my dad, but he's a company man to the core. Not to mention Andy is his best friend. I try to remind myself Dad doesn't have COVID and is fine. But a part of me remembers that my dad makes bad decisions too. Or at least rushed ones.

"I don't know," he says. "Obviously if I test positive at some point we're stuck, but . . ."

Thanks, Dad.

"It's ridiculous!" Kate says. "You feel fine. You can close the deal remotely . . ."

I know why *she's* upset. She signed up for this deal for Pops . . . not for Olivia and me. Especially me. She likes Olivia. But now she's stuck even longer without a reminder of *why* this neurotic teenaged boy is sitting at her dinner table. I can see her eyes flicking to me.

"I'm sorry, everyone," Dad says. "I have to stay for a while longer. It'll be fine."

It'll be fine. I hate that saying . . . probably because it's the antithesis of anxiety's go-to mantra of: You're fucked. And

I'm thinking now. About Dad catching COVID in Spain. About Olivia getting it here. About what I would do if either of them got really sick or worse.

I can feel an ache forming at the back of my head. A tickle in the throat.

"You all right?" Olivia asks quietly, while Dad tries to calm Kate down.

"Yeah . . . fine." She eyes me, and I feel myself spacing. I can't listen to Kate yelling anymore. "Excuse me," I manage, heading for my room. "Dad, I'll call you later."

I make it to my bathroom and shut the door. I had a call with Dr. Syme yesterday, but his advice seemed a couple weeks late. He wanted me to remember my breathing strategies and challenge my fears, but those fears keep changing. My routines are gone. No organized sports six times a week to get my heart pumping. No daily itinerary to keep my brain preoccupied. And now no Dad, the calmest man alive, for who knows how long. All the things I used to fight my anxiety are gone except for my breathing tools and mindfulness, and to be honest, I really suck at both of them.

Before I know it, I am retching air over the toilet, trying to breathe, feeling my heart pounding, cell phone beside me, ready to call 911 and tell them I am dying because maybe this time it's for real. There is always a maybe.

It's a doozy. The attack subsides about twenty minutes later, but it feels like twenty hours, and I sit on the bathroom floor with my back against the cabinet and try to remember what it was like before this. Before the attacks started. Before they led to . . . everything else.

The world teeters again.

Jonah: You busy?

Max: Not really. Just did my last delivery, so that's a bonus. What's up?

Jonah: You sure? I don't want to bother you if you're busy.

Max: That's uncharacteristically thoughtful. Everything OK?

Jonah: Yeah. Fine.

Jonah: Well, not really.

Max: ???

Jonah: I probably didn't mention this, because, you know, machismo. But I get panic attacks. Like a lot. I don't even know why I'm telling you. Is it too late to delete this?

Max: Yep. And I can't possibly talk to you anymore, ye of unchecked anxiety

Jonah: I'm serious.

Max: So am I. I always preferred emotionally catatonic guys who bottle up their rage.

Jonah: Oh.

Max: Even for a text, I thought that was pretty obviously sarcastic. You can talk to me.

Jonah: My dad's stuck in Madrid. Maybe for months.

Max: Yikes. Is he okay?

Jonah: So far. I don't know . . . it just kind of put me over the top.

Max: I know what you mean.

Jonah: Thanks again for meeting me at the park. Sorry if I made you uncomfortable.

Max: All right . . . this is way too much self-awareness. Who is this?

Jonah: Pitiable post panic attack Jonah Stephens.

Max: Well I've got to head back home. Talk soon?

Jonah: Sounds good.

The day is slowly dying as I lie back on the bed, phone propped on my chest. But a little knot works its way back in. We still barely know each other. Did I really need to mention the anxiety? Do I look like a charity case? A cry for help? I chew on a nail.

Ashley was Miss Positivity. She never wanted to talk about any of this—anxiety, panic attacks. She always redirected it to something else. "Maybe you ate something bad" or "You're probably just worried about that test."

What if that's the normal response? What if people don't want to hear about this stuff? What if I just gave Max another reason to stay *over there*?

"Shit," I murmur, flinging the phone onto the carpet.

I lie here, wallowing—yes, I know I'm wallowing—and ignore a few beeps. Carlos has been trying to get me to leave the house and come kick the ball around, despite the many reminders that my apparently hypocritical dictator won't let me leave. The phone starts to ring. I sigh deeply.

"Carlos, man," I groan, rolling off the bed and checking the screen.

It's Max. I scoop it up, fumbling it all the way to my ear. "Hello?"

"From here. Hey, have you ever heard of Windex?"

I scramble to my window and there.

She.

Is.

Max is sitting up on the hood of her rusty red Civic, ripped jeans and worn-out shoes, sunglasses on, blue mask I haven't seen before looped around her neck, phone pressed to her ear.

". . . Hi . . ." I manage.

"Were you ignoring me?"

I pull the window open, sliding the fading greeting above my head. "Definitely not."

"I figured you could use a visit. But stay up there this time. No more monkey business."

I think I'm supposed to laugh, but I'm leaning halfway out the window, and she's taking a sip of iced coffee through a straw, and I have now forgotten how to do conversation.

"You drove all the way here? For me?"

"I was in the neighborhood, as they say . . . and I needed some air." She takes another sip and leans back against the glass. "So next week is back to reality, I guess, with school and everything."

"Virtual reality. Does that count?"

"You know, I thought virtual reality would involve more hover cars."

"Yet another disappointment this year," I say.

"Speaking of disappointments, did I tell you my spring formal dress was red? I look good in red."

"I bet you do." I'm still leaning pretty far out the window, braced on my elbows. For some reason, talking like this feels closer. Even closer than last night. Her voice is in my ear, and she's right there, framed by green grass and palm trees and the fountain cherub and the bright ginger halo of the last remnants of sun.

"I'm trying to distract you, by the way," she says. "How am I doing?"

"A-plus in my book."

She sighs. "It all feels kind of petty and stupid, though. *Oh no, I don't get to wear my red dress and pretend to be in love with Rick for photographic posterity and—*"

I cough. "Rick what now?"

I'm pretty sure I can see her flushing from here. "We were supposed to go together before . . . well . . . the emoji incident. I didn't technically find a replacement yet. You?"

"I had . . . thought about finding one," I say, trying to also subliminally say . . . *you?*

"Ours was supposed to have been next week."

"I'm not really cheering you up, am I? I totally suck at moral support, FYI."

"Actually, wallowing is kind of the only thing that helps," I admit.

She stares up at the sky. "I can't believe that it's just *over*, you know? I know we get another year . . . it's not like the seniors, who don't even get a goodbye. But what's going to happen next year? What if we don't get to go back to normal? Can you imagine? Ugh. Okay, no more wallowing. I retire."

"I'd still like to see the dress."

Max laughs. "Shut up. You get me in all my work attire glory." She pushes the mask over her mouth, muffling her voice. "I get to wear this on deliveries now. If that's not fashion, I don't know what is."

"Max," I say, "will you go out with me?"

She lowers the mask. "What?"

"Like . . . be my girlfriend. You know. Formally. But also virtually, I guess."

"Is this because I mentioned Rick—"

"It's because of *you*," I cut in, leaning so far out the window, I might be joining the koi soon. "I've wanted to ask you from the second—for a while now."

She stares at me for a moment, and then takes a long sip of her iced coffee. "Maybe."

"Maybe . . ."

"I need you to meet my friends first. It's like a firewall."

"Done. Not to brag . . . but I kind of kick ass at interviews."

"We'll see about that. I trust them implicitly. If they don't approve, then we will quickly part ways. Got it?"

"I *like* you, Max."

"I think that was implied," she says, and I see a smile tugging on the corner of her lips, even from here.

"Like, *I'm about to literally fall head over heels out this window* like you."

"Please don't." She chews on her lip. "You can join our next game night."

"And if they love me?"

The corner of her mouth pulls the rest into a smile again. "Then maybe."

chapter eleven

MAX

You are now joining a meeting . . .

"You look nice," Dannie says to me. On-screen, she's tied her red bandanna around the base of a messy bun. There's something that looks suspiciously like mushy avocado stuck in her hair.

We set the Zoom meeting for ten minutes before we asked Jonah to join because obviously something like this requires a briefing. Imani has just kicked her scrawny older brother out of her chair, but Big Paw and Sweets are still milling around like background actors. Not that Imani thinks anything of it. She told me once she rarely gets to shower without someone barging in to use the bathroom. "Four people, one toilet, just how it is." She'd shrugged. "Sometimes we get into whole conversations." Was it weird to feel a tiny bit jealous of that? Like, yeah, I know, there should be a time and a place, but at least in her place, there's company.

I hold out the hem of my black-and-white striped T-shirt with its fat cat enamel pin stuck on the pocket and a damp braid draped over my collarbone. "I look regular," I say to Dannie.

"I didn't say you don't look nice *regularly*," she retorts. "I'm just giving you a compliment. You know, to boost your confidence."

Which only makes me wonder whether I look like somebody who needs a confidence boost. "Just be cool, okay?"

"I'm low-key offended," Imani says.

"Yeah," agrees Dannie. "When are we ever *not* cool? I mean, look at me." She slides on a pair of oversized sunglasses and pushes her lips into a pout.

"See?" Imani gestures at Dannie. "It's going to be fine. You act like we've never interacted with human beings before."

"I just need a second opinion. That's it." I mean, don't I? I've never been known to rush anything, let alone my feelings. I've got a good head on my shoulders. Mom says she didn't even have to babyproof, that's how careful and rational I am. But then again, apparently not careful and practical enough not to have practically held hands with Jonah over a set of monkey bars and—okay—it was only for a second, but I don't even want to *say* what I thought during that second. (Fine, I liked it.) So, yeah, maybe I've got some hang-ups. Who doesn't?

"*Oh*, okay, so something's seriously wrong with this boy." Imani leans in like this is the part where it's about to get good. "You're embarrassed of him. Is he a high school dropout? Does he wear matching sweaters with his mom? With cats? Do you remember when you had a thing for that kid who responded to questions through his puppet?"

"His name was Marcus and he was very ta—I'm not embarrassed."

"I didn't think you *got* embarrassed." Dannie pounds her puffed-out chest. "I'm Max. Don't call me Maxine. Soooooo tough."

"Actually, I think something's come up." I hike a thumb over my shoulder.

"No way, nuh-uh." Imani wags her finger. "You can't back out now. We're doing this. And don't expect to be let off easy. We're in it. This is about to be a *shared* experience."

I do not like the sound of that.

"Well, we've still got two minutes until go time," says Dannie, who is now picking at the clump of food in her hair. I make a mental note to check in with her during the day more often because Scarlett may be adorable, but at least I get fifteen-minute breaks. "Maybe now's a good time?"

"A good time for what?" I ask.

"While we're all *here*." Dannie lifts her eyebrows. "You know . . . *together*." She is overenunciating every word as though she's still in talking-to-toddlers mode.

"Are you okay?" I look at Imani to see if she has a clue, but I'm suddenly remembering how weird they were on our last call. Like they were in cahoots. "Wait a minute, what are you talking about?" This better not be about Jonah.

Imani puffs out her cheeks. "It's—okay, fine, maybe you're right."

"Of course I'm right," says Dannie, who actually usually is right.

"I—"

Just then a fourth black box materializes on-screen. "Oh, oh! Shhhhh!" Dannie peels off the sunglasses and flaps her hand.

A beat passes. The conversation dies. The suspense kills us.

And then there's Jonah. Eyes that turn down a touch at the corners. Nose that's just a little bit crooked. Freckled. A dimple peeking out from inside the smile crease of his left cheek. And I'm surprised to realize that I've noticed all these details before, that they've been mentally stored in the Jonah Stephens file that's only recently appeared on the subliminal desktop inside my head.

I don't know how to feel about this.

"Hi!" all three of us say in unison. Only we give the word five times the number of *I*'s and sound like a group of over-caffeinated camp counselors.

"Hi," Jonah says like an actual normal person.

"Glad you could join us. I'm Dannie," she says, taking the lead. "And this is Imani and obviously you know Max."

"Obviously." Jonah grins so big, his face has the vibe of a human neon sign. Honestly, if I were the type of girl who blushed, I just might.

"Do you like games?" Dannie claps her hands together. Oh boy.

"Excuse my friend," says Imani. "Dannie's been spending way too much time with her sister. She's almost three."

"That's true." Dannie nods gravely. "I'm in desperate need of adult conversation. Oh my god, I sound like my mother already."

"Funny," says Jonah. "I'm having the exact same problem. My sister is obsessed with board games, refuses to change out of her pajamas, and needs a nap to be remotely functional."

"Aw." Dannie tilts her head, all *this is adorable.* "How old is she?"

"Nineteen."

Dannie and Imani both laugh, for real, and not because I asked them to. I can tell the difference. And what I'm thinking is how Jonah Stephens actually asked me to be his girlfriend and how I'm not saying yes. But maybe I'm also not saying no.

"Did everyone download the app from the link I sent around?" Imani scans us for approval. We've come prepared because let's just say that when it comes to Imani, the apple doesn't fall that far from Sweets's tree, and we know to step in line. "Good. The game is Pictionary. Now we need teams."

"I call Dannie." Jonah raises his hand.

"Excuse me?" I cross my arms, curious about where this is headed.

"I'm sorry." He grimaces. "But some of us take game night seriously."

"*I* take game night seriously," I say.

"Don't take this the wrong way, but I have concerns," Jonah says gently.

"*What* concerns?"

"Like . . . pop culture concerns? Okay, so you'd never seen *Greed and Glory* and you had no idea who Winter Robbins even was and—"

"Wait, what now?" Imani busts out.

"Oh god, don't tell me you didn't tell them either?" My silence speaks for itself. "Max is all chummy with Arlo Oxley, one of her customers who won a freaking Oscar for producing *Greed and Glory* and allegedly dated Winter Robbins and she was completely oblivious to all of it. Seriously."

"Darn it, I knew you were just trying to make me feel better, Max." Dannie crosses her arms. "Your job *is* more fun than playing Sneaky Snacky Squirrel ten times a day."

"Thank you!" Imani raises her hands. "I've been saying this for years! I swear, sometimes it's like she's living underneath a rock. Please! Will you educate our girl? Maybe she'll listen to you."

"And hi," Dannie pipes up. "Did you not think about your—oh yeah—film crazy friend over here? Allow me to introduce myself."

"Hey, *I'm* film-crazy," adds Jonah. The two air high-five. It's ridiculous.

"I have a list," Dannie tells him earnestly. "You know

what? I've got your email now. I'm sending it to you after. You know she still hasn't seen *Inception*?"

Jonah looks at me like I've been spending my time kicking puppies instead.

"Okay, okay, I don't see how any of this impacts my game night draft score."

"Also," he continues, "I used to babysit my neighbor's toddler and it involved a *lot* of coloring. Like a lot. Dannie the sister-wrangler probably has pretty finely tuned art skills. So . . . yeah . . . Dannie."

"He's not wrong," Dannie points out.

"Yes, but aren't you supposed to want to be teamed up with *me*?"

"It's nothing personal." He shrugs. "I still like you."

"I see how it is." Imani shifts her weight, settling into her chair in front of T. rex. "This boy came to *play*. I like that. Come on, Max." She cracks her neck. "Let's show them how it's done. The category is idioms."

I arch an eyebrow at Jonah. So that's how it's going to be. *Game on.*

Dannie starts us off. She draws two trees, one with an X through it and a dog standing next to it.

"Barking up the wrong tree!" Jonah guesses in less than fifteen seconds. The two of them do some kind of completely embarrassing victory dance, but Imani and I aren't about to be scared off.

We're up next. Imani rubs her hands together. "Bring it, Mauro."

I scribble out a square with a diagonal line through one side and a pair of scissors beside it. "Cutting corners," Imani shouts louder than necessary and faster than Jonah had for his turn. We get the point and she does a *whoa* move. The gloves are off. Which, yes, would actually make a pretty good Pictionary idiom, come to think of it.

Jonah makes a truly godawful attempt at "crying over spilled milk," which causes Dannie to yell "Fudgsicles!" in frustration, making it official that she should take some time off from babysitting.

Imani crushes a drawing of "under the weather," prompting Jonah to slow-clap because, really, that's impressive. After a streak that includes "piece of cake," "costs an arm and a leg," "penny for your thoughts," and "hit the sack," Dannie and Jonah's team is up by one. If they get this next attempt, they win.

Dannie sticks her tongue out of the side of her mouth, concentrating, while she sketches a stick person standing on . . . on a cliff . . .

"Cliff hanger!" Jonah bounces in his seat.

She shakes her head, time ticking, and inks an arrow swooping down . . . down . . .

"Going overboard!" he tries again.

Another headshake.

. . . into waves.

And in the waves, Dannie draws . . . hearts.

"Five seconds," Imani warns.

Dannie holds up the picture and then she jabs her finger

and, if I'm not mistaken, it's in *my* direction. "You can't do that!" yells Imani.

Just as Jonah blurts out "Falling in love."

And Dannie snaps, and cheers, "Bingo!"

Jonah clears his throat and I find out another thing the two of us don't have in common. While I am not a girl who blushes, he is, for sure, a boy who does.

To their credit, my friends make no comment.

In fact, one might even say that they're being cool.

"That was fun." Dannie caps her pen. "We should do it again sometime."

"Absolutely," says Jonah, and he seems like he genuinely means it.

"Scarlett wakes up at the crack. I've got to get to bed." Dannie yawns.

"Or . . . hit the hay?" Jonah offers. I'd have drawn with a hammer and a stack of scratchy lines and, okay, I don't know if Imani would have gotten that. "I'm sorry. I hate myself. Ugh. Ignore me," he says.

But Imani gives him one of her signature big, toothy smiles, and it's impossible not to feel at least a little bit good after getting one of those.

One by one they leave the meeting until it's just me and Jonah looking into each other's eyes thinking this isn't a big deal, but also maybe, just maybe it kind of is.

"So?" he says with that dimple suddenly deciding to join the party.

I think I know what he's asking, but I'm not ready to

answer yet. After all, I'm a girl whose most recent relationship ended in emojis. "So . . . I've been thinking . . ."

I watch Jonah's expression lift, and my stomach knots. I'm so not good at these kinds of things.

"About what?" he prompts.

Our usual group text chain pops up on-screen, distracting me.

Imani: He's cool with us.

Dannie: I think he's cute. He's preppy, but like. Okay, he looks like he sails on the weekends, but he's definitely going to sink soon.

"About . . ." I hesitate.

Imani: Yeah. Or like he's got a sweater around his waist, but it has *Rick and Morty* on it.

"About . . . Winter," I say. And just like that I've taken the easy way out.

A flicker of something passes across Jonah's face, as quick as a shooting star, blink and I'd have missed it.

"I don't even know why it's bugging me so much," I say, building steam. "I just don't know why someone that famous, that successful, would go—poof!—missing."

He relaxes. His hair doesn't look so combed anymore. "It's definitely weird."

The adrenaline is being leeched from my body, and my eyelids are already starting to get heavy. Jonah Stephens has nice teeth. I bet he flosses every single night.

· · ·

"You know," he says. "There's only one way to find out."

"You promise that you'll do the talking?" I ask the next morning, balancing my phone under my chin as I coax open my trunk and rummage for Arlo's one paltry grocery bag.

"*Yes*, for the last time, I'll do the talking." I agreed to FaceTime Jonah once I arrived and now he sits spinning in his desk chair. It's making me kind of sick. "Since when are you so nervous, anyway?"

I slam the trunk closed and my whole car threatens to fall apart. Arlo's street is quiet. I leave my car blocking the drive knowing no one here is trying to leave any time soon.

"I want him to be happy, that's all." I peer down into the phone, a view that I have to admit I'm getting sort of used to.

"Then"—Jonah puts on his lawyering tone—"maybe this is exactly what he needs—to talk about his feelings."

"Or"—I serve it right back—"maybe he *doesn't* want to talk about his feelings."

"Some people like talking about their feelings, Max."

I adjust the bag over my wrist and stuff my keys into my front pocket. "And what's that supposed to mean?"

"Nothing." He stops spinning, thank god. "Just—you know—as a kid whose parents have helped pay a therapist's mortgage a time or two, I'm saying it can be healthy." He tries to brush it off like we don't both know what he's referring to: me talking about *my* feelings. For him.

"Right. Well," I say, cutting past this topic. "Just so long as we're clear."

Jonah has a kid-on-Christmas grin and it makes me want to roll my eyes and give him presents all at the same time. "Look at us," he says, bouncing. "We're like a crime-solving duo. We're like Sherlock and Watson. Batman and Robin. Scully and Mulder. Stabler and Benson."

"I caught two out of four." I walk the gentle slope up the drive just as a furry black streak comes bounding out to meet me.

"Chester!" I scratch the giant poodle behind his ears and, as usual, he gently stands up and puts his front paws on my shoulders because this is a dog that likes to go in for real hugs. I let my face nuzzle into his curls and breathe in his vaguely sawdust-y smell. He looks dapper in a new bow tie—navy and pink flamingo—and I don't speak dog, but I can tell he's feeling himself. He hops down and I look up to see Arlo already waiting for me on the porch. "How'd you know I was on my way?"

"I finally figured out the little app." Arlo brandishes his phone and points to the screen. "It was like watching a very slow car chase." His eyes widen. "No explosions, but still quite suspenseful. And here you are. Just like it said."

I approach and set the grocery bag on the porch, a safe distance from where Arlo stands, before retreating. "So you're finally embracing *technology*, I see." And clear my throat pointedly. *A-hem.*

"Hello, Mr. Oxley!" Jonah yells from the screen. "It's me, Jonah Stephens again."

Arlo leans forward. His nose scrunches up as he tries to

fumble for a pair of spectacles in his vest pocket. "The boy in the box?"

"A stowaway," I explain.

"Mr. Oxley, hi again. It's truly an honor to meet you, even virtually. The truth is . . ." He stumbles. "Well, I was wondering if you might indulge a few questions, from a fan?"

"Like an interview?"

"You've probably been interviewed a lot," I say. What if he's sick of interviews?

"Not in such a long time." Arlo pulls his chin in and frowns, though there's a new twinkle in his eye. I exhale, mollified. Maybe it's hard to no longer be the center of attention after so many people cared about your opinion for so long.

"Mr. Oxley, I can't tell you how much your movies meant to me and my family growing up. I've seen all of them and frankly, I think the fact that *Summer Moon* didn't win Best Picture is a national tragedy. I don't care if my dad disagrees." He takes a breath and I see that Arlo has gone soft around the eyes. "I just—I have to tell you that when it comes to my favorite, *Greed and Glory*, I—well, I went down a bit of a rabbit hole," says Jonah.

Arlo looks at me, concerned.

"He means on the internet."

Arlo nods, showing visible relief.

"And, as far as I can tell, you were the last person to have ever been photographed with the actor known as Winter Robbins." I hold my breath. Of course I knew this was coming. "You were . . . close to him," Jonah's continuing more uncertainly now, "close enough to see his talent and want him to keep working . . . maybe in one of your other films. And I'm just wondering, well, it's become a sort of mystery."

I tell myself I wouldn't keep digging if I didn't genuinely believe that when Arlo said he preferred happy endings that it meant somehow he wanted one for himself too. "I think what Jonah's asking is, did—um, did something happen between you and Winter? Were you involved, you know, romantically?"

Arlo walks back with his hand on his thinning white hair and plops onto a wooden bench beside his door. For a split second, I'm worried we've upset him and that he's going to tell us to leave.

But instead he says, "A lot *didn't* happen. That's the problem."

Oh. Wait. "What do you mean?" I ask.

His look is far away. "I guess there's no point in secrets anymore." There's a long—some would say *dramatic*—pause. "Winter was my great love. The kind movies are made about. We met shortly after he'd begun filming when I was on set and he had these eyes the color of maple syrup that—" Arlo chuckles softly. "Well . . . nobody should have eyes like that. Oh, he was this cool, macho guy, such gravitas, but he could play a mean guitar ballad, had a beautiful voice that would make your heart melt. He'd listen to a song once and play it. It was uncanny. He was a live wire. And that first day we met and we just . . . we just knew."

"Wow," Jonah says wistfully.

I have to wonder if some of this is the rose-colored glasses of years gone by, but I suppose that it doesn't really matter. "Did he break your heart?" I make my voice quieter.

Arlo's smaller than he's ever seemed before, and I immediately regret my question. "Quite the contrary," he says. "We'd only been going steady—I don't know what you kids call it these days—for a couple months," he continues, and I'm glad the screen is pointed away so that I don't have to look at Jonah right then, because we're not calling it anything, not yet. "But things were hot and heavy, I guess you'd say." He winks. "But I was being shipped off to a shoot in France that I couldn't miss. And we were trying to be reasonable. We didn't make any promises. A month before I was set to come home, he called me and told me he tested positive for HIV. This was the late eighties, mind you. Everyone was still terrified of AIDS, especially in our community. I was abroad and at that time the president was putting a travel ban that said people with HIV couldn't come into the country, and even though people should have known better, many still believed you could catch the disease from simple things like drinking out of a public water fountain. Young men got sick and would return to apartments from the hospital to find all of their belongings thrown out on the street. Just a few years earlier there had been months where

I was visiting dying friends in the hospital every weekend. I attended five memorial services in one year. And so he told me he had HIV and I felt . . . everything. You name it. Fear, first. But then I got tested . . . and I was negative. And that fear became hurt because I thought he didn't wait for me. I waited for him, but he didn't wait for me. Now I don't even know if that part was true. We didn't know the things we know now. But instead of caring for him, I lashed out. I was angry with him for letting this happen, for all of it, I cut him off. Cold turkey. Just like that. By the time I came to my senses, he'd left Los Angeles and gone home to be with family. There weren't cell phones. There wasn't email. He wasn't even Winter Robbins anymore. And I had no way to track him down. So." He shrugs. "It was kaput."

"Where did his family live?" Jonah asks. "Miami?"

"No, no, that's where he was born, but he was from the middle of the state somewhere. Swamp country. I don't remember the name of the town." He sighs, slow and rasping, like leaves over concrete. "I wished for many years to see him again. To apologize for how I'd reacted. To get that second chance. But we all must live with our decisions. I have no idea if he's even alive."

A silence falls over the porch for a moment, broken only by a rapid-fire staccato of someone typing like a hundred and fifty words per minute. On the screen, I see Jonah feverishly working away at something on his computer and I think: *Seriously, Jonah? Right now? What could possibly be so important?*

"Maybe we can find him," I say, trying to steer Arlo's focus from Jonah.

Oh god. Jonah and I went over this. *Do not say anything about looking for Winter!* Because we have zero clues and we don't want to get his hopes up and yeah Arlo is looking at me and if his hopes are as high as his bushy white eyebrows I'm screwed.

"Just . . . you know . . . we were going to try," I say. "If he's alive. I mean who knows."

I don't even want to look at my phone because I am really going off-script here, but I glance down because I need some backup stat.

Jonah looks up sharply from inside the phone. "Arlo," he says with a new kind of authority that is actually pretty attractive. "One way or another, we'll find out what happened to Winter. I can promise you that."

I fully expect Arlo to tell us to leave it alone or, you know, stop digging up his skeletons, but instead he just smiles. "That would be nice."

I exchange a furtive look with Jonah. Yeah. We're in it now.

chapter twelve

JONAH

I wake to a gentle rapping on the window. No . . . wait . . . that one was a bang. Then what might be splintering glass. I roll out of bed and run to the window, expecting a flock of deranged pigeons.

Instead, I find Carlos F. Santi.

He's standing next to the fountain in a pair of soccer shorts, runners, and no shirt, which is his modus operandi, since he has a six-pack and no sense of basic human civility. We've been best friends since we were five, and are about as different as functionally possible, but we've never even had a fight. This is the longest I've ever gone without seeing him . . . two whole weeks.

"Dude!" I shout, sliding the window up and looking down at him. "Why are you trebuchet-ing my house?"

"Why did you write 'hello from here' on your window?" Carlos counters.

I really should clean that off. "Never mind that. What happened to texting people?"

"You don't answer me."

"I do so—"

"Correctly," Carlos cuts in. "By saying yes, Carlos, I will come hang out."

"Do you watch the news?"

"Hell no."

"But you *have* heard there's a global pandemic going on."

He is now trying to pet a koi fish. He gets easily distracted. "Once or twice."

"And you do understand the gist of it? I can't just come hang out . . . Olivia's here, man."

"And she's immunally composted. I know."

"Points for effort. The fact is I can't just come *hang out.*"

"Well . . . can't we sit outside? Like sixty feet apart or whatever it is? I need to tan."

"Sixty feet might be excessive. And you already look like a bronze statue."

"How do you think I maintain the base?" he says, staring directly at the sun. "You have to treat your body like a temple. I bet you haven't done a push-up in weeks, have you?"

I pause. "Yes?"

"Come on."

He walks onto the lawn, rolls his already short shorts up even higher, and plops down onto his back, tanning in my front yard. I have a backyard with a pool and lawn chairs and am about to suggest that alternative, but I think Olivia is out there cooking another flatbread over the chiminea, and I don't want to risk bringing anyone around her.

So, I am soon sprawled out in the front yard a mere sixteen feet or so away from Carlos, feeling my decidedly unbronzed skin frying under the midday sun.

"Did I mention I hate tanning?" I mutter.

"Do you know they closed the tennis club? Tennis, bro. You *have* to stay away from each other in tennis." Carlos flips over to his stomach, where he is muffled by the grass. "I hate 2020 already."

"School starts on Monday anyway."

"I can barely stay awake when I'm in real class. Now I'll have a bed beside me! And they want me to just *not* take a nap? Maybe we should get together for classes—"

"Carlos."

"Shit. I keep forgetting. So . . . the message in the window," he says, rolling onto his back again and looking at me. "What's that about? Who are you saying hi to? The neighbor? Isn't it just some old lady who smokes like seven packs a day?"

I sigh deeply. "No. It's not for Mrs. Clodden. There's . . . a girl. Max."

"No way." He sits up, grinning. "You're dating someone—"

"No. I mean . . . I asked her out a few days ago."

"Why didn't you tell me!"

"She didn't exactly say yes."

Carlos looks at me for a moment, as if trying to work it out. "So . . . she rejected you . . ."

"Temporarily? Maybe. I'm unclear."

"Oh. That sucks, man. I thought the sign thing was pretty cute—"

"She's considering," I say with a touch of defensiveness.

Carlos lies back down, centering himself to the sun. His thick black hair is still cut into a perfect fade, and his annoyingly chiseled features are now adorned with a perfect dappling of stubble. "That's weird. Me, I like to think fast. I just follow my rock-hard gut."

"You should try using your rock-hard brain. You've had three boyfriends in the last six months."

"So what? I like selection. You know how they say 'we're like two peas in a pod'?"

"Yes . . ."

"Well, it's wrong. There are multiple peas."

I stare up at the clouds. "That's. . . . actually true."

"Listen, if you really like her, call her up. Say: Max, are you on board or not? This ship is about to sail."

"That is literally the worst advice I've ever heard."

Carlos laughs. "So you want to go play soccer or what?"

"No. Go put a shirt on and stay home. And don't talk to any strangers on the way."

"Fine, Dad. How are you doing, anyway? With the being a little crazy stuff."

I feel a pang at the word *Dad*. I think of mine, holed up in Madrid. We spoke again last night and he said he was feeling fine and would be free to leave his hotel room soon. "Nothing to worry about, buddy," he had said with his usual easy smile. I firmly disagreed.

I worry about nothing routinely. *This* is definitely not nothing.

"They're called anxiety disorders . . . but terrible. Thank you for asking."

"Anything I can do?" he asks, standing up and stretching.

"No. Well . . . yes. Don't tell anyone about Max."

"I already posted something on IG."

"Carlos—"

He grins, patting the phone in his pocket. "Joking. Let me know how it goes. Oh . . . there has been talk of secret parties lately. Just, like, people we know. Totally safe. You interested?"

"*Go.*"

Carlos laughs again and heads down the street at a languorous pace. Mrs. Clodden watches him go, smoking her seven hundredth cigarette today and leaning to take in the view as long as possible.

From: Jonah Stephens <Jonah.Stephens03@gmail.com>

To: John Stephens <johnstephens@tjm.com>

Date: April 9, 2020

Subject: Touching Base

Hey Dad,

Just checking in. Figured you're getting bored stuck in a hotel room all day. Everything is fine here. Olivia is on to painting, which is good, because I have three vases in my room now and I'm sick of flatbread. She's probably painting a Rembrandt as we speak. To be honest, the flatbread was delicious.

Why is she so damn good at everything? Clearly, one of us is adopted.

It's her, right? You can tell me.

Anyway, wish you were here . . . we could all use the moral support.

-J

P.S. What's your temp? Did you get tested again? Still negative, right?

I read it back and sigh. I was trying to keep it casual, but it really fell off at the end there. I consider sending a less neurotic follow-up, but whatever, my dad knows me by now.

I head downstairs for dinner.

Olivia and Kate are already sitting there, talking and laughing and just being the *best* of friends. Their relationship is a source of great contention between Olivia and me . . . because she's a traitor.

We've been eating outside a lot, but it's gray and misty and tonight they're at the kitchen table—a huge, live edge oak table that I'm pretty sure cost as much as a new car. My dad was going to get me said new car last year . . . and then Kate said: "Young men should work for their first vehicle" and gave him a whole speech about character. She's evil, but she's a great lawyer.

I still ride a bike.

We are having duck a l'orange tonight with walnut pecan salad . . . all of the ingredients ordered fresh today. Unfortunately Max was booked, so Claudio brought it again.

By force of habit—and extreme boredom—I did look out the window anyway when he showed up, and he saw my *hello* on the window and laughed and waved and this is my life now.

I take a bite of duck—it's utterly delicious, but I refuse to admit it—and sit abjectly on my distant end of the table. It's ridiculous, of course. Olivia may be a traitor, but that's better than a petulant toddler. But in fairness, Kate *has* quashed my dreams of a dog and a car, and generally seems to treat me with barely concealed disdain, and so it seems only fair that I disdain her back.

But truthfully, I disliked her from the second she nodded curtly at me and said: "Jonah, I presume?" She was in the picture six months after Mom. They were *married* at ten. I've heard about rebounds, but this was like one of those little rubber balls that rebounds right into your windpipe. It was just . . . fast. I needed that chair to be empty for a little while longer. Kate is sitting in it now, laughing. And she can never fill it. Not for me.

I realize they are both staring at me and I choke down a walnut. "What?"

"I asked if you're ready for classes to resume on Monday," Kate said.

"Yeah. I don't know. I have to sit on Zoom all day. Do I need to stretch first?"

"He's moody lately, isn't he?" Olivia takes a sip of red wine.

Kate nods. "He's not exercising . . . mind or body. I offered to spar with him today."

"You basically offered to beat me up. I like my fully functioning orifices."

"Why not have a daily swim?" Kate suggests.

"For your information, I fell asleep on the inflatable flamingo yesterday afternoon."

Kate rolls her eyes. "You need to utilize this time to better yourself, Jonah. Olivia is bolstering her résumé with every passing day."

"She hasn't showered in a week!" I protest.

Olivia pours herself another glass of wine, swirling it gently. She doesn't drink much usually—too much wine aggravates her GI tract—but she's been having a glass or two with Kate over dinner a few nights a week. Like I said . . . they're besties now. "I have no one to impress. It's one of the side effects of my constant exceptionalism."

"Cheers to that," Kate says, and they clink across the table. "What did you do today, Jonah?"

I think about that. Well, I lay on the grass with Carlos, played some video games, had two naps, texted with Max a little, wallowed in self-pity for an hour . . . I had a bath . . .

"Nothing," I mutter, feeling my cheeks flushing. "I didn't do a thing. And that's fine."

"Is it?" Kate asks, staring at me above the brim of her glass.

It's the tone that gets me. The passing of judgment. The implication of *weakness*. I put my fork down and feel my last little reserve of self-control take a mental health day.

"Yes, actually. It is. The world is literally shut down. Schools are closed. Sports are done. So if I want to sit around and maybe not learn Latin while mastering Krav Maga, then I think that's okay. You two can work on your résumés. Have fun."

I'm standing up, and I don't remember when that happened. Kate is looking at me in surprise. But Olivia . . . she looks angry. She downs her wine and stands up.

"Typical," she says. "This is always how it goes, Kate."

"What's that?" I snap.

"Jonah is the only one allowed to feel sad in this house. He has the exclusive right to it."

I scowl. "What is that supposed to mean?"

"Figure it out. You have plenty of free time, after all. Thank you for dinner, Kate."

She walks out, and I watch her go, stunned. Olivia *never* gets angry. I wait for Kate to yell at me. To ground me or tell me to apologize to Olivia or just kick me in the thigh.

But when I turn back to her, Kate is just sitting there, looking down at her wineglass.

"You can take the plate to your room," she says quietly.

It's not a punishment and I know it. If anything, it's an act of kindness. Which is way worse. It just reminds me that I'm a dick. Guilt and duck a l'orange churn in my guts. I meant what I said, but Kate cooked a really nice dinner for everyone and I screwed it up.

"Sorry," I say, fumbling to grab my plate and go.

"So am I," she says.

I've never heard her apologize before. I don't know what to say. So I just take my plate, retreat to my room, and decide to stick it out here for the night.

Of course, hopefully not alone.

Jonah: No pressure but I kind of just remembered we have HBO Max and you could borrow my password . . .

Max: Heart be still

Jonah: It's time for you to see Greed and Glory. Like it's basically an emergency. Stop everything you're doing and prepare to meet Winter Robbins in all his tobacco-spitting, hog-tying, terrible special effects glory

Max: . . .

Max: I'm game

Jonah: It's like a movie date but we don't even have to stand up. Call you soon.

Max: No cameras. I'm wearing flannel.

Jonah: My pajamas have ducks on them

Max: I have so many questions

Jonah: Call you in 10. But totally with a camera. I want to see my date.

Max: Two "date" references in one convo feels like a lot.

Jonah: 9 minutes. I have one leg in my pajama pants already.

Max: Are there really ducks?

Jonah: Mallards, teals, *and* drakes

Max: . . .

Max: You may FaceTime me.

I hurry to the closet. I really do have pajamas with ducks on them. I didn't actually buy them—Olivia and I get each other gag gifts every Christmas. These just turned out to be super comfy. She wears her Bigfoot slippers too, so we kind of nailed it last year.

I get in position with the laptop and FaceTime and make the call. Max pops up, hair hanging down over some plaid flannel pajamas, and I forget about the argument with Olivia and all the great things Kate thinks I should be doing. I forget about everything but Max.

"Those really are ducks," she says.

"I never lie about waterfowl."

"This is a really romantic date so far."

I cover my mouth and whisper, "Did you just call it a date?"

"It was a slip of the tongue."

"Freudian?"

"Nietzsche. Sadomasochism."

"Max?"

"Yes . . ."

"I like your pj's too."

She bursts out laughing. "What's the password?"

"It's all numbers . . . I'll text it. I still kind of wish we could actually hang out."

"Kind of?"

"I was being polite. I would give away my duck pajamas to have you here right now."

Max nods, squinting a little. "So you want me over there *after* you've given away your duck pajamas, which would leave you . . ."

"Umm . . ." I feel everything reddening. Like, I've had flushed cheeks before, and maybe even ears, but I think my nose is red too. Can noses blush? "I didn't mean it like that. I mean, it does sound nice . . ." *Shut up, Jonah.* "I mean the hanging out. Not the me naked."

"What filter are you using right now?" she asks, leaning closer with a wry smile. "The interior of a volcano? Surface of the sun?"

I clear my throat. "What I mean is, I still want to hang out. You know—within six feet of each other. Yes, I know holding hands is illegal now."

"Not sure that's a law. P.S. the password worked. Thanks. Talk tomorrow?"

"Max!"

"Joking. I need to take in the glory of your duck pj's while you still remain fully clothed."

I sling my arm around my head. "You know . . . not to brag, but I have an entire three-pack when I wake up."

"Three?"

"Yeah, not sure where the other ones are. Behind a burrito maybe. The three survivors join them after lunch."

Max pops a nacho into her mouth. "I once had an ab. Now I have nachos."

I think for just a moment about actually *seeing* Max's body and yeah, solar flare volcano filter, so I get busy setting up my laptop. I've never felt like this before. Like just touching her hand is so unlikely right now that anything else seems impossibly pent-up exciting. Which makes me think about the long term . . . what if we can't be physically close for *months*? A year. Can a relationship actually start like that? Are we even in a relationship?

"So . . ." I say with my most casual voice possible, "I liked Dannie and Imani."

She curls up into the corner of her couch, knees to her chest and one arm slung around them. "Me too. You know . . . I might just hang out with them again."

"Max."

She smiles. "Yes, they liked you. Maybe too much. They already want you on future game nights."

"I am so in." And I am thinking about the implications there but I'm definitely not going to say anything because I don't want to pressure her.

"What about your friends?" she asks. "Do I need to pass any tests?"

"Well, my best friend is Carlos F. Santi. See?" I show her a picture of us at Universal Studios two summers ago. "But he's delighted by new people in general. He'll *love* you. He's also kind of a genius in a really weird, impossible-to-describe way. You'll meet him eventually, I'm sure." My finger hovers over the play button. "Ready? Three . . . two . . . one. . . . go."

The opening score of *Greed and Glory* plays on our respective sides, just a bit out of sync.

"I guess I did make a deal, didn't I?" she says, smiling, eyes on this screen only.

I try to look confused. "I don't remember a deal."

"For the record, I haven't been purposefully avoiding the topic," she says. "Or maybe I have. I don't know. I guess I was just worried. What does dating even mean when we can't, you know, date?"

"This feels like a date."

"I agree. But how can I have a boyfriend if we haven't even, I don't know . . ."

"Kissed?"

"Kissed," she echoes. "Or even *hugged*. I just don't know if dating even means anything right now." She throws her hands up and lets them flop back to the couch.

"It could mean something." Another twang of an acoustic guitar, first on my side, then hers. I'm fumbling now. That's the problem with this new reality—there are no natural social cues. No chance for our hands to touch over a bowl of popcorn, for our eyes to meet. "It would mean something to me."

She pauses for a moment, looking off-screen, chewing on her lip, and I'm worried that I've somehow upset her. That would be a very me thing to do. Then she sits up, pushes her hair off her forehead, and looks right at me.

"Jonah," she says. "Do you want to be my boyfriend?"

"*Yeah*," I say in a rush of air, flushing, heart beating, trying hard not to shout it because that's kind of becoming a thing.

"Then we're official," Max says. "Whatever that means."

We hold eyes, and it feels *close*. It feels like she's here. It feels like the moment before we would kiss, and even though we don't get to, I think the idea still stands. Maybe a kiss is about two people *wanting* to do it, and the action is . . . secondary. Max is the first one to look at the TV.

"I have no idea what's happening so far," she says.

"I'll get you caught up. And Max?"

"Yeah?"

"I am so glad I accused you of hoarding toilet paper."

chapter thirteen

MAX

I really wish Mr. Antinova wouldn't conduct AP Lit class from his bed. It's weird. His pillowcases are extra wrinkly and I'm pretty sure that's a lava lamp I see on his nightstand. I *liked* the image I had of Mr. Antinova in the classroom with his Earl Grey tea steaming in a chunky misshapen mug, a print copy of that weekend's *New York Times* book section folded neatly on the corner of his desk, thank you very much.

I see a number of my peers have taken his lead and shown up to class today sporting pajamas, uncombed hair, and zit cream. Ellis Gardener isn't even wearing a shirt.

Mr. Antinova welcomes us back and warns us that just because we're resorting to virtual school doesn't mean we're going to get to slack off. "By the time your generation has entered the job market, most of you will likely be doing the bulk of your work remotely anyway, and so you should think of this as a good opportunity to employ self-discipline to get things done without someone standing over your shoulder."

We pick up right where we left off talking about *Hamlet*.

"What does the king reveal in his soliloquy?" Mr. Antinova asks the shirtless Ellis with his signature head tilt. Mr. Antinova doesn't bother with hand-raising in his class-room. He prefers the Socratic Method, which is a very "Earl Grey" way of saying he calls on a student and keeps asking questions until the student wishes that he or she put on extra deodorant. Lucky for me, AP Lit's one of my best classes.

By the time he's done questioning Ellis, my internet connection has gone spotty and the screen's more frozen than Elsa's underwire. I open my bedroom window, but that doesn't seem to be helping matters, so I cradle my laptop and carry it out into the kitchen. My mom's bent over the coffee table scribbling on a notepad, her own laptop open beside her.

"Miss *Mauro*." I can't tell if this is the first time Mr. Antinova has said my name or just the first time I've heard it. "Are we interrupting something? You're making us sea-sick over here. Please take a seat."

"Sorry." Then, remembering to unmute my microphone, I say it again. "Just some technical difficulties."

"Well. Now seems like a good time to turn to you," he says.

I sink down in a chair and push the computer onto our kitchen table. I tuck a strand of hair behind each ear and prepare to use superhuman levels of concentration to listen closely.

Mr. Antinova leans back against his headboard and rests his fist underneath his chin. "Gertrude screams— Polonius— What happens—"

I angle closer to the screen, as if that's the problem. "I'm sorry, you were cutting out, what was the question?"

His forehead crinkles almost as much as those pillowcases. "Excuse me, Miss Mauro, please speak up?"

"I said," almost shouting, "can you repeat the question?"

It's right then that my mom's cell phone starts playing her marimba ringtone. "Mauro Dry Cleaning," she answers in her professionally nice voice. "Yes, your statement was . . ."

I try to focus on the choppy, stop-start animation of Mr. Antinova on-screen. "—Screams— Polonius— happens— af—"

I squish my fingers into the ear closer to my mom. "I—" I'm shaking my head. "I don't know, I'm sorry. I—"

"Miss Mauro." Mr. Antinova frowns. "The assignment was— time—"

"I don't mean that—my neighbor's playing *Call of Duty* and—"

"We'll come back to you another time."

"But . . . but I did the work," I say. "All of it." At the bottom of the screen, I see that he's already muted me. I pound my fist on the table.

"I'm sure it's correct, yes." Mom seems to be dealing with her own problems. Her profile looks sharper than usual in the morning light. "I know you don't need the clothes now that you won't be in the office, but we already cleaned them— No—"

I've agreed to take an extra shift for Vons. Mom has always warned me that I can work only as long as it doesn't interfere with school. But last night, when I told her I was pulling a double the first day back to classes, she just nodded without saying a word.

A FaceTime call pops up just as I'm parking my car on my afternoon delivery route.

"Please tell me you haven't finished your shift yet," Jonah says.

"Aren't you supposed to wish for the opposite? Wow, you're already sick of me. That was fast."

"Ha. Ha. Ha. No. It's just that I wouldn't be bothering you when you're trying to wrap up for the day if it weren't *time sensitive.*"

I sit there for a beat. "Ticktock. I'm waiting."

"I found him."

"Who?"

Jonah seems to have actually managed to leave his bedroom today. He's either taken an impromptu trip to visit Buckingham Palace or that's just what his living room looks like. "Winter."

"Say what?"

"So, Arlo said that Winter wasn't actually from Miami. He was *from* some small town somewhere else in Florida. Somewhere swampy, right? So I was like, great, that's nothing to go on until I was bored—"

"You're always bored—"

"And I started just looking at a map from Florida. And right in the middle where all the swamps are is a town called Winter Haven."

"No." I bite my knuckle.

"Remember how we said that Winter was a weird stage name for someone from Miami? Well, I thought, okay, maybe. And so I started poking around and found property tax records—thanks, lawyer parents—for Ernest Ralph Robbins and . . . I found him."

"I'm scared to ask." I bite my thumbnail.

"Alive."

"Okay, so I haven't made contact with him yet, but I found a hospital where he's been working for a few years doing administrative work, and I called and said I'd come in and spoken to someone about a billing matter last week. I played it up, said I was looking for an Ernest and was trying to get back in touch and asked them to describe the person and . . . it's him."

He's talking so fast, I'm trying to keep up.

"The woman I was talking to loved him—she said he was just a really nice old man working to pass the time. The description matched too: tall and lean and apparently still a great head of hair. We got to chatting . . . And, well, okay, unfortunately he was off that day, but I'm sure—I'm *sure*—it's him."

"Wow."

"She gave me his work email address and everything so that I could follow up. Me! I have Winter Robbins's email address. Do you know how nuts my mom would think that is? She would flip."

Would. For a quick second in time, my mind flashes back to my Spanish teacher, Señora Flores, of all people. *Would* is a conditional verb. *Would* indicates "*I would if.*" But Jonah's face goes redder than normal, like a hot stove—don't touch. And I get it, the whole *don't pry in my business* thing, maybe too well. I stall a beat too long and then, I let it go. Because the way I see it: He *would* talk about his mom, *if* he wanted to.

"I can't wait to tell my dad." He bulldozes through the conversation, razing that *would* to the ground, just so we can walk over it. "And you—I can't wait for you to tell Arlo," he says.

"I mean . . . wow," I say, still processing.

"You said that already. Anything else to add?" He's smiling now.

I want to add that my heart has grown two sizes like the Grinch and that I haven't felt this optimistic about love since my faith in romance was nearly crushed by the breakup of Justin Bieber and Selena Gomez (the second time). I want to add that Arlo has been special to me in a way that I don't feel totally comfortable owning up to and that I hate how I can't afford to do a lot for the people I care about, but maybe, just maybe I can do this.

And I want to tell him—"I really like you right now." Because you know what? Jonah Stephens has been showing up for me, and that's a fact. And here I am and I can't wait to tell Arlo. After all these years. It seems so—I don't know—*right*. Especially now.

The dimple in Jonah's left cheek makes a surprise appearance. "I'll take that," he says. Which is when I notice the girl—woman?—in a plush bathrobe sitting on a bar stool in the background crunching rice cakes.

"Um." I tilt my head and nod in her direction. "I think we, uh . . ." The girl continues to eat her rice cakes. Her hair looks like it could be the home of an entire family of woodland creatures.

Jonah pivots in his spot on the couch. "Olivia! Can you not just sit there staring at us, please?"

"Don't stop on my account." She grins. Even though I'm seeing the back of his head, I'm pretty sure I can feel the heat from his eyes boring straight into hers. "What?" she says, mouth full. "*The Bachelor*'s not on. Watching you two try to fumble your way through a flirtation is just as awkward and almost as entertaining. But do you mind if I offer some notes? I think we could get some really interesting plotlines going with just a few tweaks."

"Olivia!"

"Fine." She climbs down off her bar stool. "I've got big plans to hydro paint-dip my Birkenstocks anyway." The train of her robe moves slowly off-screen.

"I've got to go too. I have to finish delivering these groceries. I'll let you know how it goes with Arlo."

"Or . . ." Jonah brightens.

"You need a hobby." But as soon as I say it, I do have a small niggling worry that Jonah does have a hobby and that maybe, just maybe, it's me. "Fine, okay, you deserve this one. But we have to make it quick."

"Oh, shoot, that's right. I forgot your—your data overages." Again, like he's just learned a new phrase.

"Yes, my *data* overages."

"I could—"

"Do not even say it," I warn. I am not some charity case, my god.

"I just don't want—" He pushes his fingers through his hair and I can tell that this is a lesson in etiquette that they don't teach in cotillion or whatever.

"Stop," I say. "I'm a big girl. I can make my own decisions. Come on. We don't have all day." I unhook my phone from the dash holder.

To my surprise, Arlo isn't waiting for me on the balcony or on the front porch.

I ring the doorbell. When he doesn't answer, I text through the app to let him know I've arrived, a couple of baby carrots firmly stashed in my pocket.

"That's weird," I say. Because I remember a lot of little things about Arlo—like how his birthday is on New Year's Eve and that when he orders chocolates it's because he wants to sit and share them with me—but never once do I remember him not showing up when I arrived.

I glance down. Jonah opens the refrigerator and pulls out a carton of orange juice.

Chester barks from behind the door and scratches at the glass.

"He's not answering." I bite my cheek.

"Maybe he's sleeping?" The juice glug-glug-glugs into a glass.

Here, on Arlo's porch, Chester's bark is deep and guttural. Then, he begins to whine, pushing his nose at the threshold.

"It's okay, Chester." I crouch down, wishing I could touch his nose. "Maybe I should check."

"You can't break into his house." Jonah hoists himself up onto the kitchen countertop. Even his cabinets look like they belong to a rich person.

"Arlo!" I yell. "Arlo! Are you home? It's me, Max!" A finch flies from a bush nearby, startling me. "He's old. He could have fallen." I don't know if I'm talking to myself or to Jonah. "What if he needs help?"

"My friend Carlos's dad is a doctor. I could call him?"

I step back to get a look at the whole house. "I think I can go around the side. Maybe through the gate."

The side of Arlo's house is shaded with thick-leaved

avocado trees. All of the shutters on the windows are closed tightly. "Arlo!" I call as I walk through the stiff blades of grass. "Arlo!"

I reach the back gate and still no answer. Through the cracks in the fence, I can see a pool. "Do you think I should go in?"

"You've come this far."

Gingerly, I unlatch the gate. It creaks open. I've never seen a backyard like Arlo's, not even at a hotel, not that I have a big database to reference. Arlo has a grotto with a legitimate waterfall cascading out of a hot tub.

"You know," Jonah whispers. "Arlo seems like a guy who appreciates a good Jacuzzi. I'm not surprised." I walk across the limestone and around the umbrella-ed lounge chairs to the glass doors.

"Arlo, are you in there? It's just Max." I'm half afraid that if I catch him off guard I'll scare him to death. He is really old, after all. I cup my hands around my eyes and press my nose to the glass. He could have gone out. As much as I've been warning him against it, I know he's still been taking trips to the dog park. But then, here's Chester, tossing his head back and forth, agitated. "No sign of him," I report back.

"He must have gone out," says Jonah, echoing my train of thought. But I really don't think he'd leave when he knew I was scheduled to come. "You'd hear him yelling for you if he was in trouble."

I press my lips together and let myself out the back gate. I trudge back through the grass. "I guess so." Digging out the carrots, I leave them on a post on the front railing.

A new voice is calling up from the main road. "Hello?"

I turn to see a woman walking a dog, looking curiously at me.

I wave.

"You looking for . . ."

I move closer to hear.

"You could—" Jonah starts, and I shush him.

"Hold on. Someone's trying to—" The small terrier mix at the end of the woman's leash is pulling hard and she stumbles forward a step or two. "Jonah, I have to go."

"Max—wait—are you sure—" I push the red button and pocket my phone.

"Excuse me," I say, coming down the path toward her. "What was that about Arlo? I was looking for him. Arlo Oxley."

"I said he's not home. An ambulance came for him this morning. Arrived about nine o'clock."

I stop several feet from her. "What happened?"

"That's all I know." She shakes her head. "Saw it arrive while I was gardening."

"Oh. Okay. Thanks for letting me know," I say, even as my heart slips slowly into my toes.

chapter fourteen

JONAH

"Shit," I manage, face-first with toilet water, feeling the alarm bells slowly subsiding into the dull aching feeling of . . . well . . . shit. I wasn't ready for that attack. I was feeling pretty good today. Great, really. I'd found Winter. I was talking to Max.

And then we got cut off and I got Max's message a few minutes later:

Max: Arlo's been taken to the hospital. Going to try and find out where. Call you later.

And yeah: Au revoir, sane Jonah. *Hospital* isn't a happy word for me. It reminds me of the one day in my life I really, really want to forget. It's also enough for my asshole brain to get to work: What if Arlo is dying? What if it's COVID? What if he gave it to Max? *What if.*

The questions always find their way to panic. To a closed-off throat and pounding heart and a very good view of toilet water because apparently I am so polite, I even throw up *air* into the toilet. I sit on the cold tiles for a bit, arms draped over my knees, slowly coming back to myself.

What was Dr. Syme saying the other day? I need to find the positives in my daily life and practice gratitude. It's like, dude, the world is on fire. It was my second virtual session since the lockdown and I'm sure Dr. Syme is trying and all, but a disembodied head on my laptop telling me to "think positive" isn't the same. It feels like I'm watching a motivational YouTube video sometimes, and I've seen all of those. My search results looks like I teach a yoga class right now: *Finding your calm while rain falls on pine needles and yes we have flutes.*

But Dr. Syme is usually on the money with these things, so I take a deep breath and try to think of something positive. I found Winter. And yeah Arlo is in the hospital, but that means he could also probably use a nice pick-me-up right about now. A nice message from Winter/Ernest Robbins saying: *Arlo, I miss you, let's fall back in love when all this is over.* Okay that might be a bit much, but you never know. And, of course, Max.

I did mention Max, and he said, "Relationships can be good and bad things when it comes to managing our anxiety." I told him I'd take the chance for Max, she's the one keeping me sane. He didn't approve of that.

I decide to go for a responsible jog. A little fresh air might do me good today. I even leave my phone behind . . . then come back to my room a second later and scoop it up. If Max calls with updates, I want to make sure I'm there for her.

We did order some masks last week—Olivia got some

crazy expensive ones that might also work on the surface of the moon—but I just plan to avoid everyone. I put one on last night to try it and my anxiety was like, *Oh this is perfect I'm totally going to pretend you're suffocating!* Carlos keeps telling me he's deathly afraid of mascne and is exploring "breathable materials," so I guess I'll see what he lands on.

I'm out the door a minute later, feeling the dry April heat fill my lungs. I wave at Mrs. Clodden and carry on, observing the mostly empty roads along with the ten thousand new joggers and gardeners and is that Mr. Wang flying a kite? It's oddly utopian, but I wonder if it's self-improvement or self-distraction. There are a few masks sprinkled around for groups walking together . . . the only real clue that it isn't a sunny Saturday afternoon during a power outage.

I just stay well clear of them. I feel caught in a strange contradiction. After isolating myself in the house for a couple weeks, part of me *wants* to see strangers. But I also feel wary of them. It's like I'm running through a zombie outbreak and I'm not sure who is about to try to attack me. I really hope this new, extra-paranoid mental state isn't permanent.

I find myself in front of my high school. I didn't plan on coming here . . . but I think I wanted to. I don't miss class particularly. I just miss routine. I miss going to school and playing soccer and when my biggest worry was my SATs and trying to avoid Ashley . . . and holy shit. It's Ashley.

I had been circling the school, thinking vaguely about

walking the track, and there she is: running laps, and jumping hurdles like a gazelle. I don't even know how she got them out of the school, but they probably just gave her a key. Everyone loves Ashley. Even me . . . once.

I stand there like a deer in headlights as she comes running over. She's wearing a sweaty white tank top, headband, and those volleyball-style spandex shorts like always. Is she going to *hug* me? I open my mouth to protest, but before I can say anything Ashley punches me in the arm.

"It's so good to see you, Jonah!"

Okay, ow. I forgot how punch-y she is. Ashley has an older brother who plays football at Stanford and I think she learned all of her social skills from him. She is a straight-A student and student council treasurer who also occasionally traps you in a headlock until you beg for mercy.

Once I hung out with her *and* her brother and I barely escaped alive.

"You too," I say, fighting the urge to rub my arm. "How's it going?"

"Not bad," she says, tilting her head toward the track. "Trying to keep my form in case the world goes back to normal soon. I was supposed to have a big meet this week, remember?"

I do. *Why* do I remember that? Oh wait . . . it's because I really, really liked her. Not Max-level-like, but to be honest, they are both *way* out of my league. Ashley is not only pretty but also fully capable of kicking my ass in *Jeopardy!* She has this ability to fit in with every crowd—she bounces around tables in the cafeteria like a Ping-Pong ball. When I found out she liked me, I laughed and said, "Yeah. Right." But she did. And we had a few good months. Even a half nelson can be weirdly romantic if deployed at the right time. And then. The ass. I take another few steps away from her.

"I should get going," I say. "I have to go . . . do some pottery."

Ashley seems to be reading something in my expression. "I owe you an apology."

"No, you don't."

"I know I hurt you."

I purse my lips and shake my head and basically hold up a sign saying "I am bad at lying."

"Nope."

She sighs. "I made a mistake. A big one. And then I tried to make myself feel better by actually starting something with Adam and . . . well . . . he wasn't you. I dumped him three weeks ago. Pretty much right at the start of the lockdown when we started talking on the phone more. I realized I couldn't take those conversations." She laugh-winces.

"Cool," I murmur, as nonchalantly as possible.

Okay, a small part of me is like *Take that, Pilates Adam,* but it's definitely the petty, illogical side. The news changes absolutely nothing . . . and more importantly, it also doesn't matter anymore. Like. At all.

I'm surprised to realize that. I had presumed I was over Ashley, but you never quite know until your first official run-in. Now that I'm here, I just wish I could run into Max instead.

Ashley eyes me for a moment. "We were friends first, Jonah. I'd like to go back to that, at least. I know it's stupid, but some of us are still getting together and you could come by one—"

"Well, A, that's literally the one thing they're telling us not to do. And B . . . I'm good anyway. Really. Thanks, though. Enjoy the workout."

I take off for the street before she can say anything else or charley-horse me goodbye or something. I actually feel pretty good about how I handled things. That was a girl I made a *photo collage* for. But there was no drama, no bringing up that night, and no temptation whatsoever to try and restart things.

That said, I do miss my friends. Being around them was the *one* time my anxiety took a break. Well . . . it used to be. Now I have Max.

I wish I could call her with some good news. Something to balance the stress of Arlo being taken to the hospital. There is one thing . . . I was trying to think of the right words, but screw it, it's going to be weird no matter what. I copy Winter's email into a new draft and start writing as I walk.

Dear Ernest Robbins,

First off: I am a huge fan. My mom and I used to watch Greed and Glory like once a week. I have your poster on my wall. The movie meant—*means*—a lot to me.

But this is only half fan mail. I'm also a friend of Arlo Oxley. He'd really love to talk to you again, and I was wondering if you might be interested in organizing a call. He's hoping you will. But if you don't, I hope you'll forgive this intrusion.

Please let me know about Arlo.

—Your biggest fan, Jonah

PS. Can I call you Winter in future correspondence? I totally understand if you'd prefer I didn't. I don't want to antagonize the fastest draw in the west, right? Okay I'll stop now.

Max is lying on her bed, hair splashed out over the pillow. "So you sent an email?"

"Two, to be precise," I confirm. She is pointing the phone down at herself, and I am pretty much in the exact same pose in my own bed . . . and it's not impossible to imagine we're in the same place. "The first one got a little . . . off track at the end. Still nothing on Arlo?"

She sighs. "Not yet. Hospitals won't give you information if you're not family."

"What about an emergency contact? He must have had someone? Some friends?"

"He never mentioned anyone. I know he was an only child. And his parents would have been long gone. Plus, Arlo's got to be in his eighties by now, right?"

"Eighty-four and a half," I recite. "It's on his IMDB page."

"So . . . he might not have a lot of friends . . . left," she continues. "But, okay, I mean, it's probably not even COVID. What are the odds of that even happening?"

I say nothing because I'm pretty sure *probably pretty good* is not what she wants to hear.

"He could have tripped on the last step and broken an ankle." She's thinking out loud. She's spinning. I get it. "That would be rough, but fixable. Or . . . food poisoning. Food poisoning is a serious thing, right?"

"Right," I say. Because boyfriends are supposed to be supportive and I want to be a good boyfriend. "How about this? I'll call tomorrow. I'm getting good at this whole tracking people down thing."

"Must be a family talent," Max says dryly.

"I'll pretend I'm his grandson. Marlo."

"Marlo?"

"It's too weird to question. They would just be like, *That rhymes with Arlo! Let me patch you right through.*"

Max rolls onto her side and brings me with her, curling up under the blanket. The phone is less than a foot away from her face. As always, a loose strand of hair trails down her cheek, past those bright green eyes. "I've been thinking about Chester," she says. "I stopped by twice today to look in the front window, but I didn't see anything. I knocked and Chester didn't come running to the door. That means . . . it means he must not be there. Right? Maybe Arlo has a mystery friend we don't know about who's watching him . . . But what if he doesn't? The next-door neighbor didn't have any news. What if we're the only two people who know? I just keep thinking about Chester in there without food or water."

I feel a pang of worry. But I don't want to add to her concerns. "I'm sure he's fine. Arlo probably broke his ankle or something and called a friend to watch Chester. He'll be home any day now and you'll get an order for foie gras and baby carrots and you can ask him yourself."

"I hope so. Thanks for caring about this. I know it's not the most romantic thing."

"We're literally trying to reunite two long-lost lovers. It's super romantic."

"You know what I mean."

I roll over too . . . left, like I am looking at her. It probably looks insane. But it's a pandemic and this is the best we can do.

"I want to find him too," I say. "Really. And besides, we'll make up for lost romantic time when the world stops being upside down. We'll go to the movies. No. We will get ice cream and then go to the movies. Now, I don't have a car per se, so you'll have to drive and have me home before midnight, I do have a curfew . . ."

Max laughs. "You're such a catch."

"I will buy the popcorn. It's like forty-five dollars, so that should be fair."

She props herself up on her elbows, raising an eyebrow. "So, to be clear, at the end of this pandemic where we can't be close to each other, Jonah Stephens's very first priority is to take me out to a movie theater?"

"Max, I am nothing if not a gentleman. I don't kiss until the tenth date."

"That's impressive."

"Or ten seconds in if you want. It's totally one hundred percent up to you."

I feel my face reddening again with that insane thought of actually kissing Max . . . I mean, yes, I've thought about it. One night I was even considering if a mask kiss would still be romantic and probably not but . . . Yeah. Max is smiling at me with her eyebrows up, all *You're thinking about it right now.*

"You really love that volcano filter, don't you?" she asks.

"It brings out my fuchsia."

Max laughs again. Man, I love that laugh. "A movie date sounds very on-brand for you."

"We're going to be able to share a large popcorn and not sanitize every time and it's going to be *wild.* Just promise me we'll never be one of those couples that calls each other *babe.* It's my only relationship rule."

"If you ever call me *babe,* I will drive over and smack you."

I look up, grinning. "You'll drive over, huh . . ."

"Don't."

"So, want to watch a movie, ba—"

"Hanging up now."

I laugh and prop the phone against the headboard,

rolling onto my forearms. We're clearly developing some sort of FaceTime dance where you just roll around until you fall off the bed or something. "Fine. So we have a plan. We are going to find Winter, and Arlo, and give them their well-deserved happy ending. And then the whole world will somehow suddenly make sense again and we are going to hold hands so much. Take that, 2020."

"You know . . . most boys try for a base hit. Jonah Stephens? A bunt. Maybe a walk."

"I like to play the numbers. I'm like Brad Pitt in *Moneyball*. Especially my looks."

She pulls her blanket up past her chin. "So that's where I knew you from! Now, I need sleep. I have like ten thousand deliveries in the morning. I just wish one of them was for Arlo."

"He'll be okay." I can't believe *I* am saying that. I sound like my dad. "Good night, Max."

"Good night, Jonah."

She ends the call and I roll onto my back and feel . . . happy. Really, scary, happy. More than I ever was with Ashley. And that makes me nervous, because I used to be happy like this.

I tell myself this is different. Nothing is going to happen. But this is anxiety. It's always the *what ifs*. It's the way it turns good things into land mines. It says, *So you found the good thing to make all the bad times worth it.*

Okay, great. But what happens if you lose her?

chapter fifteen

MAX

I wake up to the sound of footsteps and cabinet doors banging. The beep-beep-beep-hum of the microwave. It's one a.m. and I untangle my feet from the blankets and take my robe off the hook on the back of my door. Cinching its terry cloth sash around my waist, I pad gingerly out on bare feet. "Mom?" My voice is froggy with sleep. "Mom, is that you?"

When was the last time we had a real conversation? Two days ago? Last week? Recently, it's like we've returned to old times, two ships passing in the night.

It's only temporary, I remind myself.

I rub my eyes and notice her sitting at the kitchen table over a cup of coffee.

"Sorry, did I wake you?" Her voice drags, as though she's been zoned out and has just now come to.

"What are you doing up?"

"I took a job cleaning a group of doctors' offices—the lease manager at the store helped me get it—some of them are night shifts. I told you that . . . didn't I?"

I shake my head. When you've been living with someone long enough, you know all their looks just by paying attention to their eyes. My mother has a whole host of signature looks: *don't you sass me, you best be grateful, fine you're pretty funny,* just to name a few. Now those same eyes take me in too intently.

"What's wrong?" I say. Whatever it is, it's not good news. For a wild, mixed-up second, I think: *It's Arlo. She knows what's happened to Arlo.* Even though I've never even mentioned him because for one, I've never had a chance to; she's gone all the time. And for two, I might have been feeling the teensiest twinge of guilt that somehow Arlo's become my go-to for talking things out, big parental things like boys and college—*guilty* because none of that's my mom's fault; she's just working as hard as she can to get ahead.

Or, at least, that's the two-minute summary of how I know I'm supposed to feel.

Because if I'm being completely honest, sometimes in the middle of the night, I do think to myself, *How can all my mother does really be "for me" when it involves her so often being nowhere near me?* But that's just lack of sleep talking, even I know that.

"What happened?" I ask, coming back to reality.

"Nothing." She lifts the word as though it weighs a thousand pounds.

"Something's wrong. Obviously." I wonder if there is a world in which I might not have to know. Just as I've wondered over the last few weeks whether there might be a world skating alongside this one where all the normal things are happening. A switch flipped on the train track and now we're unexpectedly all aboard the wrong line headed toward god knows where.

"Sit with me," she says.

Without taking my eyes off her, I lower myself into Sir Scratchmo's favorite chair. Bracing for a crash. "Why do you look like that?" I ask.

For the first time in my life, I notice spiderweb strands of white-gray creeping out from the roots of her hair and I remind myself this is only because she hasn't had her usual dye kit.

"How much money do you have saved from working this year?"

"Three thousand and thirty-two dollars," I answer automatically.

Hatchet marks ring her lips as she pushes them together. "We're going to need that," she says.

"How much?" I stick my hands underneath my thighs.

"All of it," she says. "I have to be able to pay the landlord for the dry cleaners. All our equipment is stored there. We have nowhere else to put it. If we don't pay the landlord, we could lose every inch of it." She delivers this news matter-of-factly. She doesn't apologize and I understand why. The business, too, is "for me," for my future, as much as it's for her. Scraping by to get Mauro's Dry Cleaning may have been a group effort in peanut butter and jelly sandwiches and ramen noodles and clothes from Goodwill, but when it came down to it, my mom sacrificed the most.

I swallow. "Of course."

I push out my chair and it feels like the ground is being pushed out from underneath me too. Like I thought I'd been running someplace important, but it turns out I was just on a treadmill. My legs are hurting and I'm sweating and out of breath, but I haven't actually moved an inch in all that time. I stand, wishing to retreat to my room, back to bed, before the disappointment can move from my heart up to my face.

Mom looks up sharply. "Now?" she says. "Please?"

"Oh. Right. My phone's in my room," I say. "I'll just—"

"I'll take a check," she says.

I swallow. Hard. "Sure. Of course." I tug one of the sticky kitchen drawers open and pull out the same checkbook I'd been given when I visited the local bank branch to set up my account. And then I write the number on the second line. *Three thousand and thirty-two.* I sign my name, tear along the perforation, and hand my mom the full amount.

On my mattress, I curl up on my side and think about nothing. The nothing that is in my bank account, for instance. The nothing that my work seems to have amounted to. The way when you multiply something against nothing, you wind up with nothing all the same, and maybe that's always how it's going to be no matter what I try to do.

Sir Scratchmo slinks by on his paws and I lower my hand off the bed to call for him. He arches his back and scratches it against the dresser. I snap for him to come cuddle with me. He sneezes and turns up his tail, leaving me exactly how I've always said I don't mind being—alone.

Hours pass that feel like two seconds because nothing makes sense anymore. I could have sworn I blinked, but when I wake up, it's to the racket of my Mickey Mouse alarm. Without looking, I can feel the emptiness in the apartment. Mom's gone. I roll over and check my phone and, on it, a message waits from Jonah.

Jonah: I have an idea.

One surprisingly tricky thing about this new world in which we find ourselves is sorting out what's a good idea and what's a bad one. Like, a few weeks ago, I would have placed "breaking and entering" firmly in the "bad idea" camp, but is it crazy that just one night after my mother scooped my life's savings this feels like more of a—I don't know—*gray* area?

Before I turn onto Magnolia, I flick off my headlights and coast through the darkened streets, past occupied homes with their windows black, floodlights fanning up their stucco sides and marking the paths of circle drives. The air has cooled, but when I step out a block away from Arlo's house, the pavement still microwave-zaps my ankles.

I hook my mask loops over my ears and find Jonah waiting there for me covered head-to-toe and donning a ski mask—or at least I hope it's Jonah, or else I am in seriously mortal peril—with his bike tipped sideways on the shoulder of the road.

"Did you go out and *buy* a bank robber costume?" I ask. The sound of my car door slamming rings out like a shot. "Or does robbery just happen to be one of your many extra-curriculars? I wasn't aware that grand theft looked great on a college résumé, but I mean, if you say so."

There's a chance that I sound at least 40 percent more bitter than I mean to, but sometimes, when I haven't gotten enough sleep, I get low-key annoyed that rich kids are rewarded for playing volleyball and debating capital punishment in Spanish while no one cares that I have a 4.0 GPA and hold down an actual job with shifts and a boss and everything.

It's anyone's guess what Jonah's reaction is, given that I can't see his face, but even so, I can feel his earnest Jonah energy coming out in waves.

"We went skiing in Banff last year," he explains. I look up at the cloudy night sky and sigh. "And I'll have you know, nothing ruins a day on the slopes like getting frostbite on the tip of your nose. Plus"—he lifts a finger, no wait, a *gloved* finger—"this is just plain pandemic practical. A mask and a disguise all in one." He rotates in place to model it and I laugh even though I want to stay annoyed at how he's so casually *rich*.

"Always thinking," I say.

"So." He rubs his palms together. "What's the plan?"

"Jonah. This was your idea."

"Right. Well." He looks up the road with his hands on his

hips. "I mean, there's your classic *Mission: Impossible* where I dangle you down from a skylight. We don't really have enough people to *Ocean's Eleven* this. So . . . yeah, I mean, I figured we'd start with finding the hidden key and then I'd let you take the lead."

"Hidden key?" I ask, incredulous.

"Everyone has a hidden key. Don't you?" Jonah acts like maybe I'm an alien.

"No. Where would we *hide* it?"

"Usually under a potted plant," he says. "Perhaps a garden gnome?"

I don't have the energy to break it to him that this is not a thing in my world and besides, the only important thing is that we get in there, make sure Chester is alive, that he has plenty of food to eat, and that he gets a chance to run around. At this point, we can't assume Arlo has anyone checking on his house, so it's up to me and Jonah to make sure Chester is okay. That poor dog has probably never missed an appetizer, let alone an entrée. And even though I'm stressed and feeling annoyed, I have to give Jonah credit—this really was his idea. He's here. With me. Even if he does look like a bank robber from a high-end ski resort.

"Fine," I agree. "No *Mission: Impossible*, no *Ocean's Eleven*. I'm just relieved you didn't mention *Bonnie and Clyde*."

"I prefer happy endings, don't you?" Jonah looks at me intently.

My heart squeezes without asking my permission. "Right," I say, and if he notices the croak in my voice, Jonah's unfailing politeness prevents him from saying so. "Shall we?"

"Ladies first." He performs a small bow and I dutifully roll my eyes because we've got a good thing going here and I am not trying to mess it up.

Quietly and with plenty of room between us for Jesus—and Moses and Vishnu and Buddha and whatever other religious figures want to join the party—we make our way up the sloping path. Arlo's house is shrouded in fuzzy darkness. Not a light on in the place. Shapes shift across the front door and a prickle runs up my back. I listen to the sound of our footsteps and remind myself that Jonah's right there behind me and this is Fountain Valley.

For starters, I check beneath the elegant statue of a dog standing sentinel by the door and then stand on my tippy toes to run my fingers over the door frame. "Nothing here," I report.

"You think we should split up?"

I watch the trees sway ominously in the background. Branches scratching. The sound of crickets. "Okay, yeah, sure," I murmur, not wanting to admit that the idea of splitting up gives me the creeps. Although, it's not likely that I'll encounter anything as frightening as Jonah in a ski mask, so, on second thought, I should be fine.

Jonah takes the right side of the house, while I take the

path to the pool. The gate creaks. I'm careful not to let it bang shut behind me. Arlo's house is still quiet. Chester's probably sleeping, I tell myself. It occurs to me, though, that Arlo could have returned from the hospital by now, and I experience a brief worry that he could be resting peacefully and that my skulking around could startle him into a heart attack.

As if on cue, a floodlight snaps on, illuminating the patio with its outdoor dining set and Bermuda fans. "Hello?" I whisper. My own reflection stares back and, for a moment, I hardly recognize myself. Even with my cuffed shorts and striped tee hanging off one shoulder, I look older than I did at the start of the year somehow. Like I'm peering at a version of myself at twenty-five and wondering if that girl will have any more figured out than I do now. Standing where I am, it feels unlikely. "Arlo?" I step beneath the covered veranda and, behind me, the floodlight clicks off. I exhale. It was only me, motion-detected.

After that I check beneath flowerpots and inside the mouth of an alligator holding a bar of soap.

"Got it." I jump at the sound of Jonah's voice.

"You scared me." I clutch my chest.

"Sorry. I figured you saw the light come on. The key was dangling on a wind chime. Can you believe that? Plain sight."

Actually, I can believe that.

"So now what?" Jonah puts the key on the outdoor table and retreats to the ledge of the spa.

I try to slow my heart rate. "You go back to the street and keep watch. Text me if anything comes up. I'll make sure Chester is okay and has food and water and everything he needs."

"You shouldn't have to go in alone."

"I just . . . don't think it'd be right for us to go together. No need for us both to risk going in there." No need for us both to risk possible contraction of this stupid disease that still feels surreal to me, is what I think. "It'll be fine. I'll be in and out. No problem."

I sound more confident than I am. I still have yet to hear a peep out of Chester. It's been almost two days. Chester could have been without food, without water for almost forty-eight hours. How long can an animal survive without water? And why didn't I come earlier, because what will I do if . . . if . . .

I don't even want to finish the thought.

Jonah, too, seems reluctant to leave me. But there are no good options, which I guess could double as this year's theme. I wait for him to leave the key and stalk back into the night, thankful now that he'd worn gloves. One less thing to worry about. I take a deep breath and try the key in the lock.

It turns.

I hear the snap and test the handle.

Gently, I twist, cracking the weather seal. For a split second, I think that maybe I hear the sound of panting or the pattering of paws on hardwood, and for a second I'm sure that everything's fine. And then a high-pitched beep starts up. One long stretch of noise at a piercing din that wreaks havoc on my eardrums. The alarm.

My phone buzzes in my pocket.

Jonah: I hear something.

I call out to anyone listening. "Don't worry! It's just me, Max! Chester?" No answer. Without thinking, I jog farther into the house, looking for signs of Chester. I just need to know if he's here. If he's okay, then I'm gone.

In the kitchen, I find empty porcelain bowls sitting on a silk place mat. The beep continues, drawing out, growing louder. I pound up the stairs. "Chester!" I say, louder this time. There's a vacant dog bed in a tidy bedroom. For a crazy instant, I believe I've spotted him, before realizing it's an oil painting of Chester, standing regal, opposite a set of floor-to-ceiling bookshelves. My eyes catch snippets of Arlo's house. His Oscar encased in glass. An old movie poster. A framed picture of a much younger Arlo and a young man strumming a guitar—Winter?

My phone buzzes again. And no sooner have I bent down to examine the photograph than the beep morphs into a siren blare. The sound blasts through the house, filling the corners, vibrating inside my chest. The phone buzzes again insistently.

It's empty. The house is empty. There's nothing—*no*

one—here. I'd been counting on Chester being here. I'm realizing too late that I'd needed him to be. I feel like a kid again, a kid who's misplaced her favorite stuffed animal, the one that she needs to go to sleep. And all this is news to me, and now he's gone. I'm breaking into a house with no one here.

My mind screams. *Go.* I tear back down the stairwell—*thud, thud, thud.* My heart beats with it.

"Max!" There's a shout from down below. "Max! What are you doing?"

"Jonah, what are *you* doing all the way up here?" He's outside the open door, a black silhouette. "You're supposed to be down there!" I point.

"We've got to go. If Kate finds out—"

"Then *go!*" I'm running toward him and he's blocking the exit.

The whites of his eyes shine through the ski mask and without another word he turns and sprints. At the last second, I remember to close the door and twist the key in the lock and push it into potted soil. I'm fast. And before long I've caught up and we run through the gate back toward the street. No police sirens yet, but they're coming. They're coming and what if they don't believe that I've just broken in to find a dog? Because, I mean, really, who does that?

I can hardly see where I'm going as I follow Jonah's back down the slope, hooking a shortcut through somebody's lawn. We jump over a pair of decorative boulders like decorative boulders are an actual thing that somebody in this world needs.

It all happens fast. The sound and then what I see next, like thunder followed by lightning. A grunt and then there's a body on the ground. Dead weight on dirt. A heavy thwack.

My momentum doesn't peter out until I'm already well past the spot where he dropped. I pull myself to a hard stop. Jonah lets out a strained whine like an injured animal.

"Are you all right?" I whisper through the night, panting, more loudly than I think is wise, given our status as amateur fugitives. In the background, the sound of Arlo's alarm has begun to wake the neighbors. Lights blink on in the windows around us. I duck down, out of view.

I can't see much, but I can see Jonah, about ten feet away, rocking back and forth on what I think is his back. "My ankle," he says in a voice like a grown man is sitting on his chest. "It's fine. Just—twisted—my—AN-kle—that's all."

I don't know what to do. Because COVID has gotten us all topsy-turvy. Because in what world am I not going to close the distance between us to help my boyfriend—and the answer is this one. And when Jonah says, "Give me a hand?" all I can think is: *No*. A word that makes my blood run cold.

"Olivia," is what I say, gently though. "Maybe—" I don't know what follows. Police sirens join the night chorus and I realize we have just minutes left. "Can you stand?" I ask.

"Yes, yes, of course." The whine has disappeared from his voice. He struggles to his feet and while he doesn't make a noise, I can feel the pain in his steps. More slowly now, we make it to his bike and to my car. The sirens draw closer. If we're lucky, they'll think that the alarm was tripped by a loud tree branch or an opossum. Nothing stolen. No signs of foul play.

I stand at my car as Jonah drags his bike upright.

"Are you going to be okay?" I ask. My heart beats. My fingers feel electric. If there was ever an excuse to be alone in the same small space as Jonah, isn't this it? I could do it. Throw the bike in my trunk and take off. Just once. Stop being so responsible. Stop doing what everyone else needs me to do.

"Me?" He leans his weight onto the handlebars, breathing heavily. "Don't worry about me. Worry about Chester."

"Okay," I say with a hitch that registers the seconds ticking by, the window of opportunity, of rash thinking, closing, maybe for good. "But plenty of room to worry about both."

chapter sixteen

JONAH

"It was . . . tai chi."

Kate is analyzing her work, having set and wrapped my ankle when she saw me stumbling for a glass of orange juice this morning. I don't know if she's like an army medic in her spare time, but she pulled out a serious first aid kit in a black metal case and had me patched up before I could even finish my juice.

She decides the ankle's just sprained, which I had guessed, but it's still swollen up like a squishy water balloon and a little purple and why didn't I think of a proper excuse until now?!

She looks at me. "Tai chi?"

I nod, testing the ankle. "I took your advice . . . and you know, started exercising."

"Well, I officially retract my advice," Kate says drolly. "You should have been icing and keeping it raised all night. Keep off it for a bit."

"Thanks, Kate."

Ugh. That hurt coming out. Especially since I was still half expecting her to dramatically reveal that she knew the truth about my dead of night bike ride and deliver a karate chop to my ankle. Instead, she packs up her apparently standard-issue first aid kit, even giving me a comforting pat on the shoulder. *What's happening?* Were Kate and I bonding? *No.* Every news anchor keeps saying this is an "unprecedented time," but some precedents were there for a reason . . . like my stepmom is evil and we can never be friends.

"Want some eggs?" she asks.

What the hell, Wicked Witch of the Wills! "No . . . thank you," I manage.

"All right. I need to get back to work. Try not to tai chi yourself into a broken arm, idiot."

Well, that felt a little more natural. She strides down the hall with a distinct rapping on the hardwood—she wears heels in the house when she's working remotely because that makes sense. I check my phone, but Max hasn't gotten back to me yet. She did say she had to work this morning. We texted for an hour or two when I finally made it home last night . . . I had a bunch of messages awaiting me, since I couldn't check my phone while barely managing to ride my bike.

Max: Are you alive?

Max: All right it's been an hour! I'm going out to look for you soon.

Max: JONAH.

What can I say? It did take me a while . . . pedaling with a sprained ankle *hurts*. I should have asked if I could climb in her trunk or get strapped to the roof like a kayak or something.

Still no updates on Arlo. Max is back to work today, and I am back to house arrest . . . I basically even have the ankle monitor in ACE bandage form. I limp over to the living room and flop onto the love seat. Olivia is sprawled out on the couch—snoring—and the news is on, all talking heads and sidebars of grim, ever-rising numbers in alarming crimson. New epicenter in New York. More cases in California. Beds running out in hospitals. Death rates climbing.

I change the channel. I try to balance information with anxiety . . . and the more I know, the more I worry. Maybe ignorance really is bliss.

"Still lots of cases in Madrid," Olivia says, yawning and stretching as she wakes. "But we're rising faster now here."

"Talk to Dad yesterday?"

We were supposed to be "alternating" daily phone calls because Kate said we were driving him nuts over there. *He* never said that, mind you, but in fairness I've been asking for daily updates and symptom checks. I'm just terrified he won't pick up and that's how we'll learn he's in the hospital and everyone will be speaking Spanish and, like, what the hell will we do? But he's still answering the phone with his usual "Hey buddy! How's the weather over there—" So, it's fine. *Toooootally* fine. (See how fine?)

"Yeah," she said. "He's just working away. Self-isolation

is done but he still can't really go anywhere . . . they're fully locked down in Spain." She turns to look at my ankle. "Meanwhile, an injury in your own bedroom . . . odd."

I shift a little, trying not to look too guilty. "Boredom is dangerous."

"I agree," she said, eyeing me suspiciously above the brim of her glasses. "On an almost certainly related note, how is Max?"

"Fine. Well . . . not really. It's all just a waiting game. We still haven't gotten an update on Arlo. Or Chester."

"Is that another old man?"

"That's a dog. And nothing from Winter either."

She grunts and turns back to the TV. "Now you're just making up names."

"I thought I'd do something nice for Max tonight. To take her mind off things." I chew on my nail. The truth is, I am kind of nervous about it for several logistical reasons and maybe a few practical ones . . . but I keep thinking about what she said. That we weren't starting out very *romantically*. And, hey, I can do romantic. I mean. Probably?

"Like . . ."

"Just a little thing. Sort of a makeup event."

"Well, despite the fact that you've done literally everything wrong, she still agreed to date you . . . so carry on, I suppose. But . . ."

"From a distance," I mutter.

I check my phone and sigh. School's starting shortly,

which means I have to go watch Mrs. Walden try to explain AP Calculus on a little whiteboard while half the class forgets to mute their mikes, dozes off, or pretends they're having a power outage—which is a terrible excuse because they have online maps of that.

I, at least, have the basic human decency to screenshot myself looking studious whenever I have to go to the bathroom or want a snack.

I one-foot-hop up the stairs and I get to my desk, logging in just a bit late and finding Mrs. Walden doing a fairly half-hearted attendance check since what would she really do if no one showed? It occurs to me for the first time that if Max is working, then she's not in class. I know she's working this morning. She'll be one of the missing faces in her first class. Maybe every class, actually.

By habit, I check my emails. And . . . *Ernest Robbins*. It's short and sweet and did I mention sweet? Holy shitballs. It's happening.

Dear Jonah,

This is quite the surprise. I would like to talk to Arlo. I didn't for many years . . . I'm sure he told you the story. But time heals all wounds, as they say. And it's certainly been a lot of time. Much more than I was promised. Do you think you can show him how to do one of those Zoom calls if he doesn't already know? It would be nice to see him.

—Winter Robbins . . . still the fastest draw in the West

Okay, the last part makes me squeal and I think I vaguely hear my name being called but I am already frantically messaging Max:

Jonah: Winter got back to me!!! He wants to talk to Arlo!!! And I don't think it's to tell him off either. He said time heals all wounds AND he is still a cowboy!

"Jonah," Mrs. Walden repeats.
"Yes, hi, Mrs. Walden. The answer is six."
She sighs deeply. "Let's begin."

Max: That is amazing!!! I can't wait to tell Arlo. I almost used a smiley face, Jonah. A SMILEY FACE.

Jonah: Max don't do anything reckless . . . you have principles

Max: It was close. Honestly. I think the jazz hands are implied.

I beam at that one. And the best part? I am *just getting started*.

Jonah: It's on for tonight. You didn't kill them right?

Carlos F. Santi: No! I just got them. Would have been nice if you got *me* something.

Jonah: . . .

Carlos F. Santi: They had chocolate bro

Jonah: Are you good for the plan or not? Timing is everything. It has to be PERFECT.

Carlos F. Santi: Why do I have to do it again

Jonah: Because you have a car, apparently unfettered freedom, and because it ties into the entire virtual theme and I planned everything around it and we went over this yesterday!!

Carlos F. Santi: Unfettered?

Jonah: You got this. And then your debt is paid. Well . . . partially.

Carlos F. Santi: It was one paper

Jonah: It was a term paper! But thank you. This is going to be great.

Carlos F. Santi: You sure the address is right?

Jonah: Yeah I told her I had an Amazon thing to send her so she gave it to me.

Carlos F. Santi: Smooth. Also you know all the school events got canceled right

Jonah: . . . that's the point, Carlos

Carlos F. Santi: Just seems weird. Speaking of weird, Blake messaged me yesterday asking if I wanted to hang out. I'm like . . . A, you live in Anaheim, B, things did NOT go well last summer

Jonah: Carlos

Carlos F. Santi: Leaving

I check the time and sigh. My entire plan hinges on Carlos F. Santi. We have one hour, and a little nagging voice is still wondering if this a good idea, but too late now. We already got *some* good news today, but no one has gotten back to Max about Arlo yet and she could use a distraction. I think. Yes. She will *definitely* love this.

I go to the bathroom and check my reflection again. Dark circles around my eyes from not sleeping well in . . . weeks? Check. Ruddy hair looking overlong and hanging down over my ears and defying the polymer will of two separate hair gels? Check. Peach fuzz on my upper lip? Shaving that now. Why does Max like me again?

Max is funny and smart and gorgeous . . . that one shoulder-out-T look almost made me fall off my bike last night. And yet, she still didn't want to touch me in my hour of need. What if that wasn't pandemic related but *Jonah related*?! I try to relax. The problem with anxiety is it can be tough to distinguish rational concerns from rumination. I choose the latter.

Tousle the hair. Shave the peach fuzz. The lighting will fix the dark circles.

I got this. Like I said, it's going to be perfect.

"Bonjour, Ms. Mauro."

Max beams in from her kitchen, hair pulled back with an elastic, in a big yellow hoodie fresh off a work shift.

"Monsieur Stephens," she replies, propping the phone up in one hand while she pulls a plate of nachos out of the microwave with the other. "Just getting ready for a much needed trash TV night. I'm beat."

"Is that the world-famous Quarantine Qulassics Nacho Popcorn?" I say.

"This might look like I'm hosting a party, but nope, all for me. Like I said, it's been a long day."

I check the time and . . . three, two, one—*now*. I press play on the laptop, starting the song "Big Jet Plane." It was the most romantic song on my *Essential* playlist.

"I wish I could help you with that," I say, slowly turning up the volume.

"Did I tell you I went by Arlo's again? No sign of Chester. It's so weird. I tried asking a couple of the other neighbors. No luck. I'm getting seriously worried that he got out or something. I keep running through scenarios—Do you hear music?"

"I'm just playing something on the laptop."

She screws up her face, as if trying to hear. "It sounds like it's on my end," she says, looking off-screen. "It's getting louder. Is that . . . 'Big Jet Plane'?"

I grin. I should have known. Carlos has a reputation on our soccer team for two things: always being annoyingly optimistic no matter the score . . . and coming up big in the clutch. And here he is, right on time.

I answer his incoming Zoom call on my laptop, he shoots me a thumbs-up from his position—he's even wearing a mask and fresh gloves like I insisted so that Max could pick up the delivery—and we are in business. I turn the music up a little louder on my side, and he does the same, and then I head for my bedroom door, trying not to noticeably limp too much.

Now Max looks really confused. She heads for her front door, still looking around her apartment, but she's getting warmer. Carlos tucked the Bluetooth speaker right against the bottom of her apartment door.

"It's coming from the hallway . . ." she murmurs, glancing at me. "Jonah . . . what are you doing?"

I show her my bedroom, taking the view away from me for a second. "Me? Nothing. I'm home, see?"

As I show her the room, I pull off the button-down shirt and swing the phone back to me.

Max narrows her eyes. "Are you wearing a T-shirt tuxedo . . ."

"It's comfortable," I say, then I scoop up a vase from my desk brimming with a dozen red roses and a big open card nestled inside.

"Jonah . . . what's happening . . . where did that . . ."

I swing open my bedroom door, making sure she can clearly see what I am doing, and set the roses on the floor outside, facing me, then close the door again.

Max is looking at me like I've completely lost my mind. "Are you all right?"

Then someone knocks on her end. I see Carlos running away, giving me the *Blair Witch* view again as he bolts around the corner to hide. He shoots me another thumbs-up and ends the call just as Max opens her front door. There, sitting outside her apartment door, is what appears to be the exact same vase of roses, the same open card . . . and a little Bluetooth speaker playing the exact same song. It's off by like half a second, but it's still pretty impressive.

She opens her mouth to say something, doesn't manage it, then picks up the card. I know what it says:

Will you go to virtual formal with me? Dress code in effect (red is always in style).

I wait a beat. Two. Three. "Well?" I ask, grinning. "Will you?"

For a little while, she just holds the card. She is looking at the message and the flowers and then at me.

"How?" she finally manages.

"I had an accomplice! Don't worry . . . all safety precautions were taken."

She smiles . . . but thinly. It looks forced. "That's really nice, Jonah. Thanks."

I don't really know what to do. *Thanks* wasn't on the list of possible responses I had planned for. I would be leafing through the script right now if I had one. Line!

I just stand there awkwardly, and the music is playing just a little ahead on my side, and what the hell do I say now?

"So . . ." I finally ask. "Ready?"

She frowns.

"Um, to get dressed?" I ask.

"*Now?*"

"Well . . . yeah?" I reply. "I've got everything set up. I mean, you don't have to change—Or—we can totally reschedule—"

"No. It's okay." She tucks the card in the flowers and takes them inside and she must turn off the music, because now I only hear it on my side. She puts the roses on her table. "I'll go put on my dress. Just, um, one sec."

I hear rummaging and is it just me or is this going really badly? Max comes back on-screen in her red dress and, never mind . . . it's going great. My stomach does a little flip.

"You look amazing."

She fidgets with her dress. "I'm a mess . . . I haven't even done my hair or anything—"

"No, seriously, *amazing*," I repeat. "Like I might need to sit down."

"So . . . now what?"

"*Now*, the activities. Photos, of course, a bit of dancing, some hors d'oeuvres, which, crap, I forgot to give to Carlos, and . . . Max?" I peer closer at the screen, frowning. "Are you okay?"

Her eyes are looking a little watery. She just pats her hair down and nods. "Perfect."

But this isn't the perfect that I'd pictured.

"Max . . ."

"We really don't need hors d'oeuvres—" she says, looking around. "I already made the nachos—" Her voice lilts up too high.

"*Max.*"

She stops, takes a breath, and turns back to me. Her eyes are definitely glassy.

"Sorry, Jonah. It's really sweet. It's . . . I don't know. I think I'm just a little tired. Or something. Or I don't know, maybe this isn't exactly how I . . . pictured it." She rubs her nose with the back of her hand. "But hey, that's why we're taking . . . pictures."

"God, this was stupid. I'm so sorry. There's so much going on."

"Jonah . . . no . . . it's . . ." she says.

"No . . . it was just a bad idea. I didn't think it through."

"Jonah—"

"Someone's calling," I say, pretending to look at something that doesn't exist because I can feel pressure behind my eyes and I think I'm-an-idiot tears might happen at any moment and those are an endless cycle. "Sorry, Max. Could be an emergency. Do you mind if we talk soon?"

"O-*kay,*" she says.

She hangs up, and I stand there in my tuxedo tee for a moment, listening to the last lines of the song, and then collapse into bed.

chapter seventeen

MAX

I find Mom tipped over on the sofa, head on the armrest, neck cocked at an uncomfortable angle. Her knees are curled into her chest and the light on her face flashes blue, white, yellow, red with the changing picture on the TV screen—the TV she's watching through squinted eyes, volume turned down like we're only half listening to a conversation at another table in a restaurant. "Is that your formal dress?" she asks without lifting her head.

When I sink down on the couch's opposite side, I hike the skirt of my dress up over my knees, still dirty from grabbing items off the low shelves at Vons, and curl my heels underneath me. "Yep."

I have a secret Pinterest board dedicated to hair and makeup ideas meant just for this dress and never once did I pin an image of a greasy bun and tinted sunscreen. Dannie voted for beach waves, half up, half down, and Imani said she could do winged eyeliner because I always mess mine up when I try to do it myself and I'm annoyed that I'm annoyed that any of this matters to me.

I had felt some kind of way when I tried this dress on for the first time. My mom said I deserved it. That *we* deserved it. One big splurge. We'd never been able to splurge before. But with my socks still on and the place where my neck meets my chin slimy, I feel, worst of all, cheap.

And broke and dead tired from work and from doing homework on my lap in the front seat of my car and calling hospitals hoping to find Arlo and if there were ever a human embodiment of the notion that you can try to dress up a shitty situation but it'll still be shitty, it's me in this fancy dress that my mom and I definitely couldn't afford in retrospect.

"What's his name?" She lets her eyes close and I realize I can't remember the last time I saw her sleep. Her mouth twitches and I know she's trying to stay awake long enough to listen.

"Jonah." I hug my arms around my chest.

"Jonah," she murmurs. "Hm. Jonah. Well. Sweetie." She sighs, deep and peaceful. "Enjoy it while you can."

"What's that supposed to mean?" I suddenly feel like my dress might be too tight.

But she's already asleep. A soft snore escapes from the back of her throat. I watch her for a long moment, unable to bring myself to wake her. *Enjoy it while I can.*

But how? I've never been good at faking, and now I'm supposed to pretend to have fun at a pretend dance when everything in my actual, real life is falling apart?

Eventually, I curl up on my end, a mirror image of my mother. As I stare mindlessly at an infomercial for a wearable towel that I kind of don't hate, a text from Imani pops on-screen.

Imani: You OK?

Max: Yeah I'm fine why?

Imani: Because Jonah said that you seemed like upset or something. He's all worried and whatnot.

Imani: It's kind of cute.

Max: Why are you talking to Jonah?

Imani: Why are you not talking to Jonah more like

Max: I'm not not talking to Jonah

Imani: Don't be cute

Max: It's a long story

Imani: Moby Dick is a long story. I'm gonna go out on a limb here and guess this one is like two text messages at most

Max: Tomorrow

Imani: Smh

Imani: OK but I'll be up if you change your mind. I've got like two episodes left of this true crime podcast and like sleep, what sleep? And, hey, listen, we do need to talk. Not right now. I know you've got a bunch of your own stuff going on, but much as I hate to admit it, Dannie's right.

Max: . . .

Max: . . .

My phone wakes me up—*buzz, buzz, buzz. Buzz, buzz, buzz.*
It's slipped onto the floor and I feel around for it blindly.
Buzz, buzz, buzz. Buzz, buzz, buzz.

"Imani, I already . . ." I grumble as I heave myself into a
sitting position. My neck feels like someone tried to twist
me into human origami. The spot on the sofa beside me is
vacant. The TV's off. What time is it, anyway?

Morning light trickles in through the blinds. Footsteps
clomp from the apartment above us. My stomach growls
like a rabid dog.

The number on the screen isn't Imani's. My eyes are still
trying to adjust. I rub the heel of my hand into one of them,
then register the area code. *714.* That's Fountain Valley.

"Hello?" I scramble to get the phone up to my ear in time.
I'm still wearing my crumpled formal dress. "Hello? This is
Max."

There's a long pause. "Maxine . . . Oxley?" says a woman
on the line with a Southern accent. "Am I speaking with
Arlo Oxley's daughter? I got your message."

"Yes. Uh-huh. That's definitely me." I scoot to the edge
of the couch and hold my forehead in my palm, trying to
quickly calculate how old a daughter of Arlo's might be.
Fifty? Is that right? I should have figured this out sooner.

"I'm . . . sorry," she says. "We'd tried to locate a next of kin
but for some reason we didn't find anyone on record."

"That's . . . weird," I say, not exactly pulling off fifty.

"I'm Lucinda Welch calling from Orange Coast Memorial

Patient Services." *Orange Coast,* I mouth. *Score.* Orange Coast had been third on my list. It had been impossible to get through to a live person yesterday. I was constantly being asked whether I knew my party's extension, whether I was a provider, if this was an emergency to hang up and dial 911. "Miss Oxley, I'm afraid I have difficult news." My face falls. "Your father passed."

"What? How?"

There's rustling on the other end. "Were you not aware that he'd contracted COVID-19?"

"I—no, I didn't know."

"Oh. Again, I'm so sorry. But if you had any contact with him, you'll need to be tested."

"I—don't have any symptoms. Can I still get tested?" I scour my memory. I was always careful. Wasn't I always careful? All anyone has been able to talk about at work is how it's nearly impossible to get their hands on a test and if they do, it takes like eight days to get back, which is next to useless. My eyes travel over the spot where my mother had slept beside me.

"When was the last time you saw your father?" the woman asks.

"A little over a week ago."

"You could try asking a doctor. I don't know. We're due to get more tests in a couple weeks, I know, but for now . . ."

A couple weeks? That won't do me any good.

"When did he . . . die?" I ask. "Was anyone with him?"

"Three nights ago." I can only imagine what a terrible job Lucinda Welch must have and what a shitty year this must be for her. "Unfortunately, we're not allowing any visitors right now. Hospital policy. Social services did leave a notice in the mailbox. I'm very sorry," she repeats, and, though she could use that phrase as a shield, somehow I sense that she isn't.

"Social services?"

"Yes. The belongings he came in with will be kept in the hospital mortuary until they're picked up, and the doctor will issue a medical certificate of death. We can recommend a funeral director if—"

"That won't be necessary." I feel terrible. Weighed down. But I can't take on the responsibility of a funeral. I just can't.

"Are you—"

"I really have to go. I'm sorry," I say, and end the call.

The room spins. I feel light-headed. I can't believe—I mean, I thought somehow—but what about—

I open FaceTime and call the only person I can imagine calling in a moment like this. It starts to ring—

"I was worried I was going to have to track you down and shake that story out of you, and fair warning, I have been listening to way too much *Up and Vanished* and I'm itching to interrogate someone," she answers after the second one.

"Imani? I promise you can summarize that whole damn podcast, spoilers and all—" Imani loves relaying podcasts for me because she knows I won't listen anyway and, honestly, she makes it super suspenseful. "But—" And I know

I'm probably sounding desperate. "I need us to be in the judgment-free zone right now."

She sucks in a breath. "Okay, okay," she says, doing a sudden about-face in tone. "I'm stepping inside. Hang on."

This is a thing we do. We're too alike. And we have a tendency to go straight to tough love. So sometime in middle school, we invented the "judgment-free zone" and when either one of us asks to go there, we treat it like it's a real place with real governing rules and soft, soundproof walls. It's in the judgment-free zone that she first told me when some ignorant ass-wipe told her she should consider getting her hair chemically straightened. It was here I admitted that I'd finally worked up the courage to send my dad an email and he never bothered to respond. To an *email*. And here that Imani comes when she's about to lose her temper with her mom because sometimes that lady can have sky-high expectations and it's a whole lot better to vent to me than wind up grounded by her. Inside, we don't call each other out for throwing a pity party. We don't point out mistakes. We don't tell each other how to act.

"All right, all right. I'm ready," she says. "What's up?"

"I don't get it. I don't get anything," I tell her. "I'm trying so hard. I'm doing everything right, or at least I'm trying to. But instead of getting better, my life is actually getting worse. Worse! How is that even possible?"

I hardly ever cry, and that might sound like it's a good thing, but it's totally not. People go around thinking I'm not upset when I should be, like at a funeral, just because my face isn't leaking. But I'm plenty upset. I just don't cry. And that can be a liability, but I know Imani sees the tears that aren't coming. I guess Dannie would say she's "adding them in post."

"So this isn't about Jonah at all, then." She skips straight to it.

"Imani, my mom asked for all the money I saved up from my job. Every dime of it. She needs it to keep the business open."

"Ouch. Oh. Ouch." And this sounds like it physically pains her.

"And Arlo died."

"Amazing grace, how sweet the sound," she says softly.

"And we can't find his dog and I loved that stupid dog." My voice cracks.

"Okay, okay, I hear you. Deep breaths. You've got this." Imani is a steady force on the other end.

"And I really like Jonah, but there are certain things about . . . about all this, that he just doesn't get."

"Well," Imani says like it's a whole sentence. But then adds, "I'm not sure that's his fault."

"I'm tired, Imani. I'm so freaking tired. And all of a sudden, I'm just like, why though? What's the point?" I remember Winter's famous line, "None of this matters anyway," like—you know what?—I couldn't have said it better myself.

"Yeah. That is some serious suck."

I sigh. "I'm sorry. I know I sound like a brat. Telling you all this." I have been in a store when the clerk accused Imani of trying to shoplift a tube of lipstick that she was fully ready to pay for, and so I know what it really looks like, to feel like what's the point of trying to do right when things are always trying to go wrong. And I know that sometimes I show up sounding brand-new, acting worn-out after what's like a quarter mile when Imani's already run two marathons back to back.

"This is you and me." Imani's voice is even. "We don't have to do that. I know. Okay?"

My throat feels like it could use a plunger. I nod. "It's just, why am I running so hard if I'm not getting anywhere anyway, you know?"

She doesn't say anything, not at first.

"So," she breathes out at last, "what percentage honesty are you looking for?"

This is another thing we do because, yeah, you need friends who can be real with you, but maybe not all at once.

I consider the question carefully. "Eighty-five percent honesty."

She makes a low humming noise, which tells me she's thinking. "Okay. Well. First of all, your hard work is not for nothing."

"How?"

"*How?* Because without your hard work, you and your mom might damn well lose that business. Your hard work is holding the line. You—Max Mauro—at seventeen years old, made a real impact. You saved the day. Now tell me how that's nothing! *That's* something."

"We still could lose the business. It seems like"—I take a

gulp of air—"like I lose everything and everyone." Fine, it's a full-blown pity party, now where's my piñata?

"I heard. And I'm sorry about Arlo. That's really sad. But I bet he felt his life was better by you being in it, and yours was too."

I think about Arlo and me brainstorming my hero's journey, like my life was one of his movies. All those visits with him and I never really returned the favor. I should have asked more questions, found more time. That's hitting me hard now even as I try to listen to what Imani's telling me. "Just because he's gone," she says, "well, it's not like an Etch A Sketch, you know? He's gone but he's not erased."

"I really believed that if you just worked hard—"

"Look—" Imani interjects. "I've never known how to tell you this because I know that's some stuff that you needed to believe. But I've never been all about that whole hard-work-get-ahead shtick. In my experience that's just as easily a load a B.S. as it is not—sorry, I think I just went to ninety-five percent honesty on that one. But I mean, maybe it's not that if you work hard you always get ahead, it's just that if you don't give up, don't give in, then things still have the chance of working out some way or another. Maybe you just have to still be hanging around when luck shows up. Right?"

I take a deep, heavy breath. I don't know. I appreciate what she's saying. But I also feel like it could be just as much a bunch of B.S. I hope not. And she's usually right, we know this.

Things aren't fixed, far from it, but maybe they're a shade

better. "Okay," I say. "I don't feel it yet, but okay, if you say so."

"I do," she says with Imani-level confidence.

"What did you want to talk to me about, anyway? What's going on with you—this thing you and Dannie are doing every time I see you?"

"I—" She hesitates. "I think I better run, actually. I slept in and I'm going to get it if I don't get that dishwasher unloaded. Are you good?"

Something hangs on the line between us, but I don't trust myself to know what's what right now, and maybe it's just me reading into things. Or maybe not. "Imani?" I say, feeling my chest go all tight. "Is everything okay?"

She gives me a long look, and if we weren't in the judgment-free zone I might give her a hard time for going mushy-eyed on me. "Love you, Max" is all she says.

"A hundred percent honesty," I say. "I don't know what I'd do without you."

I call in sick from work and school, claiming that I have a family emergency. I figure if I'm going to lie, I can at least keep those lies consistent.

As far as I know, Arlo doesn't have a daughter. As far as I know, Arlo doesn't really have anyone. He would have wanted someone to check up on Chester, and I might be the only person who can. Still, it feels strange playing hooky from work just to drive the ten miles to the very neighborhood I usually work in, but it feels even stranger to consider that the last time I was here, Arlo Oxley was already dead.

I don't think he would have liked that word much—*dead*. He probably would have preferred something like *past tense*. Or better yet, *a not-so-living legend*.

It's at his house—his former house—that I find the slip from social services in the middle of a pile of magazines and junk brochures crammed into the mailbox. I hold the notice between my hands. What is it about paper that always makes things feel so official?

But there it is. Printed in black and white: *Deceased*.

I feel everything in me—my breath, my heart, my blood—go still.

I don't know anyone who's died before. Even my grandparents are alive. And, look, I know Arlo wasn't like my grandpa or anything, but I can still stand here and feel the bigness and the smallness of the world just knowing that he's not in it anymore. Something existed and now it doesn't. Someone was here and now he's not. And I don't have the right words to explain the physics and philosophy of non-existence. I can only say that "hollow" doesn't really feel like absence, and "gone" doesn't feel like space, and "futures" don't feel unwritten. They feel erased. So maybe Imani doesn't know everything after all.

I fold the slip into a square and tuck it neatly in my pocket. I have no idea what will happen to Arlo's house or to his art or his Oscar or his books or his old photographs. I guess there are lawyers who will deal with that. For now, all I'm worried about is Chester and the new address I'd read on the notice.

1 canine removed from property to Fountain Valley SPCA

Back at my car, I step on the gas and ten minutes later, I'm pulling up to the animal shelter where the parking lot is empty and the whole place has vaguely zombie apocalypse vibes. The cinder block side of the building has been painted with a bright mural of dogs, cats, and parakeets playing together in harmony. As for real dogs, I don't see a single one roaming the fenced yard out front. The thin soles of my fake faded black Keds crunch through the gravel. A handwritten sign is tacked to the glass door: *By appointment only*. I knock.

And knock and knock and knock until finally I hear the lock on the door slide out of place and a set of cowbells dangling on the other side clang.

A sunburned guy with shoulder-length hair answers. "You have an appointment?" His question is muffled by a black fabric mask.

"I'm looking for a dog. He was brought in here a couple days ago, I think."

"Yeah, but do you have an appointment?" He slouches against the door.

"No."

"Well. You're supposed to have an appointment." He points to the sign.

"Okay then, I'd like to make an appointment."

He brightens. "Hold on, let me get the calendar." He slumps off like this is the only thing he has to do today and can therefore take all the time in the world. "Okay, when would you like to come in?" His pen hovers.

"How about today at eleven o'clock?"

"Let me check, let me check. Okay, yes, today, eleven o'clock. That's available, I'll mark you down. Your name?"

"Max Mauro." I wait for him to scribble it down. "Great. Now I have an appointment." I watch him check the clock on the wall behind him. Imagine that. It's eleven. I shrug when he looks back at me. "I'm looking for a dog that was brought in. A big black poodle. Goes by the name of Chester."

"I don't know, man. I just got here." He points me in the direction of a wire gate around the side of the building. I unlatch it and enter a courtyard of open-air kennels. As soon as I enter, the dogs start barking and pawing at their cages. I'm free to roam the yard, examining each of the dog runs, hopeful that I'll see Chester.

I try not to linger at any one of the cages. A pregnant Chihuahua. An old cocker spaniel with wet ears. A pit bull mix lying sullenly with his nose in an empty bowl. Each one watches me with wet-ringed eyes and I steel myself. No one is coming for them.

The long-haired dude meanders outside. "You know they keep the newer ones over here." I bite my tongue to keep from mentioning that no, there's absolutely no way I would know that, and instead follow him to the far corner of the yard where a group of seven cages are clustered.

The stench is something terrible and I suspect it'd be much worse without the mask. "Chester?" I test out, not worried about sounding silly in front of Mr. Personality over here. "Chester? Here, boy."

I look into each of the faces of the dogs I see. A Lab with one eye. A terrier with a shaved ear and stitches. Two puppies rolling on the concrete, pushing against each other with their paws. Then, huddled in the back of a shallow kennel, I see him. A black lump hiding his face in his hind quarters. His poufs have lost all their poof and he has never looked less fabulous. My heart squeezes. "Chester." I kneel in front of the wire barrier. "Chester! It's Max, buddy."

Slowly, he raises his head and looks at me. It's like he senses it, like he knows that Arlo's really and truly gone. I take out the bag of baby carrots I've brought with me. Slowly, he rises to his feet and pads over. He sniffs at my hand, his nose wet and sloppy against my skin. His tail slowly begins to wag, then more insistently. I push the carrots toward him and he takes one carefully between his teeth. I scratch between his ears. He's probably self-conscious without his bow tie, poor thing.

"So, you going to take him or what?" The guy asks.

"I—" Of course that's what he would think. Of course that's what I *want*. "I'm sorry. It costs a lot of money at our apartment to have a dog. Plus my mom's allergic." There's a security deposit. And it's an extra fifty dollars a month at least. I'm realizing that I can't ask my mom for this. Not right now. I just can't. "What will happen to him?" I thought what I needed was to see with my own eyes that Chester was safe, but standing here now I don't feel that way at all. I just want to bring him home.

"There was a run on all the puppies right at the start of everything, but not a lot of foot traffic lately. Especially for the old ones." He stretches his back and looks around. "If he doesn't get adopted, he'll be put down eventually."

"Put *down*?"

"I know. It's a tough break."

I stretch my fingers out and Chester licks them. Arlo alone. Chester alone. I've always prided myself on being just fine on my own, but maybe that's not such a great thing after all.

chapter eighteen

JONAH

The little white pill sits on the desk. Some days they are shining beacons of hope, and others the white flag of surrender . . . a reminder that I need to have my happiness packaged in a bottle. It's my last antidepressant, but Kate is picking up my prescription today, and soon I will have another hundred days of happiness sitting in my drawer.

But this pill is also a reminder that I can't always trust my own brain. That it can trick me. That it can make mistakes, or lie to me, and it can get people hurt.

And now I might have just messed up the one bright spot with my ill-fated virtual dance. I guess I wanted to pretend things could be normal . . . and instead I reminded her that we are a million miles from normal right now. I don't know how to fix that yet. I don't even know where to start.

And it's not the only thing on my mind.

I pop the pill with a drink of stale Dasani. The anniversary is in two days. It stalks closer, a looming spectre hanging over everything, and this third round feels like it's going to hit me hard in a world of triggers. I check my last messages with Max. Still nothing since last night . . . a string of awkward apologies and awkward assurances that we're both "fine." Yeah. I made Max cry at a made-up formal. That's *fine*.

I glance at the window, at the message on the glass, written in a permanent marker because I'm an idiot, though it's fading a little more every day. Maybe faster some days. Kate has been on my case to wipe it off. She says it looks like we live in a frat house, which feels a bit overdramatic, but hey, pick your battles, I guess. I sigh and go find some Windex.

Of course, I wrote it on the outside of the window, so I have to open it up and get into the same weird, contorted pose with my back against the window frame.

"Don't do it," a sarcastic voice says.

I twist around and see Olivia standing on the front lawn, inspecting some new item she has ordered. She actually looks somewhat composed today. Her hair is still a frizzy auburn supernova, but she isn't wearing a housecoat or silk pajamas, and she seems to have mustered up some capri pants and an actual T-shirt, which is a small miracle.

"What's your deal?" I ask, flipping myself back into scrub mode.

It must have been a damn good marker, because it's just smudging more with every wipe. I spray some Windex and end up getting half of it in my mouth.

"Virtual classes have resumed," Olivia says. "I have an evening class later."

"Does this mean you're going to stop building pergolas and opening pottery barns?"

"I suppose. I just bought this processor so I can try my hand at bitcoin mining."

I groan, managing a last good scrubbing, and then check my progress. The message is gone. I already miss it.

"If you're going to space out, dearest brother, try not to do it while hanging out a window."

I grunt and slip back inside, peering down at her. "Is it rude if I close this now?"

"Yes. What are we going to do this year?"

"With—"

"With Mom. You know it's in two days."

I look away. "Yeah. I remember."

"I would like to do a memorial. I thought maybe we could plant a tree in the yard."

"No, thanks."

She stares up at me, slipping the box into the crook of her arm. "Kate thought it was—"

"*Kate* doesn't get a vote. I don't want to do anything."

"So you're going to lock yourself in your room? Not talk all day again like last year?"

"Probably. Is that allowed?"

"Well, *I* am going to do something this year and plant a tree. *I* want a place to talk with her, since I can't exactly go walk around the cemetery right now. *I* want to remember my mom. And it would be nice if my little brother would join me. I have already prepared a few words."

"And I am sure it's a masterpiece like everything else you do. *I* won't be there. *I* just want to get through the day."

"You really are selfish," she snaps, shaking her head. "It's all about you, isn't it?"

"Yes. My mourning process is about me. Because mine is different from yours."

She rolls her eyes. "I know . . . it's much worse—"

"It is!" I shout, which I apparently like to do these days.

"This is what you do. You make up little narratives in your head and we're all just characters. You narrate. You choose what happened. You disregard whatever facts you want. Hop over to my story for a minute or two, Jonah."

"You are fine! Look at you. You're about to mine freaking bitcoins."

She smiles thinly. "Of course. I'm fine . . . you decided that. Why bother asking?"

Olivia walks inside, leaving me alone with my head out the window, and I see Mrs. Clodden across the street smoking and eavesdropping and I just scowl and close it. No more hopeful words. Just the steady midday sun beating in through the glass.

I close the blinds and flop into bed, checking my phone. Still nothing from Max. So instead, steady scrolling through TikTok. Little intervals of happier lives. Choppy fragmented glimpses into all the things I don't feel like doing. I toss my phone aside.

Carlos F. Santi: Do you ever think about the meaning of life?

Jonah: Do you???

Carlos F. Santi: No but I did today. I figured it out

Jonah: . . .

Carlos F. Santi: See I thought it was about being happy. But it's not

Jonah: Thank goodness

Carlos F. Santi: It's about love

Jonah: oh god

Carlos F. Santi: Because it's HARD. You experience all these emotions and it makes you question like why am I even here? But then it works and it's the greatest thing in the world

Jonah: Are you dating someone

Carlos F. Santi: Maybe. But just on the computer. I promise

Jonah: SO WHAT IS THE MEANING OF LIFE

Carlos F. Santi: To love one special person!

Jonah: I thought there were *multiple* peas

Carlos F. Santi: You just pull the other ones out! Throw them away, man! Then there are only two left, and sure, the pod is kind of messed up and maybe they'll fall out but still

Jonah: please stop

Carlos F. Santi: What I am saying is, you just need to show her how you feel

Jonah: I just invited her to a virtual formal and she wept!!!!!!!!!

Carlos F. Santi: Honestly I thought the idea was pretty cute. It was like magic.

Carlos F. Santi: But maybe it just needs to be simpler?

Jonah: . . .

Jonah: I just wish I could see her

Carlos F. Santi: So do something special for her. But, like, not so complicated. SHOW her how you feel, dude. Take your shirt off . . . well not you, but like in a metamorphosis sense. Like play to your strengths

Jonah: Metaphorical, Carlos. It's metaphorical. What are my strengths again

Carlos F. Santi: You know a lot of words. And you got that dimple. *Use the dimple, Jonah* (like imagine that in Obi-Wan's voice!)

Jonah: We're done here

Carlos F. Santi: Think I should make an IG post about all this? Like my meaning of life

Jonah: Yes. Move over Confucius . . . Carlos F. Santi has this covered.

Carlos F. Santi: What's a Confucius?

Jonah: goodbye

Jonah: . . . but call me later I want to hear about the new guy

I wish Kate would just surrender family dinners, but here we are. Here we always are. How was your day, Jonah? Completely useless? Super. Olivia? Oh . . . you built a time machine? Very nice.

I am shoveling down a vegan meat loaf so I can flee back to my room, but it's like eating sand and Olivia is glaring at me from across the table while Kate looks between us like a boxing referee.

"Is something the matter?" she asks finally.

"Are we vegan now?" I ask, forcing another mouthful down. "I didn't get a vote."

She exchanges a knowing look with Olivia. I hate that look. It says: *What* ever *shall we do with this boorish young gadabout?* And yes it's in an olde English accent. Kate smiles.

"I thought we would try something new. We have discussed a lifestyle change."

"Vegan? *Now?* Shouldn't we be storing canned goods or something for the apocalypse? The rest of the world is hoarding toilet paper and we're going to secure the bok choy?"

Olivia taps her finger on the table. "You know," she says, voice drier than the meat loaf, "the kitchen is open. You are more than welcome to use it."

I want to yell but I probably am being an ass and I just take a breath. Picking a fight with everyone when you are trapped inside a box of emotions is probably not a good idea.

"Thank you for dinner, Kate," I grumble. "I love soy and chickpeas and . . . soy."

"It is rather dry," she says, smiling through a sip of wine. "So . . . Wednesday."

Okay, never mind, this isn't going to end well. "I won't be there. I'm sorry."

She nods. "When I got divorced—"

"*Please* stop talking about your surfer ex-husband. It's not relevant. Did you reconsider what I asked you about this morning? Like at all?"

"It's just not the right time for a new addition—"

I lay my fork down and sit back, folding my arms. "It's the *only* time."

"I'm sorry, Jonah," she says, shaking her head. "I know it's been tough on you. I know you were looking forward to Paris—"

"I'm stuffed," I cut in. "I'll do the dishes . . . just leave them."

"Spending the day with Max?" Olivia asks.

I'm already heading for my room, but I stop, wary all of a sudden. "I planned something for the evening. We'll be way apart from each other, though . . . so you're both safe."

"Does this really make sense right now—" Kate starts.

"I don't know. I haven't planned it all out yet. Are you going to forbid me from going? Lock me in my room? You wanted me to do *something*. So, I will."

Kate sighs. "I'm just going to ask that you make the mature decision."

"Much appreciated," I mutter, hurrying upstairs and closing the door safely behind me. I managed to keep it together, I guess, but I feel my blood boiling. Not about

Max . . . they have every right to ask. But I don't want to talk to Kate about my mom. Ever.

I grab my phone. I feel like I'm fighting with everyone right now . . . but at least one of them is definitely my fault. Possibly all. But right now, I just need to make amends with Max.

Jonah: Okay I need to make a confession. I have terrible instincts. I get things wrong like 99% of the time and the other times are when I ask Olivia what to do. And the dance thing? Totally, inexcusably ill-timed. The world is on fire so let's wear dresses and drink bubbly yay! But please know that despite any bumbling, stupid miscues (past and future) I really just want to play any small role I can in making this bad time a little better for you. And if we can share a popcorn one day . . . well, that would be nice too. You know how I feel. I wear my heart on my sleeve except I take it from there and throw it at people. I guess, in summary, I'm sorry, let's never speak of virtual dances ever again, and I would love to watch TV in elastic-waist pants with you again soon

I send it before I read it over because I know I'll write fifty drafts otherwise. But then I do read it and yeah less was probably going to be more in this case. Though, in fairness, I started the text by admitting I suck at everything. I sigh and put the phone aside, figuring I'll see if Carlos wants to play some *Call of Duty,* but my phone pings. I quickly scoop it up, seeing *Max.*

Max: I could really use that right now

I let out a long, relieved breath. But it also doesn't really sound like Max . . . I was pretty sure I was about to get a comment about my melodrama, at best.

Jonah: I'm ready anytime. Everything okay?

Max: Not exactly

Jonah: Can I call?

Max: I'll call in a sec. Just let me get myself together

Jonah: Okay I'm freaking out a little

Max: . . .

Max: Arlo passed away. The hospital called me earlier.

I sit back down on the bed, feeling numbness settle over me. I didn't know Arlo very well. But I had bought in, hook, line, and sinker. I'd convinced myself there was a happy ending en route. A love story gone right. A little win for Arlo and my mom's favorite cowboy.

My anxiety rides the wave. I can feel the questions starting. But I push them away.

For once, I realize this is absolutely not about me.

Jonah: I'm so sorry, Max. Take the time you need. If I can do anything just let me know

She calls me a minute later, and she's in her pj's, hair bundled up in a messy bun, big green eyes just a little red and puffy. I open my mouth to say something, but Max speaks first.

"Can we watch really awful TV and eat everything?" she says.

I smile. "Absolutely. Should I put on my duck jammies?"

"That would be perfect." She pauses. "There is one other thing you can do."

"Anything."

"Can you send me Winter's email? I . . . I think I'd like to be the one to tell him."

"Of course. I really am sorry, Max. I know Arlo meant a lot to you."

She nods, and her eyes look a bit glassy as she drops onto the couch. "Me too." Max glances at me, brushing loose strands of hair from her face. "And . . . you do, by the way."

"Do what?"

"Make it better," she says quietly.

I just nod too, because that means everything, and I don't know how to say that.

"But, yeah, I'm really going to need you to change into those duck jammies," Max says.

"Max, if there is one thing I was born to do, it's to spread happiness via flannel waterfowl."

chapter nineteen

MAX

I blame Baader-Meinhof.

I have no idea if that's a person or what and, even if it is, let's face it, he's probably dead, but that won't stop me from deciding that this is basically all his fault.

I wake up to the sound of my mom's coughing.

Baader-Meinhof is basically that phenomenon of having a frequency bias. Like I hear a song for the first time and suddenly I'm hearing it everywhere. It's driving me crazy, I'm hearing it so much. But am I really or am I just suddenly aware of it?

Through my thin bedroom wall, I listen to the staccato bursts of my mother's coughing. Baader. Freaking. Meinhof.

I kick off my sheets and nearly trip over Sir Scratchmo, who doesn't seem to be aware of anything other than a diamond patch of sunlight on the carpet. My mom is a lump in her bed, shifting in the dimness of her bedroom.

"Mom?" I murmur from the threshold. The room smells stale. She turns and her eyes shine in the gray light. "Are you okay?"

She scrunches up the pillow underneath her head. Her black hair splays out into veins on the pillowcase. "Are you leaving for work?" She sounds like my mom and I don't know what I'd been expecting.

"In a little while." My shoulder leans on the doorframe. I'm still in my favorite pair of gray sweatpants, the ones that are fuzzy inside and that my mom sometimes tries to steal when she thinks I won't notice because they're really that comfortable. "Are you sick?" I ask, not sure I want to know, worried that if I do, I might realize that I already did.

"Just allergies." She looks relaxed, calm, like she's getting ready to drift off to sleep, and I try to let some of that energy rub off on me.

"You're sure?"

There's a long beat. "The pollen's been terrible the last few days. You haven't noticed?"

"Maybe I'm immune," I say, meaning one thing and also something else entirely. I've been careful, I remind myself. I never got too close to Arlo. Though, I was, I realize, inside his house. Not to mention the grocery store, day in and day out. If anyone is the weakest link, it's me.

What I wouldn't give to have a cotton swab stuffed up my nose just to know what's what. In a perfect world, I might have. In a perfect world, even without a test, I would have locked myself up for fourteen days and thrown away the key. But my world's so far from perfect, we aren't even neighbors.

My feet are tired from jogging up and down people's driveways. My arms are sore from carrying grocery bags. Every morning my back hurts from sitting in my car for too many hours. And I still haven't got the slightest clue how to help poor Chester, who, let's be real, is not cut out for anything less than a five-star hotel.

"When's your next paycheck?" Mom asks, and I wish she would try to hide her eagerness from me, but she doesn't.

"Friday. I'm supposed to have school today." I've been racking up absences, and the weirdest thing is, my mom has been pretending not to notice.

"I can write you a note," she offers in a tone that suggests this is perfectly normal Mom behavior.

I understand that I do have a choice in the matter, but it's not a good one. So I promise to check on her and she insists that she's fine and I figure I have to believe her because if I don't, we're screwed. It's so obvious that, clearly, neither of us needs to say it out loud.

Up until now, I've always thought of myself as a pretty honest person—but maybe just not with as high a percentage of honesty as I thought. *You will go to a four-year college. You'll get a fancy business degree. If you work hard, you'll get ahead. Everything is fine.* Well, maybe if I'd asked myself for 100 percent honesty, I'd have realized that all that was nothing but a lie I told myself to get through the day.

But I'm in too deep now.

I wash my face. I pull on overalls. I brush my hair and my

teeth. I lace up my shoes. I put in my earbuds. And it's then that I see a missed text from last night.

Jonah: Are you free on Wednesday? Want to get together? (like totally outside and careful etc.) I have a thing. A nice thing. Not a big thing. I can explain later.

A good lie is like a good magic trick. To pull it off, the person has to believe, has to not think too hard, has to look-over-here.

Max: Sounds good, I could actually use the distraction.

Welcome to the Twilight Zone, I think when I arrive at Vons, where the hottest club in town is now the grocery store. A line snakes around the corner and a bagger-turned-bouncer stands at the front of it, controlling how many people get to go inside at once. He waves at me as I cut the line and step right inside like I'm the least cool VIP that ever existed, but, hey, I'll take it.

I've already got a list of five orders to fill and the managers have been encouraging us to make it snappy so we can try to help out more people. The idea makes me tired before it's even lunchtime. I like to start with produce so that my customers aren't left with slim pickings. I am getting up-close and personal with the cantaloupe when a call rings through my AirPods.

"Thank god." Dannie's talking fast even for her. "Please just give me two minutes of non-toddler conversation. Please, please, please. Please. I need to talk to someone over two."

"Scarlett's rubbing off on you." I sniff a cantaloupe, checking for the sweet scent beneath the rough outer rind. I still think of Dannie as Dannie Quincy, but she's actually got a whole other name since I first met her—Dannie Ngujo. It happened when her mom and stepdad, Jake, had Scarlett and Jake was all: *Do you want me to adopt you?* And she said "Yes!" so they could all share the same last name. He gave her tulips when he asked and Dannie told us afterward that he was sweating a lot, he was so nervous. It was really sweet.

"Don't say her name," Dannie hisses. "I don't want to talk about the kid, Max. Isn't there anything to discuss anymore other than My Little Pony and *Paw Patrol* and Princess Dairy Wiggle or whatever the hell her name is?"

"I'm sorry, I'm sorry. What about school?" I move down the aisle, palming a pair of lemons and shoving them into a plastic bag. I already know their product number by heart and so I weigh them on the little scale and wait for the bar code to chug from the printer.

"You mean that thing I try to listen to in between trips to the pantry for snacks or when she-who-shall-not-be-named isn't hanging from my neck or saying she's too hot or—look, I'm doing it again. Save me. Have you talked to Imani yet?"

"I . . . did. But—" Damn. I knew something was up with Imani. "I didn't want to . . . you know, be all up in her grill, or whatever. She wasn't exactly forthcoming." I sound a tad defensive.

"I know." I can practically hear Dannie chewing the inside of her cheek.

"What's going on with you two, anyway? You're being super weird. Are we breaking up?" I try it as a joke.

But Dannie doesn't laugh.

"Be careful out there," she says. "No, not you. Scarlett! No, Scarlett!" Dannie's voice goes shrill, stabbing my eardrums. "Not in your mouth. Hold on, I have a toddler with a death wish. Just talk to Imani. Time is running— No!" Before she can finish her thought, the line goes dead.

I wait until I'm outside loading the bags into the trunk of my car before calling Imani. "Grand Central Station," she answers. "Hang on. Let me go find a closet to sit in again." You have to be real friends with Imani to know that she's not joking. We have had a lot of deep conversations sitting on quilts in her linen closet—surprisingly comfortable. "Okay, I'm here."

"So we never got to your thing. Spill. What's going on? Why are you and Dannie scheming behind my back?"

"We're not scheming," says Imani, clear-voiced because closet acoustics are really good.

"I thought the three of us agreed, no secrets."

"We were twelve." Like that should matter. "Okay, look, are you sitting down?"

"No, I'm holding two dozen eggs, a cantaloupe, and a couple of lemons."

"Maybe set those down," Imani says as though she's a hostage negotiator. My skin is going all tingly and I have a horror movie voice inside my head saying: *Don't go in there.* I remind myself it can't be all that bad. It's Imani. Imani's been there for me since Day 1, back when a four-year-old me accidentally tried sitting down on a toilet with the seat up and fell right in. Imani pulled me out, brought me paper towels, and even though she was just a tiny kid, she didn't tell anybody, not even our teacher. Snap to fourth grade, when I drew her some (pretty terrible) pictures—puppies, butterflies, hearts, stars, all the basics—every day of fourth grade when her family had some stuff going on. I happen to know on good authority that she still keeps those in a box in the back of her closet, and speaking of that, we always share clothes because two puny wardrobes makes at least one halfway decent one. So, that's about us in a nutshell.

"Okay," I say. "I'm listening."

"I don't want you to freak out. And just so you know, I would have told you sooner, but I know how hard you've been working, and your mom and then Arlo and, well, I know how you are about . . . well, about things changing." Even though Imani's not wrong, something about hearing her say that about me out loud hurts. She and Dannie both know how unstable things used to be for my mom and me, how our phone number was always changing, our address, my school, her job, and even how I was taken away. But I didn't know my friends saw all those things as, like, this open wound. "We're moving."

"Who?" The question comes out with a gust of relief. Between the three of us, we've all moved too many times to count on two hands.

"My whole family. Even Sweets and Big Paw."

"Okay. Where? Did you guys buy a house? Oh my god, you guys bought a house, didn't you?!"

"Not exactly," she says. "Actually, Sweets has a sister who passed away that I never knew. But that sister left her a whole house in her will and it's big enough for all of us to live in and I can even have my own bathroom."

"Wow, moving on up." And now I maybe see what Imani meant . . . her family worked at it long enough for luck to show up.

"There's a catch."

"Yeah? Like what?"

"It's in Kansas."

"Kansas?!" I shriek, and a lady passing by with a full shopping cart turns to stare at me.

"I know. I . . . we had a family meeting about it. It's a lot cheaper to live there, plus we've got the house that we can fix up even nicer with all of us pitching in and my dad found a job out there already."

I have that shaky feeling in my knees like I just threw up. "When?"

"In three days."

I lean against my dirty old car for support. All this has been happening right underneath my nose. Imani has a whole new life, she's moving on, and I'm moving backward and I don't know what to say because none of this is up to me.

"It's bad timing," she says. "Because I deserve a going-away party. Obviously. But you guys will just have to be all about my virtual housewarming party. And I'll be back to visit. After all this is over."

I really feel like I'm going to be sick now. "That's really . . . exciting."

"Come on. Don't be fake with me."

All around, there is the rattle of shopping cart wheels, the rumble of car engines, hot black pavement and birds hopping around picking for scraps and none of it feels real. "It's not fake. I'm trying to say the right thing because that's how I want to feel about it, and I know that's how I should feel about it. Sixty-six percent honesty." I hope it doesn't take too long for my heart to catch up.

"I hear you," Imani says.

"I really should get through these deliveries," I tell her. She knows better than to object.

But truthfully, I don't have it in me to get back to work. Not yet. I thought I'd been through the hardest part—with my mom, back when I was younger. You know, things suck. The heroine struggles mightily. And in the end, she wins. But life isn't a movie. The lovers aren't even united. *None of this matters anyway.*

And that reminds me.

I pull up the message Jonah forwarded me from Ernest, a.k.a. Winter, and I know that just like you shouldn't drive while drunk, emailing while in the middle of an existential crisis probably isn't such a great idea, either.

Ernest,

Jonah Stephens passed along your email address to me. I was a friend of Arlo's. Listen, sorry we bothered you and got your hopes up. Turns out it was for nothing. When we set out to find you for Arlo, I thought: hey, it's worth a try. But actually trying is kind of a waste of time, I've learned. There actually is no "A for effort." And you can think you have everything all lined up perfectly and—poof!—it's gone. In this case, I'm talking about Arlo. I'm sorry to inform you that he died. I know, it sucks. I'm actually pretty heartbroken myself. But, hey, that's life.

All the best,

Maxine Mauro

I reread the words I've typed out on-screen and think: *They're perfect. I've said it all.*

But . . . too much maybe. I don't mean to be cruel. I delete it and write another.

Ernest,

Jonah Stephens forwarded me your email. Arlo was a good friend to me. He passed away a couple days ago. I'm so sorry.

Maxine Mauro

chapter twenty

JONAH

"Alexa, are you still allowed to have a picnic in California?"

I'm pacing again and I can probably just google this, but she's my go-to these days because she talks and I think it counts as communication. I'm kind of freaking out. Today's been a write-off. It's been a bad anxiety stretch with Arlo's death and Chester in the shelter and general concern for Max, and tomorrow is the anniversary. I can't take all those things on at once. I need something good for tomorrow. I need *Max*.

"I'm sorry. I'm not sure about that," Alexa replies, and she sounds genuinely regretful.

"Hmm. Alexa . . . can I get a fine for being in a park in Fountain Valley?"

She seems to consider that. "You can find all sorts of things in a park. Like—"

"Thank you, Alexa."

Yes, I thank Alexa. It's just good manners, and also I am losing it. It's too late anyway. It's all planned out now. A sunset picnic. The crimson sun in a clear sky (I checked the weather). And we can just be together outside of everything else that's happened and happening. Just me and Max. She already agreed to it, so I know she's still in.

I check the time. It's nearly midnight. I'm restless and anxious and thinking about Max and Arlo and Winter and the anniversary and . . . everything. There's definitely no point trying to sleep. I go to find snacks instead.

Olivia has beaten me to it, eating straight from a tub of ice cream while reading. She looks up at me over the brim of her glasses. "I put the chips in the cupboard over the fridge."

"Thanks."

It's still a little weird between us. I thought that was impossible, because Olivia doesn't usually do social barriers or polite indifference. She just says something deeply cutting and we move on from there. But for some reason, she has sheathed her knives.

I grab the bag and eat leaning against the counter, popping ketchup chips into my mouth and thinking I should go upstairs . . . but I also really want us to be normal again. So I linger, watching her read, noticing the aquamarine bathrobe has returned in all its crusty glory.

"What are you reading?" I ask.

"Chomsky. And simultaneously recalling why ice cream is my late night snack of choice."

"Why?"

"It has an audible advantage."

I sigh and try to chew more quietly. It just sounds louder. "I'm going to bed."

"Good night." I am halfway out the door when she adds: "Change your mind?"

"No."

She leans back, closing the book. "I'd like you to attend. I made a playlist."

"No, *thank you.*"

"You didn't do it, Jonah. You just made a phone call."

"I don't want to talk about this."

"You just want to close your eyes and hope it will all fade away, right?"

"Actually, I want to open my eyes and realize that it was all a bad dream."

Oliva stares at me as she scrapes out the last of the ice cream. "Been a long dream."

"I'm happy you're doing what you need to tomorrow. Honestly. I just won't be here."

"Still hanging out with Max?"

"Yeah. Someone who doesn't know what day it is . . . and who won't remind me."

Olivia nods thoughtfully. "And you're still being careful?"

"Not so much as a kiss, masked or otherwise."

I didn't tell them about Arlo. That he just *died* of the coronavirus. They didn't really know about Winter and the search, and I guess I told myself they didn't need to know about any of it. But I know Max was very careful. It's not worth mentioning it . . . mostly because I know what they would say. If they thought there was contact, Kate would lock me in my room and throw away the key. But Max told me she never even went within ten feet of Arlo, and I saw firsthand how cautious she was around him.

Olivia just shakes her head and goes back to the book. "Well, have fun."

I linger for a moment longer, because nothing has changed, and then I pop another chip into my mouth and go back upstairs to my fortress of solitude. I figure we'll let the anniversary pass, she can eulogize, I can extricate myself, and we'll be right back to normal. I flop onto my bed and find a message from Max.

Max: Normally I would never message someone at midnight but you did claim you never sleep so hi?

Jonah: Correction. I lie here eating chips until three in the morning, sleep fitfully until sunrise, and then fall into a deep slumber until 11:30 when I wake up with deep self-loathing. So . . .

Max: So same idea

Jonah: You know . . . we could be insomnia buddies

Max: Did you really just buddy me again

Jonah: . . .

Jonah: I retract my text. But I think we're onto something. Insomnia is usually a lonely activity. A time for pondering whether the shirt you wore that day was too mauve after all. But we can play games!

Max: If you say truth or dare I'm going to do the unthinkable and go to sleep

Jonah: Max

Max: Yes

Jonah: I have riddles

Max: zzzzzzzz

Jonah: Magic tricks? I will require both FaceTime and a complete lack of expectations

Max: I do my best not sleeping in pitch blackness. Better for existential dread

Jonah: Of course. I know they say get up and do something instead but what do scientists know, I slept fine once. A few months ago. I think we had turkey

Max: Can I ask you something

Jonah: Anything. Unless it's about magic tricks I don't know any I was bluffing

Max: Do you think we would work, like, outside of all this? That we would actually stay together

Jonah: Yes

Max: Is that your master's thesis or . . .

Jonah: I know what you're saying. We are kind of rocking the distance thing. Minus one or two slight miscalculations. But we haven't done the other stuff and it's possible that we'll suck at that

Max: That's direct and slightly alarming

Jonah: NO I meant like meeting parents and stuff. I assure you . . . I can hold hands the best of them. I don't even get clammy palms. It's genetic

Max: As always, so many questions. So you think it'll just be lockdown lifted, we run into each other's arms and be the normal couple who met over toilet paper what a cute story but also it was all so very awful

Jonah: Wow you really do get dark past midnight

Max: What if we are that pandemic couple Jonah? The ones that just needed a distraction and when and if we get out of this we don't have a connection anymore because it was built on anxiety and insomnia

Jonah: That's how I build everything. Of course it does all come crashing to the ground . . .

Max: JONAH

Jonah: Honestly, I think building a relationship during the shitty times is kind of genius. It's like the world is on fire. I can't even go near you, everything is terrible and . . . we're still here. We're texting each other at midnight because you are the one person I want to talk to when everything is terrible

Max: I truly can't decide if that's romantic or not

Jonah: I don't want things to go *back to normal.* It's not like things were perfect before. I WANT to come out of all this different, and, ideally, with you

Max: Okay that was slightly romantic. Also terribly cliche. Is that from a movie?

Jonah: Yes it is. *Max and Jonah's Infinite Essential Playlist*

Max: Yeah I'm going to bed. I have to wake up at 6 am

Jonah: There's a 6 am?

Max: goodnight

Jonah: Still on for tomorrow?

Max: Just have to pick out the right cocktail dress. Also are you sure this is a good idea?

Jonah: All required safety protocols are being implemented. Plus spare utensils. But this is going to be totally low-key. No music. No accomplices. Just a nice simple evening.

Max: All right . . .

I lie there for a while, vaguely considering some sort of healthy distraction. And then I down a whole bag of chips and watch *Contagion* because I am a masochistic idiot and go to bed full of salt, grease, and fear, and that always leads to a productive sleep.

I lie there and think, and I don't know where the dreams start and the memories end. It can't be a dream because it happened exactly like that. But it can't be a memory because I can see it. I can *feel* it. I am at school and then I am in the hospital and I can smell the Lysol and taste the dry air and I can see the doctor walking toward me and I sit down. *I sit down.* I remember that perfectly, or dream it, because I can feel the hard plastic.

"I'm sorry," she says. I don't hear the rest.

Olivia is crying. My father is crying. And I am sitting, silent, staring at the wall. Someone's touching me, hugging me, but I don't remember who, or my dream doesn't care, because I just remember the cream-colored wall and the sound of my dad crying. I had never heard him cry before.

And then I see her casket. I see the priest talking, but I didn't hear him then, and I don't now. Then she is in the ground, and I am at home, staring at the ceiling in the darkness.

No. Light is forming a halo around my blinds. It's morning, and it came so fast, I know it was at least partly a dream. I feel bile stinging the back of my throat. Olivia wants me to plant a tree and remember. She doesn't get it. I *always* remember. Today, this one annual day in particular, I need to forget.

I give myself a game plan as I crawl out of bed. It's not the anniversary. It's my date with Max. It's a picnic in the park at sunset. Of course, sunset is a long way away . . . but I planned that out too. Classes all day. Clean my room because I saved that job for today and it needs it. A long run. A protracted shower. An early departure to set things up for Max. Stay scheduled. Stay busy. The thought of seeing Max gives me something to look forward to, keeps me focused on the future. I go to get breakfast and get changed and sit down for school and everything is fine.

Today is my date with Max. It's going to be a good day.

chapter twenty-one

MAX

I've heard stories about people with bad gut feelings. That one person who, at the last minute, didn't board the plane that later crashed. The woman who got weird vibes from that nice guy asking for help with his groceries who totally turned out to be a serial killer. The identical twin who knew the moment his brother was killed in a car accident.

For the record, I've always thought that was a load of baloney. Something I've been reminding myself of for the last two-plus hours.

"Hi, Mom? Just checking in. Text or call."

"Hi, Mom? Getting your voice mail again. Can you call me back?"

"Hi, Mom? How are you feeling? Call me back when you're up."

"Hi, Mom?"

No answer. It's important to remind myself what I believe. Or rather, what I don't. I don't believe everything happens for a reason. I don't believe in signs. I don't believe in having no regrets. I don't believe in karma. I don't believe I have a superhuman Spidey sense that something is wrong. I am not a Marvel character.

I drive my shift on autopilot, letting the comfortingly posh voice of the GPS lady tell me what to do. I think logically. That queasy feeling in the pit of my stomach is probably just indigestion, a normal response to the fact that my mother believes expiration dates are a conspiracy and last night we ate hot dogs. That tightness in my chest doesn't mean anything other than I should really try to do cardio more than once a year. That tingle creeping up the back of my neck—

"Hi, Mom?" I try again, and get her voice mail: *Sorry I missed you—*

Two more grocery orders sit in my trunk. I check the map. It will take me at least thirty minutes to deliver them both. Screw it. I pull a hard U-turn.

I have a bad feeling.

It's five o'clock. My mom's keys are on the hook. I thought she might be on a cleaning shift at the doctors' office plaza by now. Her laptop is closed on the kitchen table. The microwave door hangs wide open.

"Why weren't you answering any of my calls?" I yell out because I'm suddenly sort of pissed off. We need that money. She's the one who said so. And now where am I? Not where I should be, that's for sure.

But the apartment is quiet. No TV on. No sound of my mother talking on the phone. Just the buzz of our air-conditioning unit. "Mom?" The light's off in her room. I flip it on. For a solid five seconds I experience a sense of relief like I've never felt before. Her shape is so familiar, lying with her back to me, the covers pushed down to the bottom of the bed, the wrinkles puckered on the bottom of her bare feet. Gently, I shake her shoulder. "You had me worried." I roll my eyes, because just try to imagine if I pulled a stunt like this. She'd straight up kill me.

She doesn't move. Her breath rattles like a lawn mower starting up. Like my rickety old car.

"Hey." I nudge harder. "*Hey.*"

She stirs. Her legs bicycle-pump in her sleep and slowly, she rolls onto her back and stares up at me glassy-eyed.

"Max?" Strands of hair stick to her forehead. "What . . ." She gives up without finishing her sentence.

"Do you have a fever?" I touch her skin with the back of my hand. Heat radiates. "Hang on." I back out of the room quickly and go to the kitchen to wash my hands and retrieve my mask from the table, which I put on for the first time ever at home. Next I rummage through the bottom cabinet of our shared bathroom, tossing aside half-used bottles of lotion, a box of tampons, Walgreens samples, and nail polish remover until I find what I'm looking for.

Back in her bedroom, I place the ancient thermometer under her tongue and command her to hold it there. Her chest swells and contracts, swells and contracts. After two minutes, I hold the thermometer up and turn it in the light until I can make out the thin line of mercury.

Shit.

"It's one oh four." My tone comes out scolding.

She pinches her eyes closed. "It'll be okay."

"Okay? *Mom.* You clearly have COVID," I say, matter-of-factly because *come on.*

"You don't know that."

Except that I do know that. "Mom," I say. "I've been at work. I've delivered people's groceries. I've been inside Vons. *You've* been at work. Cleaning doctors' offices. Where there are sick people." I pace, flapping the thermometer against my thigh.

"We were really careful. You're always . . . so careful, Max." I glance away from the look of desperation I see reflected back at me. Deep breath in, like her lungs are strapped to a massage chair set to vibrate. "Even if I do." Exhale. "Most people . . . recover fine . . . at home."

"We should go to the doctor."

"I don't need to go to the doctor." We've been here before. Doctors are expensive. There are always bills that come after a doctor's visit. Tricky ones. Ones we're not expecting. Even with our insurance.

"You do." I try to remember everything I've heard about coronavirus in the last few weeks, but it feels like a giant lake of information. I can't hold any of it in my head.

"No." I know she means this word to be final and that she thinks she's giving me her scary Mauro Mom look, but really, it's just sad.

"I'll make you something to eat."

I take it one step at a time. Raid the cabinets for a can of Campbell's Rice and Stars. Turn on the stove and shake out the congealed contents. It holds the shape of the can for a solid thirty seconds. I add water and stir. For once, I don't put in my headphones. Instead, I listen closely for the sound of her breathing. I know we don't live in a palace or anything, but a kitchen to a bedroom is still a long way to be able to hear someone's breathing who isn't Darth Vader.

She eats soup. I eat nothing. Somehow two hours pass and I'm still in the clothes I wore to work. She naps. I pace. I question everything. I watch TV with the volume turned down. There are whole half hours that pass during which everything seems fine. My mom laughs. It makes her cough, but it's still laughing, which has to be a good sign. This from the girl who still definitely, probably doesn't believe in signs.

I slink away to call work and apologize. I get someone to restock the two deliveries still sitting in my car. My customers will be mad, but I can live with that.

"Do you need anything?" I ask just after nine, too wired to sleep yet still exhausted.

It takes my brain a moment to process what I'm seeing. My mom slouched on the floor beside her bed, her head drooped between her knees. She's panting, panting, panting.

"I . . . can't . . ." She wheezes, a sharp, high-pitched whine with every breath. "Breathe." Her fingers spread out, clutching at the fitted sheet. Her eyes are wild, whites showing the entire way around her pupils. "I . . . can't . . . breathe." Her fingernails scratch at the carpet. She fights for air. It's like she's underwater.

"Mom. Try to relax."

She's tossing her head. Gulping. She reaches for her chest.

This time I don't ask. I'm almost glad my mom can't argue. I grab my phone and I'm dialing 911 before I can think through what I'm doing.

"Yes." I press my finger into my ear, listening hard to the steady male voice on the other end of the line. "Yes, my mother. She can't breathe." I glance through to her bedroom and then wish that I hadn't. "Her fever was one oh four last time I checked. . . . Yes." I remain calm. Panic does not create solutions. My mom taught me that. "Okay . . . yes. I can do that." I give him our address, and just as the operator asked, I unlock the door to the apartment, run a dishcloth under the faucet, and place it on my mother's forehead. Then I wait.

My mom takes far fewer breaths than she should in the space that follows. I haven't even told her yet. I don't need to. Her fist pounds the floor. For the first time in more than ten years, I wish I had a dad.

"It's going to be okay," I say, not that either of us is listening. Sir Scratchmo meows for his food nearby. The statistics are in our favor. That's key. Most cases are mild. Some people don't even know they have coronavirus at all.

I really wish I were an idiot and that I could believe that nonsense. Rainbows and fluffy clouds and unicorns. But I am not that kind of girl. I know better.

When the paramedic pounds on the door, when they clomp through with face shields and latex gloves, patches sewn to their sleeves, when they Velcro the blood pressure cuff to her arm, and place a stethoscope under her shirt, when I miss all the words they say into their handset radios, when they wheel in a gurney, I am thinking one word and that word's *Arlo*.

"I'm coming with her." I trail the female paramedic, a redhead with a severe ponytail.

"I'm sorry." She holds out her gloved hand like a stop sign. "But there are no visitors allowed."

"But she's my mother."

"I understand." Her mouth moves beneath the mask. "But no visitors. It's protocol right now."

I twist my fingers together and try to come up with something to say. I've never been good at talking my way out of anything. I have never been called "charming."

"Let me come in the ambulance at least," I say.

"Miss. I need you to step aside."

Out of some preconditioned behavior, I do. "I'm a minor," I attempt.

"Miss," she says, this time with more emphasis. "We can call CPS on the way to have someone check on you."

"No!" Her words shoot through me like a lightning bolt. "I'll call someone. I—"

"Your mother is crashing. She needs to get to a hospital. Now." It all happens so fast. And also in slow motion. Like a time warp. A galaxy wormhole. An alternate reality.

They leave the door open. Dazed, I shut it and sink onto the couch, understanding without meaning to that tonight might be the last time I see my mother alive.

chapter twenty-two

JONAH

I step out of the shower with a burst of steam, scrubbed raw and pink, smelling like a—I check the bottle—alpine breeze, and smile into the mirror because I am doing a hell of a job so far. I went to virtual school and sat at my desk and I even participated and never once left for a snack. After my last class, I went for a run and made it six miles before my apparently atrophied lungs made me choose between home or death. To cap it off, I showered far longer than should ever be allowed in the parched state of California: six reckless minutes of steaming hot relaxation.

And, most importantly, I avoided Olivia and Kate all day and no one asked me to sing "Amazing Grace" with Olivia on the bagpipes or help with a ten-cannon salute or whatever else she had planned. And now I've made it. It's after dinner and I ate alone in my room and no one yelled at me. I have my picnic supplies ready to go in a basket I found in the basement, which is plastic instead of wicker but close enough. And now I get to go see Max.

Take that, brain. Make me sad and I will just run until you have no oxygen and then plan picnics. I'm vaguely aware that I am acting insane, especially given the fact that Arlo's passing is hanging over this particular anniversary as well, but it's kind of just making me more intent on ignoring everything. There's just too much. I need distraction. I also realize I need a blanket. Rookie mistake, Jonah. Seriously, since I've never planned a picnic.

I hurry downstairs to the main linen closet, looking for something suitable.

"Plush, but not too warm," I murmur, sorting through options. "And it has to be big. Like ten by ten. Maybe she would prefer her own blanket—"

"Jonah."

I yelp and fall into the closet, then turn to see Olivia standing behind me. "What?"

"Are you leaving?"

She is wearing black. Like . . . c'mon, Olivia. You're killing me. Black pants and a black shirt over that and a black *headband*. Just seeing the outfit makes me angry. This is a girl who wore the same bathrobe for two weeks straight and now she has a handy memorial outfit?

I tuck a blanket under my arm, scowling. It's a bit coarse, but whatever. "Yes."

"I would like you to come out. Even for ten minutes. Just for the actual planting."

"No. Thank you."

I start for the door. I'm a bit early, but I have to bike with the basket and the blanket and everything. I want to have it all set up when Max arrives. I do a quick inventory even though I feel Olivia staring at me.

1. Bluetooth speaker for casual but slightly emotive music

2. Various sweets and a charcuterie set for two

3. Two bottles of wine because I think meeting in the park is already a felony so why not make it two

4. A candle, which in hindsight is a terrible idea on a blanket

5. Two masks to be prudent, though I have officially decided mask kisses will never be a thing. Probably. I mean, if she leaned in for one I would totally mask-kiss her back

Nodding in satisfaction, I swing open the door and start outside.

"Do you know what my last words to Mom were?" Olivia says quietly.

I pause halfway across the porch, basket in hand. "No."

"I told her to get out of my room."

I don't know what to do. I glance back at her, wondering if there will be tears, but instead, her hazel eyes are narrowed, her cheeks flushed.

"It would have been nice to work through this together. I gave you space because I knew you needed it. But with all this going on, I thought maybe we could try this year."

I can feel something shifting in my gut. My whole day of wall-building is starting to crumble and there are dark things beyond the walls and now I am angry because I tried so *hard* today. I don't want to be selfish. But when the options are to be a jerk or fall into a chasm that might not have a bottom, well, it's pretty easy.

"See you later," I say.

"You really are a coward, aren't you?"

I don't answer. I just flee down the steps, from my house, from her. Then it's a mad dash on the bike, pedaling furiously, pushing the air from my lungs until I can only focus on that pain and nothing else. I'm angry at Olivia, even though I know it's petty, because I was trying and I was *making* it. I was almost there. But it's fine. It's done now.

I can't wait to see Max. To forget everything else. I bike up a little hill in the park and set up there, out of sight of the road, and wait, and fix the blanket and adjust the spread and change the song, and wait. And wait.

I check my phone and sit down again, watching as another definitely-not-Max's-car drives by. It's 9:15, which isn't *that* bad. We agreed on 8:30. The sun is kind of, well, setting. It's forging stained glass behind the hills to the east and the forecast was right; it's perfect out here. I sigh. No big deal. It wasn't about the sunset. She'll be here soon. I've had about a third of a bottle of wine to calm my nerves and I'm starting to feel a little tingly. I should stop.

I check my messages, which are rapidly becoming a tragic monologue.

Jonah: All set! Just up on the first hill with the oak on it. See you soon

Jonah: It's really nice out. You close? Thought I saw a red car

Jonah: Max? I hope everything is okay!

The last one was from five minutes ago. I cringe as I read them, but it turns out that sitting on a hill by yourself is great for introspection, which was the exact opposite of my plan.

I keep thinking about Olivia. I should have said something. I should have given her a hug. I should have done literally *anything* but run away. I'll make it up to her tomorrow. Maybe I can do something nice for her. I don't think she set up her bitcoin-mining operation yet . . . maybe I can help with that? Yeah. That should make up for not being there as she plants a tree for our dead mother and *where is Max!* I check the road and try a call and there's no answer and I just fight the urge to text her again.

I'm worried that something is wrong . . . but I'm also wondering if this was just another addition to my growing list of missteps. I said I wasn't going to pretend things were normal and now here I am planning a *picnic*. And maybe Max agreed to come at first because she didn't want to hurt my feelings, but has now changed her mind. Maybe she doesn't know how to tell me that I am being a complete idiot again. Maybe she's wondering if I am, in general, a complete, irredeemable idiot. And this pinot grigio I "borrowed" from Kate's wine fridge seems to be tipping the scales, because the latter argument is making a lot of sense.

I try to stop the snowball. Dr. Syme always says I need to validate my negative thoughts with evidence . . . otherwise they're almost certainly just anxious thoughts. Better yet, counter them with evidence to the contrary. For example: Max told me that I make the bad times a little better.

Of course, I also helped create the bad times by pushing her into finding Winter Robbins and promising her a happy ending on several different occasions, which probably made Arlo's sudden passing even worse. Oh my god . . . I really am pushy. I shouted *I like you* at her. I held her to a stupid deal about going out. I asked her to put on her formal dress on a random day after work when she clearly didn't want to. And now because I am trying to avoid a mental breakdown on an anniversary she doesn't even know about, I have invited her to an in-person picnic when she *just* lost someone to COVID and okay, yeah, we have a snowball. I am the worst.

I try another call to apologize. No answer. I consider a text but I really want to talk. Maybe I should just come out and explain . . . But the thought of actually talking about Mom today of all days seems beyond me. Another twenty minutes go by in the failing light. Maybe one more try?

I fight that urge for a long time. Like a bottle and a half of pinot amount of time. And now the sun is down and I am sitting on a blanket in the dark, repeatedly lighting and blowing out a candle feeling . . . drunk. Yeah. We'll call it what it is. I'm drunk, I'm alone, and the wine has spoken.

Max bailed out on our date. And, to be honest, I don't blame her. But . . . now what?

I check my cell phone: 10:45. It feels like my stomach is trapped in a slowly tightening vise. It feels like I really am a complete idiot, sitting on a blanket that is a little too small, a little too coarse, with my now-empty bottles of wine and a charcuterie board for two. It feels like I am sitting on a hill, and that today is, of course, the anniversary of my mom's death, and that I am all alone in the darkness to think about what I did.

I don't know if I can go home right now. I don't know if I can stay here. I sit in limbo, trying to decide what to do, teetering on the edge of that deep dark hole without a bottom.

And then my phone buzzes, and I scoop it up instantly.

It's not Max.

chapter twenty-three

MAX

I cease to exist. Just like that, there's a blank spot in the tape. The line goes dead. I'm canceled. Gone to the world.

Peace out.

And here I stay. In this place where I don't exist for either seconds or minutes or hours or eons and think the empty thoughts of nothing in particular from which I have no plans to escape, no plans at all really, this until my consciousness is punctured by a persistent, annoying buzz. Coming from somewhere underneath me. Pardon the interruption.

There's a wet puddle of drool by my cheek. Exhaustion sticks to my bones. My head feels as though it's been stuffed with sofa cushions. Actually, the sound is coming from inside the couch and I squint and dig around in the seams, coming up with two quarters, a lot of cat hair, and eventually my cell phone.

"Hello?" My voice is groggy. I'm trying to process where I am and why I'm sleeping on the sofa, but I'm not doing it very quickly.

"Are you with Jonah?" comes a loud, brusque voice. I have to hold the phone away from my ear.

"What time is it?" I rub the heel of my hand into my eye socket and groan. The questions are coming out in the wrong order. Take two. "Who is this?"

"Olivia Stephens. And it's eleven thirty."

"P.M.?"

"Yes, P.M. Obviously."

Is it obvious?

"I'm looking for Jonah," she says impatiently. "Can you put him on?"

"Jonah? I'm not with—Oh. Hold on." I frantically scroll through my phone to our text message chain where I'd been intending to type out a message and had gotten as far as *So*— It sits there unsent.

In my defense, I did have a few important things on my mind, which are all crashing in on me at the moment and suddenly the phrase *a rude awakening* makes a whole lot more sense.

"As a reminder, telephones are a medium that require verbal communication," Olivia says.

"Right. Sorry. It's just that . . . No, I haven't seen him at all."

"But you two were supposed to be engaged in some highly gag-inducing lovey-dovey stuff." There's an accusatory note to her statement, and under normal circumstances I would argue her semantics, but truthfully, we did probably have a bit of lovey-dovey stuff planned.

That, however, was over three hours ago.

I download the evening for her in as neat and tidy a

package as I can manage, from the time I returned from work to the time the ambulance took my mother away, not just for efficiency's sake but so that reciting the details doesn't present an opportunity for fear to reach in through the cracks and seize me. Don't look down, my mom used to tell me on the jungle gym. So I don't.

"And he has no idea?"

"I don't see how he would." I cringe to think about Jonah waiting for me at our agreed-upon meeting spot. Alone. On a hill. But Jonah will understand. He'll know I had a good reason. That I wouldn't just stand him up. "I'll try calling him. Hang on. It'll only take a minute."

It takes even less than that. Thirty seconds for Jonah's phone to quit ringing and switch over to voice mail. So I try it twice. "No luck," I report back to her. "But I'm sure he's fine."

"I'm not," she says. "Max, I think Jonah might be in real trouble."

Okay, so I'm glad she can't see me rolling my eyes. "I've seen Jonah wear a braided belt. How much trouble can he really get into?"

There's a person-chewing-the-inside-of-their-lip-till-it-bleeds energy coming across loud and clear. "I should go," she says. "I need to look for him. Will you call me back on this number if you hear anything?"

I know I'm a little slow with processing things right now, but I'm starting to realize that she's serious. She's actually worried about Jonah.

"Wait—" I stop her before she can hit end on our call. "You can't go."

"I've always found the idea of legal adulthood to be at best arbitrary and at worst offensive, but in point of fact, I can."

I catch about 3 percent of the words coming out of her mouth. "Jonah said you have some kind of condition. That you have to be extra careful," I explain as if this is brand-new information to her. Why do I get the sense that feeling like an idiot around Olivia is sort of par for the course?

"Crohn's. The gift that keeps on giving. But as the great Greek physician Hippocrates once said, 'Desperate times call for desperate measures.'"

"Let me go. I'll go instead."

"You've got your own family to deal with," she says with a gentleness I imagine is out of character.

"Yeah. But I can't do anything from here." No visitors allowed at the hospital. Therefore, somewhere my mom is in a hospital room without me. "Listen, I'm used to being out and about for work. And besides, it'll give me something to do besides sit here and worry."

Olivia sighs. "Max, do you know what day it is?"

"Wednesday, I think."

"No. I mean yes. But what I mean is, today is the anniversary of our mother's death."

My stomach clumps, an uncomfortable mass of regret taking shape there. "I swear, Olivia. I had no idea."

"Yes, well." She clears her throat like a professor in a lecture hall. "It gets worse," she says. "Much."

Five minutes and I'm back in my car.

"So," Olivia says, her face appearing on the screen and—god—if I squint and the lighting's just right, she really looks like Jonah. Their eyes are the same shape. "It's like the *Amazing Race* only instead of a million dollars, the grand prize is a somewhat bougie, anxiety-riddled teenage boy."

I have my foot on the brake, hand on the gearshift. "Lucky for me, I like somewhat bougie, anxiety-riddled teenage boys."

"I'm going to pretend that wasn't actually kind of adorable."

"That makes two of us," I agree. FaceTime had seemed like a suitable, albeit possibly expensive compromise for her not coming, though now that we're in it, I'm feeling like we're at the start of a bad buddy cop movie. "One problem, though. Aren't there clues on *Amazing Race*?"

At some point, and I legitimately do not know when, Olivia changed into a Lycra unitard and neon sweatbands. It's a lot of spandex. "Okay, so perhaps less *Amazing Race* and more Nate the Great," she says.

"I'm sorry, *who?*"

"Famed child detective. Keep up."

I'm not sure I like where this is going.

"We need a Theory," she says.

"Okay. Well. I think we need to try to be in Jonah's head."

"That sounds like the absolute worst Airbnb I could imagine."

"So the question is," I say, ignoring her, "where would Jonah go?"

"Ah, my trusty crime dog, Sludge." Literally, what? "But that means we're assuming that he ever left."

"You don't think . . . you don't think he'd still be there?" I say. "That would be—"

"Pathetic?" Not the word I was thinking. "Good work, Max, now you're in his head."

And with that, we're off. Olivia disables her camera just for while we're moving—"Safety first!"—but somehow manages to be a very involved back-seat driver from clear across county lines, wanting to know if I've come to a complete stop and if I'm going the speed limit and also when I am going to get there. It might be impressive if it weren't quickly driving me insane.

"Do you mind?" I say as I'm pulling into the place where Jonah and I were meant to meet tonight. I park and turn my camera back on. "One button," I warn her. "That's all it takes."

She frowns and I think I detect something like respect in her expression. After all, she's not the only one who can be salty.

"I'm unhooking you from the dash," I tell her as though I'm walking her through a potentially painful medical procedure. "Now I'm getting out of the car. Now I'm looking around. I don't see his bike. All right." I bend down and tighten the laces on my shoes. "Climbing now. Here I go." Up the small hill I begin to climb, the grass damp and knotty beneath my soles. I peer into the phone. "Are you okay? Why are you breathing so heavy?" She's making a show of puffing her cheeks in and out.

"Vicarious cardio," she says. "My preferred form of exercise."

But as I near the top, my heart is already on the descent. Looking around, it's pretty obvious: Jonah's not here. And I'm realizing now how I really thought that he might be, that it'd be that easy. "Dammit." I sink down into the grass. "Where could he be?" I'm trying not to feel like this is my fault, trying harder not to worry. Not yet. I rest my chin on my knee and listen to the breeze through the palm trees. The twinkle of the sleepy city lights when my knuckle knocks against something hard. I pick up a candle, the wick blackened. I touch the wax in the center of the crater. It's not warm, but it's still soft and my finger leaves an indent. "He was definitely here," I tell her. It would have been a nice spot—Jonah was right. "Olivia," I say. "You said it gets worse." Even though the punctuation's all wrong, the question hangs in the air.

"I'm not sure that it's my place to tell you." Olivia sits down, nestling into position on a giant fuzzy rug that's bigger than my whole room.

"She was your mother too."

There's a long pause and I worry that maybe I've said something wrong.

"Thank you." Her fingers go to the necklace at the hollow of her throat.

"And also," I continue, thankful that the whole FaceTime

thing makes it less awkward not to make eye contact if we don't want to. "It might help. I mean, two heads are better than one."

"Fair enough," she says. "In that case, I'll tell you on the way to the soccer field."

"Oh! Good idea," I say, frustrated for not thinking of it myself.

By the time we return to my car, we've worked up a mild sweat, albeit Olivia's vicariously. She doesn't like the sound of the air-conditioning and since it hardly works anyway, I reluctantly concede. I focus on what's important, which is getting to Jonah before it's too late. Too late for what, I don't know, but something tells me that whatever Olivia's about to say will convince me that he is in dire need of finding.

"I should probably mention that my dad's a lawyer," she begins at a place I'm sure can't be the beginning. "He's always involved us in his work and treated us like grown-ups. We often talked legal theories at the dinner table. Eggshell skull, positivism, and the one that stuck with Jonah, *sine qua non*."

"At the risk of sounding dumb, what's that?"

"It's a fancy word for saying 'but-for causation.' One thing wouldn't have happened but for another thing happening. Are you following?"

"I'm with you."

"Okay, so I will preface this by saying that I don't believe my mother's death is Jonah's fault." A chill works its way up the length of my spine. "Jonah was getting ready to take the PSATs. He was in the school parking lot when he had his first full-blown, balls-to-the-wall panic attack. Seriously, I think he truly thought he was dying. Didn't know which way was up. He did what any kid would do. He texted his mom."

My heart tugs. Because, truth be told, I would very much like to be able to text my mom right now.

"No one can blame him for that. She rushed over to him immediately, which is exactly the sort of thing our mother would do. Drop everything to help us. But she was texting him, ran a red light, and the next thing any of us knew, she was dead. Jonah believes that he is responsible because but for his call, she wouldn't be dead."

I stare out at the dark soccer field at which I've arrived and already I know in my bones that Jonah's not here. "And Jonah wouldn't be missing right now," I say, "but for the fact that I didn't show up for him."

She says nothing. As much as we'd like, there's no use arguing with logic.

"School parking lot," I say. "That's where he was when he sent the text, right?"

"Bingo. Yes." Olivia claps. "Let's go. And step on it."

Surprisingly, I think we make a pretty good team. The

school's a two-minute drive. And still, no dice. Each time we show up somewhere, the two of us try harder and less successfully to stave off the panic setting into our voices. We try the beach. Olivia even checks the roof of their house. Until eventually, we're out of ideas. I sit in the darkness of my car, the crash of an inky ocean like a slow roll of thunder in the distance.

"You can't misplace a whole seventeen-year-old boy," I say.

Neither of us wants to acknowledge the scary possibilities that have begun to seem more like probabilities. Jonah's missing.

A text message dings on my phone. It's late for that. I look at the name. Dannie.

"You've paused me," says Olivia.

"Sit tight," I say, reading the message. "I think I've got something."

"Is it him?" asks Olivia. "Is that Jonah? I'm going to kill him."

"No. My friend Dannie sent me a link to a TikTok video." I furrow my brow. "She says, Isn't that Jonah?"

"Isn't what Jonah? Who?"

I click the link and my phone starts to play a video. "That's not Jonah," I mutter. "That's Ashley." Definitely Ashley, who I know from brief Instagram stalking, so sue me. But not just any Ashley. Ashley in a bikini. Ashley on a boat. Ashley doing one of those viral TikTok videos I have definitely not learned except that one time in my room that absolutely nobody needs to know about, like, ever.

"Text it to me." Olivia is so commanding. I don't bother arguing the point. I just forward it straight on. The video keeps replaying until . . . Olivia says it first—"Oh my goddess, that's Jonah."

It is. Behind Ashley, sitting on an upholstered leather bench beside (if my instincts are correct) Carlos F. Santi, drinking a beer. Unless they've started serving lemonade in aluminum cans.

"I know where we have to go," says Olivia.

Fountain Valley Yacht Club is the closest thing I've ever seen to the White House in real life. Olivia gives me the code to the front gate because did I really believe Jonah Stephens didn't belong to some sort of club that involved boating? (No, I did not). I am all, "Are you sure, you have really not seen my vehicular transportation; it is absolutely going to look like I'm casing the joint," but Olivia doesn't care about my one-of-these-things-is-not-like-the-other defense and bosses me right through the gate and onto the off-season set of a Ralph Lauren catalog.

"I don't see his bike," I say.

"Park near the water."

I obey. The mood, however, has shifted. The tension travels the distance between us. I cut the engine because I can't afford the gas to keep my car idling plus the data overages, too, and I manually roll down the window. I don't feel like having a witness, so I turn Olivia to face out the windshield.

"Nice view," she murmurs. "You know, my dad used to take us here."

There's a vaguely sulfuric smell of seaweed, traces of gasoline, and freshly cut grass. The dock creaks. It's way too quiet.

"Maybe it's an old video," I say.

Olivia doesn't answer.

We wait, together at least in trying not to think about our respective mothers. It's enough in common for now.

Sound travels faster across water. Or something like that. Science isn't my best subject. But there's something about sound and water, because I hear peals of laughter before I see the headlights on the boat. Peals. There's a word I've never used before, but that's exactly what it is.

"Do you hear that?" I whisper.

After another second—"I do."

Waves begin to slosh between the planks on the dock, and then a white-hulled boat—I don't know what kind; I don't own clothes with whales on them—begins coasting up to it at an angle. Carlos F. Santi jumps out with a rope in hand and now the odds of the video being old feel astronomical. I keep my breathing even and try to channel Nate the Great and his dog Sludge the way Olivia had suggested. They probably wouldn't jump to conclusions. So I don't either.

I wait. I've been waiting, but I can do it some more.

Actually, you know what?

Screw that.

I twist my key hard in the ignition and my car is a beast roaring to life. The headlights sweep across. Jonah looks up the moment he's caught in the spotlight, which is just as he reaches his arms out to help Ashley off the boat. Her arm is tossed easily around his neck and, as she steps down, she swings around and kisses the grand prize, that somewhat bougie, anxiety-riddled teenage boy I could have sworn I'd been promised.

"Found him."

chapter twenty-four

JONAH

I always hear about the deer in headlights thing and I know the headlights are probably metaphorical but these ones are actually scalding my eyes. I can't move. I pull away from Ashley and just *stand there*. It's hard to see who it is in the blinding light.

But I know. I know the car and the wheezing, ticking motor that just sputtered back to life. The moment feels endless. I hear Ashley saying, "Oh shit, the cleaning staff is here," and Carlos saying, "Fiddlesticks," and Lane up on the flybridge shouting, "Is that my dad? Oh man, I am so dead!" but they all feel really far away, like I just drifted out into the vacuum of space.

I try to justify things to myself, like a defense attorney going over some last notes before the trial. I didn't kiss Ashley back. I didn't ask her to kiss me. I definitely shouldn't have gotten close enough to help her off the boat, but I was just being polite, and I pulled away the second our lips touched.

But I know what it looks like. It looks like a yacht club prep is partying on a boat with his ex-girlfriend during a pandemic lockdown and, well, that's because he is.

I start for the car, and the questions flood my wine-soaked brain. Where was she? *How* is she here now? *How* could she possibly know where I am and oh my god Sara promised she was not going to put anything on TikTok.

The engine roars again, the car turns, and Max speeds away in a screech of tires and a last plume of smoke and sparks. I suddenly feel a lot more sober. And a lot shittier. I grab my phone to text her and . . . it's dead. I spent so much time playing games and numbly staring at the screen on the hill, I must have drained the battery. It's probably been dead for hours.

Carlos drapes his arm around my shoulders, pulling me in. "I presume that was—"

I step away. "Yeah," I breathe.

I'd called him when I got Ashley's text for "a last-second boat party just in case you change your mind (I hope you do)!!" followed by like a thousand emojis because *it wasn't Max, you idiot*. Carlos, of course, had already been going to the party, and he had sped over to pick me up, and I got in his car like I hadn't spent a half hour lecturing him about social distancing on my front lawn a couple weeks ago. I feel like I'm emerging from a haze. What am I doing here? Why are there so many people?

"Lane, tell your dad that the cleaners are speeding around in here," someone complains.

"My dad doesn't know we're here," Lane snaps. "So why am I seeing a TikTok on my dad's freaking boat, *Sara*. Take it down!"

"It already has two hundred likes!" Sara protests. "I can't."

Carlos pats my shoulder. "Well, she did abandon you tonight. Though I did say—"

"That anything could have happened and I shouldn't jump to conclusions," I mutter.

"Yeah. *Or* she was with some other dude and just realized the time."

"Carlos!"

"Just being the devil's aristocrat."

I rub my forehead in exasperation. I should probably go home and face the Reaper, but I know I won't be able to sleep. I know I need to explain myself. I know that in the world of the block button I might not get another chance to see her. And I really shouldn't be doing anything that is happening right now, but I think that metaphorical ship has sailed too, so I turn to Carlos. "Can I get another ride?"

"We're not going home, are we?" he asks, grinning.

"No."

Carlos hurries to his car. "I am *loving* all this drama. Max, she just fell onto my lips!"

"Shut up!"

"This is it," Carlos says, nodding at the low-slung apartment building.

It's three stories and curved around the driveway like one of the cheap highway motels we see on the way to San Antonio to visit Dad's family. Kate would rather die than let us stay in one, of course, and she would probably say the same for this place. Most of the exterior lights are burnt out, the concrete entryway looks ideal for murder, and two dudes are smoking out front.

On the plus side, I think the fact that I am afraid they are going to murder me confirms I am fully sober again. I need to explain myself, and I already downed a water bottle I found in the back of Carlos's car and a decent amount of that charcuterie board. So I'm definitely a little more sober and *definitely* sick with guilt, and both explain why I almost threw up five minutes ago.

"Wish me luck," I say. "Unit 237, right?"

"Yes, sir. Do you have a plan?"

I pause. "Lay out everything in a desperate rush and hope she understands?"

"Perfect. Can I listen in?"

"No! Are you okay to wait? I can get the bike out of the trunk and ride home."

Carlos looks at me like I am a sad, lost little child. "I'll wait for you in the car, dear."

"Stop having so much fun with my misery."

"I'm sorry," he says. "But if you need a witness, call me up."

I sigh deeply and step out of the car, then pause. "Wait . . . how did you get in last time? I never asked."

"Lock's broken," Carlos calls. "Just press any button and it'll buzz you in."

"That's not safe," I murmur, heading for the partially illuminated lobby.

It does work, though, and soon I am up on the second floor hurrying down some paper-thin, bright yellow carpet checking door numbers and 237 appears and it doesn't have a peephole, so maybe she'll even open the door.

I stand there for a moment, trying to get my thoughts together. I need a clear, coherent explanation. But my brain isn't working right and I feel so sick about everything that I just knock and fidget and try to slightly compose myself.

The door opens to the length of a chain and half of her face, which is more than enough to recognize that she is *not* happy to see me. In fact, it's even less than half, because she's wearing a mask. She must think I'm a risk now. I'm so stupid. I fumble into my pocket and pull out my own, looping it around my probably bright red ears.

"Are you serious, Jonah?" she snaps. "Get out of here!"

"Max, I can explain—"

"Step back," she says coldly. "I don't want to risk giving you anything."

I take a few steps back, holding my hands up. This is starting badly. "Max—"

"I spoke with Olivia. I'm sorry about your mom. I am. And—no, you know what? Not going to do this. Just . . . bye."

"Max, she kissed me. I pulled away immediately. There is nothing going on with her."

Her eyes flash. "We're dating and we've only *touched arms*. *By accident*. We've been careful. I haven't kissed my own boyfriend. And then I show up and you're just making out with your ex—"

"We weren't *making out*—"

"I don't care! What was the point of all this? What was the point of us being careful? What was the point of telling me you liked me in the first place?"

Her voice cracks a little as she says it, like she is balancing between anger and tears. I feel my heart shredding.

"Max, I just had a lot going on and needed a break and—"

"And thought you'd go hang out with a hundred people and make out with Ashley."

"We weren't making out," I repeat, starting to sweat. "And the party was really stupid. I know. It was meant to be a little distraction. The whole lockdown thing is hard on the brain—"

She laughs derisively. "Is it? Why? Because you don't get to go on your free trip to Paris? Or are you bored sitting in your mansion drawing on your window? Oh no. I have to go lounge by the pool again today. This is *hard*."

I open my mouth, close it again. I'm so shocked by the vitriol that I can't even form a response for a moment and I finally just change tacks. "You left me sitting on a hill all night, Max. And I don't blame you at all. But . . . a text would have been nice."

"I am *so sorry*," Max says. "How dare my mom get rushed to the hospital! I will take it up with her if they ever let me see her."

I step toward her, feeling all my arguments fall away. "What? Is she okay?"

Max closes the door even more. There is just a sliver of her left.

"No, she isn't. Go home. And stay away from Olivia, you selfish asshole."

She closes the door, and I hear a dead bolt slide into place. And then it's just me on some old banana-cream carpet with the lingering smell of cigarettes in the air and a moment to reflect.

Ashley kissed me tonight. Lane hugged me. I clinked drinks with ten different people and probably sloshed them all together. I've been with Carlos all night and . . .

And Olivia is at home.

I shuffle back to the car, and Carlos just pats my arm and turns the ignition.

"Can you stop at the gas station?" I murmur.

"Why?"

"I need to get some supplies. Like . . . two weeks' worth."

"I'm coming in," Kate says, knocking again.

"No," I say loudly. "The door is locked."

"What happened last night? Why is Olivia acting so strangely? Why are you locking yourself in your room?"

I am lying on my bed, still fully clothed, the bedding untouched beneath me. Winter stares judgmentally down at me from my wall. Fine, I deserve that.

I didn't even close my eyes all night. I just lay there, looking at my enormous gas station haul that is supposed to keep me alive for the next two weeks. It's a lot of chips and peanuts. I did get some sandwiches, but I don't have a fridge, so I kind of need to eat those today. One case of water. Two cases of soda. Why did I buy so much soda?

"I . . . had someone cough on my face," I say. "A stranger. While I was jogging."

It's a vain lie, since Olivia clearly knows the truth, but if I tell Kate outright that I went to a boat party she might break down the door, and I need that thing. I already put a towel under it to create a better seal, even though Alexa didn't seem to think that was necessary. I came into the house last night with my mask on and yellow dish gloves I bought at the gas station and just hurried straight to my room. Bubble commenced.

"Why would you jog so close to somebody?"

"Poor spatial awareness."

She grunts. "I can believe that. Did it sound like a sick cough? Was he smoking?"

"It doesn't matter!"

"I'm sure you're fine."

"I'm not going anywhere near Olivia. I have a bathroom and all the food I need."

I check my phone. It's the same ten-minute routine I've been practicing since I sent Max a message last night. Well, three messages.

Jonah: Max I am so sorry about tonight and your mom please talk to me

Jonah: I just needed to get out. It was dumb. I wasn't thinking

Jonah: I won't bother you anymore. Just . . . I'm sorry. I hope you're okay

She didn't reply. Won't, I suspect. And a life without Max messages seems really, really shitty. And I will have two weeks of self-imposed house arrest to drive that point home.

"So you're going to sit in there for what . . . two weeks?" Kate asks, snorting.

"Yes!"

She sighs deeply. "Fine. Wait a couple of days. Then I'll take you to my friend who's an oral surgeon. She has tests."

"Wait." I look up at the door, frowning. "You have friends?"

"Her nurse will test you there if you want. You'll need to wait a couple of days before she'll test you, I think, and then a couple days after that for the results. But it will still be faster."

"I thought there weren't enough tests and you had to be sick to take one and all that?"

"Yes . . . or you know someone. But I doubt your therapist wants you locked up in a room for two weeks."

I really can't keep up with this woman. "Thanks, Kate."

"Thank me when you have a cotton swab poking your brain."

I actually do feel a little better. Maybe my fervent promises through the night that if I just didn't give anything to Olivia I would be really good and never go to any stupid boat parties ever again have paid off. I slide off the bed and help myself to a breakfast of Doritos and Pepsi, almost throw up, and then frantically brush my teeth, eyeing myself in the mirror.

My clothes are filthy. My hair is everywhere. I am spitting out orange toothpaste. I look completely insane.

But I guess I made it through another anniversary.

chapter twenty-five

MAX

Dannie says I'm keeping vigil. I say I have nowhere to go, so I might as well be here . . . in my car . . . waiting . . .

The end of that sentence is "just in case." And I know I'm not fooling even myself by lopping off the end like that.

Case has become such a loaded word lately. The number of them is growing so fast the reporters can't keep up, and after my mother's positive results yesterday, she's another one of them. I wonder who tells the CDC, I wonder how they keep tabs at all, I wonder if somebody expects me to do something that I don't know I'm supposed to do. I've heard all sorts of crazy things. Like one minute it's all about how almost everybody who gets the virus is a-okay, and then the next I'm hearing how some twenty-five-year-old triathlete in the best shape of his life is dead. I heard a rumor that in New York they're going to start loading bodies onto moving trucks. I heard kids don't get it. But then again, I heard that maybe they do.

I remember when my mom and I used to sit around watching people in the mall. Only she taught me that the phrase for it goes the other way around: *people watching*.

That's what I'm doing now. People in scrubs carrying thermoses. A police officer with a clear plastic shield over his face who I can tell wants to sit down on that bench so badly. There's a card table sitting out front of the sliding glass doors and it looks as if these two nurses manning it are selling lemonade when really they're checking temperatures. I've only caught them sending one person away so far and I had so many questions I couldn't get answered. I have no idea if people around here are happy or sad or what because it turns out it's a whole lot harder to read people's eyes than novels would lead you to believe. But I assume most people are sad. Or at least tense.

I can't help thinking how Arlo didn't even have someone sitting in the parking lot waiting for him. All of it makes me feel like a failure. I'm failing my mom. I'm failing Chester. I already failed Arlo, even failed to organize—I don't know—a memorial or something. I have never felt more useless in my entire life.

Inside my car, I've got my phone to keep me company.

Dannie: But did you even explain to him what happened?

It's still fresh. I mean, Mom didn't get a hold of a phone charger until last night. She's had a chest X-ray, tubes in her nose, an IV drip, and they've been checking her oxygen levels on the regular using a squeezy thing (not the technical term) over her fingertip.

Max: Oh he knows

Dannie: You're sure?

Max: YES.

Max: Also what does it matter?

Hold the phone. I'd been pretty sure that my friends were required to switch to hating Jonah posthaste. It's written in the Girl Code right between Don't Be on a Diet on Your Friend's Birthday and Share Thy Hair Ties.

Because you know who makes excuses for boys' bad behavior? Dumbass girls. And I am not a dumbass girl. Here is the only fact that matters: His lips were on her mouth. I repeat: On her mouth. His ex-girlfriend. During a pandemic. Any additional information can only be offered as a reason, of which there are—let me check, oh right—no good ones.

Imani: Well.

Max: You're not seriously making excuses for him, are you?

Imani's moving tomorrow, but for now, we're pretending that she's not because—hello—I've already gotten all the reality checks I need, thanks.

Dannie: No. I'm not

Max: Good. Because it couldn't be more obvious that I was just a distraction

Imani: It could be a little more obvious

Max: How do you not see what I'm saying? OK. It's like you're marathon training and closet organizing, only picture this: Jonah's corona-hobby was . . . me

Max: He needed a warm body. I could have been anyone. I was interchangeable. Fungible.

Imani: Ooo that was a vocab word last year!

Max: But great news, I deliver! So, you know, that was real convenient for him.

Dannie: I hate seeing you like this

Max: I'm not like anything. Really. I don't even care. I'm simply trying to point out how messed up his logic is. The second I was unavailable to him, he was on to the next thing

Imani: More like on to the last thing, to be fair

Max: Exactly. And it's not like I care, really. I have way bigger things to worry about than Jonah Stephens

Dannie: Uh-oh. She first and last named him

Imani: Shoot you're riiiiiight

Max: What's that supposed to mean?

Dannie: It means that you must really like him because you used his first and last name

Max: That is the stupidest thing I've ever heard. That's his name.

Imani: You know, for not wanting to talk about him, you sure are talking about him a lot

So. I didn't say my phone was *good* company.

I switch the ringer off and passive-aggressively ignore my best friends, who will understand because get this: That's why they're my best friends. They're not just like, *Oh hey, Max didn't respond for an hour, guess it's time to go find a new best friend.* See how that works?

Not that I'm sour. It's just that the one annoying part is how I got used to talking to Jonah during the day, which in hindsight was my bad. Time to recalibrate. To detox. Go cold turkey. Imani's moving on. Jonah *moved* on. And I'm here. Right here.

I watch the hospital doors slide open and closed. I put my headphones on. The moment I realize that the Mountain Goats are playing and that the Mountain Goats are from *his* playlist, I turn it off. Or at least that's precisely what I'm going to do, after this song.

chapter twenty-six

JONAH

Well, I've lost it. I stand back, looking at my bedroom window, an uncapped marker in my right hand like the smoking gun of insanity. Two days locked in my bedroom has finally tipped the scales.

I am playing Pictionary with myself. On a window. I did get a washable marker this time.

I guess in a perfect world, I thought Mrs. Clodden would play along across the street. No. In a perfect world, Max would be sitting outside on the hood of her old Civic, sunglasses resting on the bridge of her nose, hair blowing in the breeze.

But this is not a perfect world, which becomes more apparent with every passing day.

"In the weeds," I murmur, guessing at my own picture, because, as mentioned, I'm nuts.

It was a subpar picture, to be honest. My weeds look like flowers, and the dog I drew looks like a chair with a tail.

I wipe the picture away with my sleeve and rewrite my *Hello* . . . though from the inside. I've mastered writing mirror script now, at least, so I'm basically as smart as Da Vinci.

It's probably just going to remind me how much I screwed up everything and that Max hates me and that I have now been imprisoned for my sins. I might even be facing capital punishment—Olivia hasn't spoken to me once, and she could definitely build a guillotine in two days. Or maybe Kate will just snap my neck and save the mess. Winter still stares at me in grizzled disapproval all day, which is yet another handy visual cue that I let literally everybody down, even one of my *heroes*. That takes a special kind of failure. I guess Dad still likes me, but he did send me a relatively scathing message about responsibility: "Jonah I expect more out of you . . ." *Why*? When did I ever give the impression I was a functional human being? I throw up air into toilets, people.

I did send Ernest another email yesterday. I guess I felt too guilty after getting his hopes up about Arlo, and told myself I wouldn't ask . . . but I've had a lot of time to think. About all the ways I screwed things up, for sure, but also that last lingering question: What did it mean, that line?

I *may* also have included that Max broke up with me and my life was in shambles . . . I have a real issue with moderating my emails lately.

I've also sent ten messages to Max. No replies. I did manage to get through to Imani and Dannie and start a little group chat, and at least have been able to check in on Max's mom that way, who is still in the hospital while I am locked in my mini Bastille.

"Hello, is it brie you're looking for," I murmur as I write.

I should exercise or something. Clear my head. I have

been watching YouTube workout videos . . . I just haven't been working out with them. I've also been eating chips three meals a day. Why did I go to a gas station for supplies? Why did I go to a boat party in the first place? Why do I do all of the things that I do because they are all wrong?

Okay, a little workout. Or a shower. It's almost noon . . . I could have a nap . . .

There's a knock on my door. It's stiff rapping, but not the wood-crunching power of Kate's iron fists, so I step closer, making sure the towel is firmly wedged beneath the door.

"Hello . . ."

"Having fun in there?" Olivia says, her tone still slightly acidic.

"It's swell," I mutter. "I thought you hated me."

"I hate raucous laughter and the sound of someone eating an orange. I dislike you."

"I really am sorry. I just—"

"I also hate rationalizations. Apologies should never require an addendum."

"So . . . you forgive me?" I ask hopefully.

I could really use a win. A small glimmer of redemption.

"I do not," she confirms, dashing that hope. "But I did notice you drawing pictures on the windows and thought a mental health analysis was in order. I also recommended a virtual appointment." I feel the door shift as she leans against it. "Kate is taking you to get a test today. Then if all goes well, you can hopefully return to society as a reformed—read, less idiotic—offender."

"That's something."

"Is Max speaking to you?"

"No. I think she legit hates me."

"Understandable. Mom goes to the hospital and boy-friend goes to the ex."

"The ex was coincidental," I mutter. "It was the *distraction* I was after."

"The memorial was nice. I planted that Japanese maple. I even had a plaque made."

I lean against the door as well, silent for a moment. "It sounds nice."

"Was it worth it? The grand distraction?"

I consider that. "I don't know. I made it through . . . so maybe."

"At a pretty high cost, I would say. You are minus one girl-friend, correct? And made it through what exactly . . . being sad? Acknowledging the facts? Mourning your mom?"

"It's worked so far."

"Has it?" she counters.

"It's all I have—"

"It's all you *choose* to have. If you never say goodbye, they can never be gone."

I feel my eyes burning. I stare at the window and the message I wrote to no one.

"Kate will be ready soon," Olivia says softly. "Get changed."

I listen to her walk away.

• • •

"Just tilt your head back a little and . . . there."

"Ugh," I manage, feeling the swab poke something that can't be far from my brain while the nurse's eyes smile encouragingly at me from behind a plastic face shield.

"Very good," he says through his mask. "You're all done."

I must look really pitiable, because he's been talking to me like I'm a toddler since I walked in. He's probably in his mid-thirties, with some square-framed glasses, a comb-over, and a neck tattoo poking over his collar that kind of looks like an AK-47, so he's really throwing me off, especially since this clinic had a fountain in the lobby and possibly a real Caravaggio.

I keep thinking about what Olivia said, and about Max, and about where I went wrong.

"Did you always work here?" I ask him while I do a weird rabbit thing with my nose.

He shakes his head. "Used to be in emerge. Down at Huntington."

"Must have seen a lot of stuff, huh. Like . . . mental distress?"

"Yeah."

"Can I ask you a serious medical question?" I say as he puts the swab in a tube and writes some notes. I check his name tag again. "And can I call you Craig?"

"What else would you call me?"

"If you did something bad to someone . . . okay, that sounds awful. If my girlfriend caught me kissing my ex at a boat party—"

"So that's why you're here," he mutters. "In fairness, it still sounds awful."

"I know. It gets worse. Her mom is sick and she's alone and I've just . . . screwed it all up. Bad. Probably irreparably, she-never-wants-to-see-me-again bad. But I'm worried about her."

Craig looks up from the notepad, furrowing his prodigious eyebrows. "So what's the question?"

"Is there anything I can do for her? Like . . . what do people need at times like that?"

I know I have a therapist and all, but Dr. Syme didn't have any openings this week and I really need sound medical advice before next Wednesday.

"Hold still; I'm taking one more temperature reading." Craig shoots me in the head with a laser and writes something down, then puts a stethoscope to my chest. "Well, if her mom is sick . . . she's scared. And do you know what people really need when it's scary?"

I think about that. "Distraction?"

"They just need you to be there for them. No questions asked."

I chew on that one for a moment. No grand gestures? No flowers or music or candles on a hill? It's basically the opposite of how I try to fix everything . . . with Band-Aids made of charcuterie and good intentions. Even my simple gestures are over the top. And, to be honest, it hasn't worked. I guess Olivia was telling me the same thing, and Carlos, and maybe I should have listened. Or maybe I just needed Craig and oh okay he's already left.

I sigh and sanitize my hands and go to meet a masked Kate in the car. The back seat is separated from the front by a drop-sheet sealed with duct tape . . . I brought my bubble with me.

"Did he say you're screwed or what?" Kate asks dryly.

"I guess I'll find out in two days. But also . . . yes," I reply, buckling my seat belt and lowering the windows further.

"So it's back to your cell."

"Back to my cell," I say, sighing. "I wouldn't be averse to some vegetables. Can you throw some in later?"

"Sure."

We ride in silence for a little while, my head pressed against the cool glass. "Kate?"

"Yeah?"

"Thanks."

She doesn't say anything for a moment. When she does, her voice is weirdly quiet. "You're welcome."

Imani: She's at Huntington Beach Hospital. Five days now.

Jonah: Any updates?

Imani: Stable, as far as Max knows. She just sits in the parking lot half the day. Can't go inside.

Dannie: She was finally able to get tested a few days ago. Negative.

Jonah: I was wondering about that . . . I just got mine back today too. Good to go.

Imani: So you can go make out with Ashley again?

Dannie: Whoa escalation much

Imani: Yeah I know. But I had to say something. This already feels too covert

Jonah: I deserve it. And you told her I said hi?

Dannie: Which of the last four hundred times

Jonah: Right. Did you talk to her today yet? Is she doing okay?

Imani: Oh she's super

Dannie: IMANI

Imani: Sorry. Got some stuff going on here. I really was rooting for you Jonah

Imani: *Am*

Jonah: Thanks guys. I got to run

An email popped up while we were talking . . . from Ernest Robbins. I open it eagerly.

Dear Jonah Stephens,

Sorry to hear about you and Max. I hope it still works out between you. Take it from me . . . giving up is not the answer.

As for the infamous line, it's probably less exciting than you think. Arlo was incorrect; it wasn't about acting. I was a moody sort, but even *I* wasn't that melodramatic.

I ad-libbed it on purpose. The original line was: "I won't

rest till he's dead." I was supposed to say it around that campfire the night before the battle, grim and quiet, lit up by the flames. But I didn't like it. It felt empty.

My character had found so much along the way: a new sidekick, a new horse, and all those beautiful, quiet moments riding through the plains. I said "None of this really matters" to imply that maybe he could just ride off with his new friend, and forget the entire vendetta, and live happily ever after in the wild.

Of course, we had a script. So I still had to go to town and kill that land baron. But I insisted the line stay . . . just as a hint that my character had found some perspective along the way. I suppose it was jarring. I know the writer hated it. But he was never going to get an Oscar anyway. I'm glad they used it.

I hope that helps.

—Winter

I read it again. And again. I feel a steady pressure building behind my eyes.

Mom would have loved it.

She wanted a little optimism in her cowboys. And I can think of nothing better than a secret wish to ride off into the sunset with a friend. I just wish I could tell her she was right. And maybe I am a bit of a mess lately, because my eyes are watering as I look up at Winter's poster.

Wiping my face with my sleeve, I consider the first part

of his email too. The quarantine is over—my bedroom is a testament to that. I finally cleaned it this morning, vacuuming up a truly disturbing amount of Dorito dust and cookie crumbs.

I also hugged Olivia, who claimed that I was making her emotionally ill and should be confined again, but I'm like 99 percent sure I felt a little squeeze back.

In total, I spent five days in semi-complete isolation. And I was lucky. Really, really lucky. I guess I knew that before. But I've had a *lot* of time to think. And I kept going back to Arlo. To how happy he seemed when Max told him about us trying to find Winter. To how young and energetic he seemed, and how that was stripped away so quickly. How his death left so much unfulfilled, and Chester without a home, and Max heartbroken. And what's really happened to *me* during this quarantine? Just a string of inconveniences . . . a delay for Paris, a distant but healthy dad in Madrid, more time with my sister. My brain is good at inventing problems. But I missed all the real ones.

And, of course, it all brings me back to Max. To how giving up doesn't feel like the answer to me, either.

But how do I fix this? How do I say sorry? I have no idea.

I do have a bunch of markers, and me, for whatever that's worth.

Maybe nothing, but hey, it never hurts to say hello.

chapter twenty-seven

MAX

There's a breach in my force field. More on that in a minute, I guess.

For now—now being the moments when I studiously ignore the breach—I'm considering the idea of reincarnation and surprisingly—*surprisingly*—this philosophical journey has nothing to do with a sudden need for a more optimistic take on death, but by my own slow, blank-minded evolution into a reptile.

Ten minutes ago, I unpeeled my back from the windshield of my car and rolled over to draw a diagonal line across the four tally marks already written in the dust of my hood. Day Five. I should probably be worried that I haven't been able to work, that I haven't attended any of my classes, but I have enough worries at the moment and so those will need to get in line.

After that, I pulled my hair up off my neck and lay back against the windshield again, face to the sun. On either side of me are rows of similar windshields, picture windows of blue sky and white clouds, light bouncing off them.

I'm tanner than I was a few days earlier. I've got sock

lines. And yesterday, I reached the end of the internet. So now I just lie here.

Lie here and think about useless things like how similar I've become to a lizard and whether it might be possible to become one when I'm dead. And I don't like being interrupted.

Which returns me to the force field breach.

I did take safety precautions. I de-friended him on Facebook, blocked him on Instagram, put a do not disturb setting on his phone number, but the one place I apparently neglected to safeguard was my inbox. And even though it still sits unread, the email is there. I know it's there. It's only a matter of time. A popped balloon cannot be un-popped.

I sit up, sighing. Pushing my sunglasses into a headband, I tuck my ankles underneath me, cross-legged on the hood of my car, and hunch over to cast a shadow across my phone screen. I prepare myself for the world's longest, multi-syllabic, thesaurus-irrific list of excuses. Pardon me, but it's Jonah, so you know he's bound to call his B.S. "extenuations" or some similar nonsense.

From: Jonah Stephens <Jonah.Stephens03@gmail.com>
To: Maxine Mauro <tothemax448@gmail.com>
Subject: Hello (From Here)

Okay, so first off, it's funny how Jonah thinks that "Hello" is going to automatically spark a conversation when all it makes me want to say right now is "Goodbye."

I think it goes without saying that I'm an imbecile.

Ugh, dear god, see what I mean? Why does he have to say "imbecile" when we all know he was an idiot?

I know this is reaching you at a stressful time and if I am adding to your stress by sending you this email, then please, delete it, no hard feelings.

Like I need his permission, right?

Still reading? Okay, great. So, here's the thing: I have a theory that time is one long string of moments stacked up between disasters and we never know how many moments we've got until that next Bad Thing pops into the lineup. And you might think that my mom's death would have made me less afraid of disaster seeing as how I've already seen the worst and lived through it. For a different sort of person than I am, that might work. But the truth is, ever since my mom died, I've been living in fear of the next disaster. I wake up feeling like I'm in a horror movie (my least favorite film genre, BTW) and I'm watching through my fingers knowing at any second, there's going to be a jump scare. Lately, it's been even worse than that. All I've been able to see is one long string of disasters. Disaster, disaster, disaster, as far as the eye could see. That is, until you came along and

suddenly I was cooking disgusting food and playing
Pictionary and spending more time on the phone than
I ever have in my life and suddenly I was living in the
moments *you* made. You invented spaces where there
were none . . . it was like . . . it was like you made little
gaps where I could come up for air and breathe. And if I
haven't said thank you for that, thank you.

But somewhere along the way, I guess I forgot you had
your own string of moments and disasters and started
thinking you were here just to fill mine. I know your mom
is sick and you're scared and—newsflash—things aren't,
like, normal. But I guess you knew that already. And
for the record: Olivia says I am an "asshat" and based
on some preliminary projections, I'd say there's a high
probability she's correct.

I send a silent thank-you to Olivia.

Also I wrote a whole three more paragraphs and just
deleted them because I could practically hear you telling
me to end it there and imaginary you, like the real one, is
usually right. The End.
Oh, and P.S. Look up.

I read the last line two more times. *Look . . . up?* My eyes
travel to the sea of cars in the parking lot, to one of the
white-brick half-walls that form little castles on the concrete, guarding hydro boxes and garbage bins. And there he

is, sitting on the lip, shoes dangling down over the leaning bicycle beneath him, holding a sign against his stomach, written in blue marker.

IF YOU NEED ME (I'M HERE)

I've watched a lot of movies and, look, I know how there are probably an actual *million* think pieces about the myriad of ways entertainment affects our, like, lizard brains or whatever (wow, so we're back to reptiles so soon), but you don't realize how right those mommy bloggers are until you're sitting on the hood of your car with a tiny, disembodied voice that sounds suspiciously like Bridget Jones narrating your next moves to you in your head. *There. He. Is. Run to him. Leap up in the air and straddle him around his waist like every girl who has ever been on* The Bachelor. *Spin around. Profess your love. Now kiss him, for god's sake.*

But yeah, no. I don't do any of that. I delete the email, get in my car, and leave.

chapter twenty-eight

JONAH

I guess, in a sense, Carlos was right, if only accidentally. Not about the grand gestures or the push-ups. But about the shitty part, where love punches a hole in you, and you're lost, and you look at the world differently, and maybe, if you're sensible, at yourself. And possibly even the push-ups, though I'm still not doing those.

But I did do a little introspection, and I found *space*. It was like I put a puzzle back together when my mom died, and somewhere along the way I got lazy, or negligent, and just left some of the pieces in the box. Maybe I figured it was close enough, like you could stand back and look at the puzzle and say *Yeah, that's probably Jonah . . . just don't look too closely.*

But when Max drove away and I realized that it was undoubtedly over between us, I think I lost another piece. And it must have been a corner piece or something, because the whole picture kind of fell apart. I didn't expect her to forgive me. That wasn't even the point. I meant what I wrote . . . I was there if she needed me, and that was it. I didn't message her again after that day. That, at least, I did right.

But I had panic attacks. I spaced. I kept in contact with Imani and Dannie for updates about Max's mom, but otherwise, I shut out the world. Even Carlos, who seemed to understand. I think I needed time to focus on that puzzle again. To shake up the box, pull all the pieces out, and rebuild Jonah Stephens.

So, long story short, that's basically why I am sitting cross-legged on the grass in front of a tree. Kind of like a quasi-Buddha, except I'm wearing soccer shorts and a plaid button-down because I haven't gotten to the fashion piece yet. The Japanese maple really is a beautiful tree. Squat and shapely and a deep, ruddy red, it's also surrounded by a wall of round black stones that my sister built, and there is a little plaque set into the dirt in front of it, which reads:

In memory of Janice Stephens. "Take a moment. Take it in."

She used to say that all the time. Especially to me. She had lots of wise little sayings and good advice. I left those pieces out. But this tree and this plaque reminded me that I left out a whole lot of other memories too. Memories that I had stored away because they didn't really involve me.

Mom and Olivia in their ridiculous plastic poker hats playing Uno every Saturday night. Mom and Olivia screaming madly at the TV during *Jeopardy!* with their hands poised on their imaginary buzzers. Mom and Olivia bringing whiteboards scribbled with idea webs and diagrams to their two-person book club. Mom and Olivia in the sunroom, sprawled out in the fading daylight, reading together because they didn't want to part even for that solitary activity.

Olivia had a rough time growing up. Bullies and bad encounters. She didn't have a lot of friends . . . even as a kid, she was brilliant and reclusive and, well, Olivia. She preferred to stay home. No sports. No real outside hobbies. It was a lot of her and Mom. A whole life of shared activities.

"Have you unlocked the mysteries of life yet?"

"Working on it."

Kate steps up beside me, aerating the lawn with her heels. "Keep me apprised."

"Talk to Dad this morning?"

"I did. He's still on track for next week."

"One more test, right?"

"Then it's home sweet home," she confirms. "We'll do something nice for him."

"Well, Olivia did build a pergola. We can just say that's for him."

She smiles. "True. How's Max doing? Haven't heard you talk about her in a little while."

The name still has a kick to it. Not like Ashley's. Hers was just a reminder of one bad night. *Max* reminds me of the lone bright spots in a bad couple of months, which is somehow worse. Her smile on a glowing screen. A playground close enough to Paris. Big blue words fading on my bedroom window.

And more than that, all the things I thought might

follow. All the things that won't. Turns out our story really was a lot like Arlo and Winter's after all. I wasn't there in her time of need. I ran away. And once this is over (if it is *ever* over), we won't be reunited.

"Her mom is still in the hospital."

"Well, give her my best."

I feel a dry spot form in my throat but nod anyway. "I will."

It's silent for a moment, and I expect Kate to sweep back inside again. She stays.

"You've been sitting out here a lot."

I lean back, digging my hands into the grass. The sun is beating down today, and I can feel it prickling the bridge of my nose. "Yeah. Olivia did a good job. Not that I am remotely surprised."

I *am* very surprised when Kate sits down beside me. She's in a freaking pantsuit.

"She sounds like she was a wonderful woman," Kate says slowly, as if waiting for me to react. "Olivia was telling some stories during the memorial. I'm sorry I didn't get to meet her."

I do feel a twinge. A little voice that says, *You wouldn't have met her*. But that voice is kind of an asshole, and it keeps causing trouble. I just nod. "You would have liked her."

She kicks her heels off and sits cross-legged too. "I could have learned a thing or two. About trying to be . . . motherly. I wanted kids more than anything, you know. It just didn't work out with Greg."

"The surfer dude?"

She smiles thinly. "We didn't break up because he wanted to surf, Jonah. He wanted to surf and travel the world . . . and not have kids. The rest I could have dealt with, but not that. We were going to have a family, but he changed his mind. So I left him."

I don't really know what to say to that, so I just turn back to the tree. "Oh."

"Yeah. I wondered for a long time if I made the right choice. Love the person . . . hate the narrative. Do you just go with it because you love them and love conquers all and all that shit? I don't know. And then I was so damn picky I didn't remarry until your dad, and then, because life is indeed shit, it was too late for me. And your dad. He is an old fart now."

"Can we skip this part?"

"Sure. Well, I love your dad, so it worked out, and I got two stepkids in the process. I was excited . . . and then one of them just put up with me and the other one truly hated me and I guess I figured I didn't have the chops after all. And maybe I was lucky I never got my own."

I glance at her. "Now I really feel like a dick."

"We were both dicks." She sighs. "But I was technically supposed to be the adult."

"In fairness, you've kept us all sane and alive through six weeks of almost complete isolation. I would say that was pretty damn good parenting. And you only kicked me once."

"That was an accident. But thank you."

I hesitate. "And . . . maybe a little bit of my anger toward you was misdirected."

"What do you mean?"

My eyes drift back to the memorial. "It all felt too soon," I say finally, "you coming into the picture. But that wasn't your fault. I was angry at Dad, but I was already down a parent. I . . . So I gave him a pass. I took it out on you."

Kate is quiet for a moment. "I figured that might be part of it. It *was* fast."

"But I should have talked to him. I'm sorry."

"*He* should have talked to *you*. He still should. Both of you," she says, leaning over to bump shoulders. "It's too late to get rid of me, but it never hurts to talk things out. I know it can be tough with that man—"

"He's almost *too* cheery sometimes, right?"

She laughs. "Absolutely."

A breeze rustles the claret leaves, and I get the weird thought that Mom would have liked it here, sitting in front of her own living memorial. I've never gone back to her tombstone since the interment. It never felt like her anyway. Cold stone. A name and a couple of numbers that were too close together by fifty years at least. A thousand, if I had my way. And bouquets of cut flowers on either side, replaced every few weeks, living and dying in brief splashes of color.

But the tree will stay. It will, in fact, only grow.

"Did you see the paperwork I left out for you?" I ask.

"Already signed. You're sure about this?"

"Absolutely. Thanks, Kate."

"Anytime." She glances at me. "You know what Greg told me the last time I saw him?"

"What?"

"He said he loved me, but that he understood, and that he hoped I got my family, and my dream job—I was paying him alimony, so that made sense—and that he was sorry he changed."

I think about that. "To be honest . . . he kind of seems like a nice guy."

"He was. But I guess it takes more than that."

We sit there for a while, until the sun slips behind some clouds, and go inside together.

I don't know what happens when an unstoppable force meets an immovable object. Or I didn't, rather, until Kate decided to play Settlers of Catan with us tonight. The two most competitive people on the planet have squared off at the kitchen table, and I am caught in the middle, just trying to build a happy little village while two empires take shape around me. I'm kind of afraid.

Kate is staring at the board at the moment. Her left eye is twitching. "It's the roads," she whispers, sounding disconcertingly intense like she has since the moment we started. "You keep getting all the damn roads."

I clear my throat. "Typically we try for like a one-minute

shot clock—" She looks up at me, and I force a smile. "But take your time."

Olivia looks outwardly relaxed, but I know she too is stressed. She's not winning, at least, not cleanly, and at the moment it's anyone's game. Well, not mine. I am firmly in last.

I really must stop recommending this game.

Kate rolls . . . and it's a good one. She reaps the rewards and builds another city, and I think I see Olivia's eye twitching now too. Kate only needs one more Victory Point to win.

I roll and collect a few logs and some iron ore like usual, which I use to do absolutely nothing because I am a poor and destitute villager. Olivia scans the board. Scans her cards. Scans the remaining pieces. She needs two Victory Points. She rolls and gets one.

Kate takes the dice, and fate, into her hands.

Both of Olivia's eyes are twitching. Kate plots. Then she rolls. Then she reaps. And for a moment, it looks like she is just short of triumph.

But then the cards go down, a village is razed in the name of progress, and a new cobalt city arises in the desert, and one empire rules them all.

I look at Olivia. As far as I know, she has never lost anything. At least, not since she was little, playing Uno with Mom, and even then, I doubt she lost from the age of seven. And she just . . . sits there. She eyes the board, as if in disbelief, counting the ten Victory Points in her head.

Kate is grinning maniacally, almost sure to plunge the

world into a new dark age. She says, "Good game, kids . . . let's play again soon," and then clacks out again to the theme song of her own percussive footsteps like a true conquering dictator. Olivia is still quiet.

"I fucking lost," she says finally.

I sit there for a long moment. "Yeah."

She puts her cards down, and for a second, I am terrified she is about to cry. Instead, she starts to clean the board, which she definitely doesn't have to do because I was the clear loser. I help her, and we pack it up, and when she goes to stand, I stand with her.

And then I give her a hug.

She stiffens . . . and then she hugs me back. Fully this time, squeezing me tighter.

"I'm sorry," I say quietly.

I don't mean the game, and I should probably say it, but I don't have a clue how to apologize for two years of self-absorbed pity. Of not being there when my sister lost her mom and her best friend on the same day, and with her, an entire lifetime of pre-planned activities.

But Olivia is the smartest person I know. And she just rests her head on my shoulder.

"I miss her," she whispers.

"Me too."

When I let go, she just nods at me and goes to her room, and I put the board back in the closet. I was, undoubtedly, the loser. But I'm glad we played.

chapter twenty-nine

MAX

www.facebook.com

Max Mauro

May 20 at 8:00 p.m.

 Hi, I'm having a memorial service tonight and will be doing an Instagram Live. Please tune in to pay your respects if you can. I'll start streaming at 8:45 p.m. Rest in Peace.

Imani Jackson

Hugs. I wouldn't miss it.

Carlos F. Santi

Prayers up, girl. You know I'm in.

Dannie Ngujo

Love you. You know I'm here if you ever need to talk.

Olivia Stephens

"Death sets a thing significant" ~ Emily Dickinson

 Sometimes, when things are hard, I think of how I could have been born into a thousand different families, in a hundred different countries. I think of how I could have been born into wealth or into the kind of poverty that can't afford shoes, and, amidst all those possibilities, I'm grateful I was born near an ocean.

When the voices in my head are loud, the ocean is louder. When my worries feel too big, the ocean is always bigger. When I meet the ocean with heartache, it gives me somewhere to drown it.

And though the ocean doesn't take insurance, it doesn't have to, because it's the cheapest form of therapy you can find, free for everyone.

I've abandoned my shoes at the top of the beach, which is officially closed, but liberties have been taken.

The sand holds on to the day's sun and I trudge awkwardly through the small, warm dunes until the place where the beach is packed and hard and the lapping water leaves behind froth and seaweed. The moon's reflection bounces over the black sea and I drop my backpack onto a dry spot beside me, before kneeling to unload it.

I give myself time to get situated, only a few more minutes until I go live. Part of me would still prefer to do nothing at all, but I guess the whole point is that this isn't about me. My mother always believed that every life moment deserves its moment. Didn't matter if it was a first day at school, a good report card, even a business loan, she said you had to pause and give it its due, otherwise time had a way of getting too slippery. I guess that's why she made me "cheers" with ice cream the first time I got my period, but I digress.

I have everything I need here, which isn't much. I plan to keep it simple and from the heart. Really, it's the best I can do given the circumstances. I walk back out toward the water and, no, this isn't some Victorian tragedy where, because of my grief, I just keep going and let the ocean take me. It's a normal tragedy where I shed some ugly tears as I begin to carve big, capital letters into the packed sand.

Once I'm finished, I wipe the grit from my hands and the tears from my face and retrieve my phone from the towel I've laid out. I reposition so that the breeze isn't blowing strands of hair in my eyes. I don't look like Beyoncé in a wind machine or anything, but it's an improvement.

Signing on, I try not to freak out. "Hi, guys," I say uncertainly into the camera as the live feed begins to play. "So, I'm, um, here at Huntington Beach." In the bottom left-hand corner I see that people have actually begun to join. Dannie sends up a bunch of little hearts. Imani types *Hiya* from her new home in Kansas. And soon there are others. "Okay, wow, thanks. I—look, this won't take long. I just thought I needed to do, you know, something. So, I guess I should start by saying a few words."

I dig my toes deeper into the sand. For a whole two breaths, I'm not sure I'm going to be able to speak at all, but sure enough, I find my words like I've written them right there on the beach.

"Mr. Antinova asked us to pick out a poem that encapsulated the experience of quarantine and everything, so in light of it all, I picked this one by Emily Dickinson—thanks, Olivia—and figured I would read it to you all now. Here goes nothing." I clear my throat.

"*Hope is the thing with feathers, that perches in the soul, and sings the tune without the words, and never stops at all, And sweetest in the Gale is heard, and sore must be the storm, that could abash the little Bird, that kept so many warm, I've heard it in the chilliest land, and on the strangest Sea, yet never in Extremity, it asked a crumb of me.*"

I fold up the scrap of paper I've been reading from, unsure of what else to say. I take a long look at my hands and try. "If I've learned anything these last few weeks it's that nothing's a given. Nothing's permanent. Not our dreams. Not our . . . life. And definitely, not even all this.

"Now, if you can just give me one second I'll set up the memorial . . . thing. Hang on." I fumble around for a hot second and the picture on the phone goes topsy-turvy. "Sorry. Here." I prop it up on the towel against the backpack. "Everyone can see me?" There's a smattering of thumbs-ups in the comments below. I return the gesture, but in real life.

I fiddle with the drone camera that Dannie lent me. She didn't even make me sign over a kidney as collateral, which was nice. She did insist on giving me a thirty-minute FaceTime tutorial on how it worked and I'll be honest, I was hardly listening.

"There's the on switch," I murmur. Three red lights spring out of the dark. "And, let's see, let's see—" I glance up.

Dannie's comment pops up: *We went over this!*

"Spotlight. That's it." A white light flicks bright and settles. I point it away from my face.

"Hey."

With a start I look up to see a silhouette in the beam standing at a distance.

On the live stream comments burst out of the left-hand corner:

I heard someone

Who is that?

Are you about to be murdered? Blink twice if you need help!

"Jonah?" I squint to see the shadowy figure, illuminated only by the floodlights in the distant parking lot. He steps just a foot closer so that I can see him. Here. In person.

"Yeah, hi, I didn't mean to freak you out. I just—I thought there was someone else who should be here."

A great poufy ball of black fur bounds across the beach, kicking up sand. "How did you—what—" I can't finish my sentence because Chester's tongue is lapping at my face and I'm basically French kissing a dog and I like it. Chester looks like his old self again and I see why—he's once again sporting a bow tie. He stands up on his hind legs and shakes his ears. His tail wags madly. I press my forehead to his and feel his wet snout nose against my throat. "Jonah!" I shriek like a girl at a boy band concert, but who cares?

"I was able to negotiate Kate and my dad into letting me get a dog since I'm going to be around this summer after all."

His voice is slightly muffled behind the mask and I notice the gloves. "I think Kate was thinking I'd choose something small and fluffy like a teacup Pomeranian, but considering she didn't specify . . ." He shrugs. "I learned that from you."

"Verbal contracts are binding, I hear." I smile, and when I do, I feel a full body ache, but it's good, like stretching and—

"Think you could send that thing over here?" Jonah's hair flops to one side. Something's different about him. He seems more at ease.

Chester curls up on the towel because he is fancy, obviously. I pick up the drone and, using the remote controller, manage to fly it at least close enough to Jonah that he reaches out and catches it. He pulls something out of his back pocket—a sheet of paper maybe—and waving it for me, he proceeds to tie it onto the side of the drone.

"Incoming." He gently lifts it up and I bring it back for a smooth landing on the towel. Chester lifts his head, only mildly interested and ultimately unimpressed by twenty-first-century developments in technology.

"What is this?" I crouch down beside it, and when I turn the paper over I see that it's not a paper at all, but a photograph. A young woman with brown hair stands in front of the Pont des Arts. She looks like Anne Hathaway's character in *The Devil Wears Prada*, only this young woman isn't playing Andy Sachs; she's real. On the back, someone's scribbled in old cursive: *Esprit Brillants, Sorbonne, Paris, 1993.* "Oh" is what

I can manage as I study the picture more closely. *This* is why Jonah wanted to go to Paris so badly. *This* is why he needed that scholarship. His mother did it twenty-seven years before him.

"I'm . . . sorry for your loss," I say. This is a memorial service after all.

"I'm sorry for your loss too," he echoes.

I give a small shake of my head. Jonah lifts his chin and looks at the stars.

"Right." I take up my phone again, more uncertainly. "Well, here it goes." I link the drone camera feed to show on the live stream and then carefully, I lift off.

Up, up, up, the drone rises like it's floating, like it's a modern-day sky lantern, bright and glowing in the night. I check my phone screen. Not yet, not yet, and then there they are. The words on the beach.

ARLO OXLEY (1936–2020)

"You will be missed," I say because it's true. For most of my life I've either been missing someone or worried about missing someone. I take a deep breath. "Arlo was there when I needed someone to talk to more than I even knew that I did. For a brief time, Arlo was a constant, and anybody that knows me knows I love consistency. He was funny when I needed a laugh or at least a good story. He was big-hearted in the way that I wish I was. His presence will be so missed."

Slowly, I bring the drone back to earth. I turn the live stream back on me. "So, okay—wow, a lot of comments here. Sorry I missed them, how—"

I begin to read through the scroll of comments rising from the edge of the screen.

Dannie Ngujo: Oh my god, this is so romantic

Carlos F. Santi: That's my boy! It's like a movie!

Olivia Stephens: Officially I want to puke. Unofficially . . .

Rick Hutton: :) <3 ;)

Imani Jackson: Tell him you LOVE him already

Imani Jackson: Seriously, what are you waiting for?

Dannie Ngujo: OMG, mayday! Mayday! Use your words, Max!

Ernest Robbins: That was beautiful. But remember, not everyone receives the gift of a second chance.

Dannie Ngujo: You guys!

Winter Robbins made it and he's right. If he can forgive the man he loved for abandoning him in his time of need, then what am I waiting for?

I start to say something, but the second I do, I realize that Jonah's gone. His footprints next to Chester's leave a small path in the sand. Behind me, the tide's begun to crawl, nipping at the tail end of the words written on the beach.

I falter, unsure of what I'm supposed to do here. "Thanks, everyone, for coming. Good night." A wave crashes in again.

chapter thirty

JONAH

I wake to a gentle kiss on the lips. Soft. Wet. Hairy.

"Chester!" I sputter, wiping my mouth. "A little personal space, please?"

He obediently backs off the bed and sits down, staring up at me with a very expressive look that says: "It's like ten, dude, can I go grab a pee?" Groaning, I throw the covers off and scratch him behind his ear, muttering vague apologies because we are roomies now and I'm the only one with an opposable thumb. With great power . . .

"Let's go, boy."

We make our way to the backyard, and Chester runs off to do his business behind some boxwood because he is nothing if not a gentleman. I didn't know Arlo Oxley well, but he definitely knew how to train a dog. Olivia fawns over him. Even David Copperfield likes Chester, and that cat hates everybody.

It took a while to convince Kate . . . she kept saying we didn't need "any new additions." But let's be honest . . . I was going to save Chester one way or another. If I had to snatch him from the shelter and live a life together on the rails with a bindle, I totally would have done it. A) I have always wanted a dog. B) He wears a *bow tie*. C) I knew Max needed something good.

I take a breath in the morning sunlight, and then notice Olivia sprawled out on a lawn chair with a book. I park myself on the one beside her. The house has fallen back into a quiet routine. Dad arrived home safe and sound, finally, and we had a little barbecue and a little tearing up and a game of Settlers, which he now claims he will never play again out of fear for his life. And so we now have two new members of the Stephens Family Bubble, and both are chipper fellows and make for easy additions.

I haven't spoken to him yet about Kate. But I will. At the very least, he probably deserves to know why I was so vehemently anti for so long, if he hasn't worked that out already. Kate thinks he has and just hasn't wanted to address it. She says he needs to. She's going to give him a nudge.

And I figure I'll just keep trying this new thing where I actually face the uncomfortable things in my life and see what happens.

I feel like I'm busier than ever. School and self-tutored French and all the usual stuff, but Olivia and I have also been mining bitcoin and making vases and working on our mini-winery and I guess I am doing a puzzle too. It's coming along. Still getting panic attacks and insomnia and those great space-outs where I float around in the ether for a while. But I think rebuilding yourself takes time. I think, unfortunately, there is no great big fix. It takes a lot of pieces, and a lot of patience, and they don't always fit together the first time around.

"Have you been reading?" Olivia asks, her eyes fixed on the book.

Oh yeah. We also have a book club. She really is tireless.

"Yes?"

"Hmm. I have already prepared a few discussion topics. We meet tomorrow."

"I'll be ready," I grumble.

Olivia lowers the book. She's wearing a white tee and khaki shorts; her aquamarine bathrobe still makes appearances, but it's no longer petrified, and her hair has been conditioned and combed out of sentience. She was the better actor. I was the better costume designer. But it turns out we both had some pieces missing. We're working on it together these days, and to be honest, it's a lot easier. Olivia was right. Obviously.

"I've been thinking about Max," she says, eyeing me over the top of the flap.

"That makes two of us."

"You heard the news, I presume?" she asks quietly.

I nod. "Dannie told me yesterday. You spoke to Max?"

"She called me last night."

"Lucky you," I say, sighing. "Honestly, I was so relieved, I almost ran over to Max's to hug them both."

"And then you remembered that your sister would have killed you."

"Precisely. And that Max doesn't want to see me anyway."

Olivia is quiet for a moment, and then turns to a page she has earmarked and reads: *"But that afternoon he asked himself, with his infinite capacity for illusion, if such pitiless indifference might not be a subterfuge for hiding the torments of love."*

"I really wish you didn't choose *Love in the Time of Cholera.*"

"It was thematically relevant."

"So are you saying I'm deluded? Or that Max is feigning indifference to hide the torments of love? Or both?"

"Just a quote I enjoyed," she says absently. "I already gave you my advice, if you recall."

"The whole heart-numbing isolation thing?"

She goes back to her book. "Oh, the heartache you would have avoided."

"So your whole book report is basically: Don't love in the time of cholera."

"No. It's that love is, unfortunately, an inevitable pain in the ass. Cholera, as it turned out, had very little to do with it."

I close my eyes, feeling the midday heat on my cheeks. "I look forward to the diagrams." Then I open them again, frowning as I look at her hand. "Are you wearing a ring?"

It's on her right hand, but definitely on the ring finger. Olivia *never* wears jewelry.

"No," she says, not looking up from her book. But her ears go just a bit pink.

"Is that a *promise ring*?" I ask incredulously, trying to grab at it. "Oh my god. Does Delaware actually exist?!"

"Of course not!" Olivia says, snatching her arm away. She pauses. "Her name is Nya."

"So your whole lecture was hypocritical? And why did you make up a different name?"

"Dramatic effect. And it wasn't hypocritical . . . she *is* far away. Well, in San Diego. And she bought me this ring online and had it delivered, and I gave it the requisite time before opening it. We are simply, well, *promising* to try and resume things as soon as the world allows."

Her ears are bright pink now.

I grin, squeezing her arm. "I'm happy for you, Olivia."

She tries to look disdainful, but I catch a twitch at the corner of her mouth.

"It was nice what you did with Chester and showing up there and everything," Olivia says after a moment. "I know she appreciated it."

I glance at her. "You're almost done, right?"

"Last few pages."

"Does it work out? Do they . . . get together eventually?"

"Oh, my dear, cheating little brother. Go finish the book."

Carlos F. Santi: I broke up with Marcus today

Jonah: the guy you were computer dating?

Carlos F. Santi: yeah

Jonah: I'm sorry to hear that

Carlos F. Santi: I've been thinking again

Jonah: oh boy

Carlos F. Santi: the meaning of life was never love man

Jonah: . . .

Carlos F. Santi: you see love is shitty and stupid and I hate it

Jonah: I thought that was the whole point. The pod thing.

Carlos F. Santi: I was wrong. The peas just fall out, bro.

Jonah: So what's the meaning of life?

Carlos F. Santi: I don't know. You should have listened to Confusedness

Jonah: Did you hear me sighing from there?

Carlos F. Santi: I can imagine. Want to hang out later?

Jonah: dude!

Carlos F. Santi: Joking! But could I like sit in the front yard and yell up at you?

Jonah: I mean . . . we have phones.

Carlos F. Santi: I'm coming anyway

Jonah: Fine. I will wait by the window with bated breath.

Carlos F. Santi: Still got the message on it?

Jonah: . . .

Jonah: yeah.

I glance at my bedroom window. The words are fresh as ever, of course . . . the benefits of an inside job. But Dad was asking about it and didn't seem overly thrilled that I was drawing on his windows, so it's probably time for another cleaning. I guess I have been working on goodbyes.

I grab the Windex and a cloth and go to work, squinting against the glare, cleaning the words away to reveal an unfettered view of that awful cupid statue and the curbside where she used to park for deliveries . . . and a really old red car parked in front of Mrs. Clodden's.

I freeze.

Max is walking back down the driveway, mask on, carrying the now empty delivery bag whose contents she has left on Mrs. Clodden's porch. She reaches her car and strips off the mask, her long brown hair breaking free from her messy bun as ever, ripped jeans, worn-out sneakers, headphones jammed into either ear, mouthing all the words.

Whether she would have checked anyway, or whether she feels my gaze, she looks up at me. The words are gone. It's just me with my Windex bottle and a cloth. I wave. She smiles and waves back, and for a moment, I think she might stay. Might walk over. Might sit and chat on the hood of her car.

Then she drives away, throwing off a trail of smoke and stray sparks, and I watch her go, and I suppose it was my infinite capacity for illusion all along.

My phone pings. I check it despondently, figuring Carlos is pondering life again.

Instead, I see *Max*.

I open the message in a rush, lay my forehead against the windowpane, and smile.

Max: FYI. If you need anything, I deliver.

EPILOGUE

See, the problem with conventional wisdom is that it really needs context. For example: avocados. With most fruits, you want them in the early stage of ripening. Maybe even pre-ripe: green bananas just keep getting better. The longer a fruit sits in the grocery store, the less people want it.

And then we have avocados, which is why I'm standing in the middle of the very busy produce section trying to find the old ones. If your goal is tonight's guacamole, then you have to search for the ones with a little bit of squish.

It's busy, but not crazy busy, which I've learned is a different vibe entirely. Everyone has a mask on and there are still arrows on the floor and dividers at the registers, but the state-wide shelter-at-home order is gone for now, and the general population has returned in search of non-canned sustenance.

My orders have decreased a little, which is nice, because I can attend online classes and help out a bit at Mauro's Dry Cleaning. It was looking bad for a little while. But with the government loans, we put in a new drop-off system and some plastic barriers and, hey, people are still spilling stuff on their duvets. It's slower, but I think we're going to pull through. I mean, maybe. Conventional wisdom really does fall apart in a pandemic. I still have lots of petty grievances. My bank account balance barely warrants a bank account. I'm terrible at math. Logan Bennett is still a dick. And spending time with loved ones? Well, I guess that's still relevant too. Except it's loved *one*, Me and Mom. I almost had two for a little while. But I guess it's hard to hold people close from a distance.

I pick up another avocado and squeeze. Old and mushy. Perfect.

"You know, avocados actually have more potassium than bananas."

I drop my perfect avocado. Shit. I look up. Double shit. "Hello."

He's basically in disguise. Glasses and a big blue mask and he's had a haircut, but not a particularly good one (I suspect Olivia). Still, he is like a pandemic Clark Kent, except a little skinny and holding toilet paper and, yeah, he's still really, really cute. He's smiling. I know how his eyes change.

"Hello," he says.

"Your avocado knowledge never ceases to amaze."

"I almost went with that one the first time, you know. It was close. I spent fifteen minutes deciding."

"That checks out. No more personal shoppers?"

"Depends. But I get geared up now for the essentials and so far so good." He crosses his fingers.

"So that explains why I never got another order."

Wow, that sounded bitter.

Okay, confession: I thought he was going to order. Like I sent that text and was kind of looking at my phone for the next hour (or three) thinking, *Here it comes* . . . but, nope, nothing.

"I thought ordering groceries from an ex was morally questionable." He clears his throat. The tops of his cheeks redden. "And . . . I didn't know if you were just being nice."

It goes silent for a second. I mean, not really, someone is yelling at their kid and an old man is complaining about moldy lettuce and there's an announcement over the PA and actually it might be the loudest place on earth.

"I'm not that nice," I finally say, because someone should probably say something.

He picks up the avocado I dropped and is about to hand it to me, seems to think better of it, reaches for the bin, seems to think better of that, and then just holds it.

He's nothing if not polite.

"You know, I have a couple blankets," he says.

"Con . . . gratulations?"

"Parks are cool." He shoves his hands in pockets and rocks back, peering over the produce stands. "People are allowed to hang out in . . . parks. Like . . . at a distance and whatnot."

"Jonah . . ." I say. "Are you asking me out on a picnic?"

"I was actually asking you out on a date. Was that not clear? I thought it was clear."

"Always so mysterious. Never know what you're thinking."

"Oh, I'm sorry. Did you want me to shout it? I can do that." He takes a big, heaving breath and—

"No, no, no." I wave him down and he lets his chest fall. "I mean—what I mean is . . . When?"

"Tonight?"

"I can't," I say.

He deflates. "Oh. Yeah, okay, no problem. I get it."

"My mom and I are trying out this new thing. It's called 'actually hanging out'? Have you heard of it? It's pretty cool. You know, we got some inspiration from you. We're doing a movie night thing. More March Madness bracket than fantasy football draft, and I'm not watching anything old-timey, but there may even be a trophy at the end."

"Good for you two." He nods thoughtfully. "So . . ."

"So . . ."

Well, what now, conventional wisdom? The world's still hanging on. Love ain't the last one standing. There are griev-ances and bad timing and all the things that came before. There's the memory of tears when I put on my dress, and the red swell of anger when he went to that party, and the hollow loss when I drove away from a too-perfectly roman-tic apology and . . . yeah, maybe there's Love. So I guess you just get to pick your avocado or . . . whatever.

"But I could do it tomorrow?" I say.

"Wha—wait, seriously?" he says in a rush of air.

I love it when he does that.

"Seriously."

"Yes. Tomorrow. Fantastic." He puts the avocado in his basket and basically skips toward the dairy section—okay, he doesn't skip, that'd be cheesy even for Jonah, but at least knowing him, it'd be artisanal.

Someday, I think, we will look back at this moment and see that there were good times to be remembered—long phone calls, new hobbies, elastic pants. Someday, there will be BuzzFeed quizzes with headlines like: "You Might Be a Pandemic Kid If . . ." And it will be like how Maroon 5 always transports me to the feeling of having a crush in fourth grade or the smell of gingerbread brings me back to my grandma's house, and for me, no matter what happens next, this time will be him. Jonah.

And since the world's not really ending, Jonah and I can begin. Again.

ACKNOWLEDGMENTS

If we were to write something in permanent marker across our own windows, it would be: THANK YOU.

Thank you to our Writers House agents, Dan and Bri, for bringing us together and helping us to navigate this uncertain time.

Thank you to our editor, Jessica Dandino Garrison. Your first email about our work bubbled with the type of enthusiasm writers can live off of for years. Ever since, you have proved to be the smartest, most thoughtful, and, yes, still enthusiastic advocate and guiding light we could have hoped for. We are also incredibly grateful for the efforts of Rosie Ahmed, Regina Castillo, Kelley Brady, Jeff Östberg, Felicity Vallence, James Akinaka, Shannon Spann, our expert readers Sharifa Love and Lily Malcom, and the rest of the Dial and Penguin Young Readers Team for turning our story into a book.

HELLO (FROM US)

Chandler: Our story, like Jonah and Max's, started with a simple "hello" from our respective heres: Wes from Nova Scotia and me from Austin. It was April 2020 . . . early enough that we had no real idea what was coming, but far enough along that we knew we were in the midst of a life-defining moment. Quarantine was just so *weird*. We were all sort of ravenous for human interaction and, wow, people were Zoom-happy. I think it's in that spirit of human connection that our agents set us up on a platonic blind date with each other.

Wes: At the time, I was dealing with the loss of Kobe Bryant, a friend and collaborator, and I was eager to channel my energy and uncertainty into a new story. Like Jonah, I was looking for a bright spot.

Chandler: We're writers. Put us in a room, literal or virtual, and we're going to start spinning story ideas.

Wes: I think that's how we both process the world. The idea of writing something of the moment, *in* the moment felt like burying a time capsule for ourselves. We had no idea what our lives would look like by the time the book came out. Our characters' ambiguity is our ambiguity.

Chandler: Unburying the time capsule for a second, looking back I can clearly see what I was trying to process. I'd had my second baby on New Year's Eve and my husband, daughter, and I were supposed to take our newborn to see my parents in Florida the week of the lockdown. It was months and months and months before my parents saw my son, and my in-laws still haven't been with him. I'm very thankful that my family is healthy, but there's still some sadness that our parents have missed out on these irretrievable first few months (and now a full year) of our son's life during which he has changed so much.

Wes: Yes, one thing Chandler and I agreed on right away: the little things still mattered. There was this constant need to contextualize our grief over these missed moments. I'd hear Chandler say, "I know I'm so lucky and can't complain," which is understandable. We knew people all around us, including teens, were losing parents, grandparents, aunts, uncles, friends.

Chandler: And we could see how existing issues were turned upside down by the pandemic—struggles with housing, food and money insecurity, systemic racism, mental illness.

Wes: Some degree of pain sprouted up in every community. And we were both seeing this impulse in many teens—a reluctance to feel bad about feeling bad for missing the more "trivial" things like prom and graduation and sports seasons and trips abroad. Big moments they expected would mark their lives and now just . . . wouldn't.

Chandler: Jonah and Max appeared to us when we started thinking about two people who connect because of the pandemic, but are also kept apart by it.

Wes: They're seeing the world through each other's eyes. They're trying to figure out how to feel. They're *in* it.

Chandler: Totally. Jonah said that everything about 2020 sucked except for Max, and that's how I've felt about this process. Nothing about the past year has been easy, but writing this book with Wes was so joyful and, yes, easy.

Wes: Did you just get sappy? Is that a thing that happened?

Chandler: I know, I know, I'm usually the one cutting out laughing and smiling and, you know, *nice* things for my characters. Let's pretend this never happened.

Wes: Well, we *did* write a love story. It was a bad year . . . sometimes you just need a good love story.

Chandler: I completely agree. I hope *Hello (From Here)* reminds readers, like it did for us, that good things can still happen in the worst times.

Chandler Baker is the author of five young adult novels, including *This Is Not the End*. Her adult debut, *Whisper Network*, was a *New York Times* best seller and Reese Witherspoon Book Club pick. Chandler lives in Austin, Texas, with her husband and two young children. She can usually be found listening to audiobooks at two times the normal speed, overspending at bookstores, or obsessing over true crime.

@chandlerbakerbooks
@cbakerbooks
chandlerbaker.com

Wesley King is the #1 *New York Times* bestselling author of eleven novels, including the Wizenard series with Kobe Bryant, the Edgar Award–winning and Bank Street Best Book of the Year *OCDaniel*, and the Junior Library Guild selections *The Vindico* and *The Feros*. He lives in Nova Scotia, as well as on a 1967 boat that he's sailing around the world.

@wesleykingauthor
@wesleytking
wesleytking.com